PRAISE FOR

ASTRID SEES ALL

“Guiding readers on a descent [illegible] of a certain Musto.”

—*The Millions*

“*Astrid Sees All* is so fun to read you might miss the grief that fuels this novel. . . . Phoebe is a feminist heroine as complicated as she is compelling.”

—Darcey Steinke, author of *Flash Count Diary* and *Suicide Blonde*

“A new wave coming-of-age story, *Astrid Sees All* is a blast from the past, taking the reader back to the ratty Bohemia of the Lower East Side of the early ’80s, complete with squatters, cold-water sublets, white punks on dope in the trashed bathrooms of trendy clubs, and even a cameo by the king of downtown, Lou Reed. Sharp-eyed and light on her feet, Natalie Standiford is the perfect tour guide for one young woman’s leap from the ivied halls of college into another, even more unreal world.”

—Stewart O’Nan, author of *The Speed Queen*

“*Astrid Sees All* zooms us back to the 1980s in the most delightful and nostalgic way: New York in all its craziness and magnetism is alive again through the clear-eyed observations and adventures of our witty and generous narrator.”

—Martha McPhee, author of *An Elegant Woman*

"*Astrid Sees All* is an unforgettable story: a Lower East Side nightworld full of damaged young dreamers, all kids who want to be stars, but end up just breaking each other's hearts along with their own. Only Natalie Standiford could bring these girls to life with so much tender wit, street-wise compassion, and brilliant soul. She gives this novel the beautifully fragile strut of a Lou Reed guitar ballad."

—Rob Sheffield, *New York Times* bestselling author of *Love Is a Mix Tape*

"*Astrid Sees All* has the startling vibrancy of a Nan Goldin photograph and the heartbreak and wit of a film by Preston Sturges, which is to say Natalie Standiford's vision is an original one. I loved Astrid so much that I didn't want this funny, sad novel to ever end. Standiford has the storytelling charm!"

—René Steinke, author of *Holy Skirts* and *Friendswood*

"The author's glee in evoking the zeitgeist of the 1980s is infectious. . . . Smart details, lively digressions, and spot-on period snapshots."

—*Kirkus Reviews*

"Standiford captures a beating, smoky world. . . . There is page-turning plot aplenty here, dealing with the pains of grief, addiction, and simply growing up, all made endurable by love and friendship."

—*Booklist*

ASTRID SEES ALL

A NOVEL

NATALIE STANDIFORD

ATRIA PAPERBACK

New York London Toronto Sydney New Delhi

An Imprint of Simon & Schuster, Inc.
1230 Avenue of the Americas
New York, NY 10020

First Atria Paperback edition February 2022

ATRIA PAPERBACK and colophon are trademarks of Simon & Schuster, Inc.

For information about special discounts for bulk purchases, please contact Simon & Schuster Special Sales at 1-866-506-1949 or business@simonandschuster.com.

The Simon & Schuster Speakers Bureau can bring authors to your live event. For more information or to book an event, contact the Simon & Schuster Speakers Bureau at 1-866-248-3049 or visit our website at www.simonspeakers.com.

Interior design by Kathryn A. Kenney-Peterson

Manufactured in the United States of America

1 3 5 7 9 10 8 6 4 2

Library of Congress Cataloging-in-Publication Data

Names: Standiford, Natalie, author.
Title: Astrid sees all : a novel / Natalie Standiford.
Description: First Atria Books hardcover edition. | New York : Atria Books, 2021.
Identifiers: LCCN 2020034560 (print) | LCCN 2020034561 (ebook) | ISBN 9781982153656 (hardcover) | ISBN 9781982153670 (ebook)
Subjects: GSAFD: Suspense fiction.
Classification: LCC PS3619.T364736 A94 2021 (print) | LCC PS3619.T364736 (ebook) | DDC 813/.6—dc23
LC record available at https://lccn.loc.gov/2020034560
LC ebook record available at https://lccn.loc.gov/2020034561

ISBN 978-1-9821-5365-6
ISBN 978-1-9821-5366-3 (pbk)
ISBN 978-1-9821-5367-0 (ebook)

For Eric, always

We hardly ever see the moon any more

so no wonder

it's so beautiful when we look up suddenly

and there it is gliding broken-faced over the bridges

—Frank O'Hara, "Avenue A"

CONTENTS

1	Going Underground	1
2	An Apartment	17
3	The Tale of Attila and Caledonia	31
4	The Gatsby Party	39
5	Chanterelle	53
6	*Don Giovanni*	59
7	Shadow	65
8	Examination Room	75
9	The Dietzes' Party	79
10	Roses	91
11	What Time Is It?	95
12	Café Lethe	109
13	So Bored of Having My Picture Taken	121
14	Junkie Heaven	131
15	International With Monument	135
16	Purple Footprints	143
17	Wake	149
18	Wreck Room	155
19	Expanding Universe	161
20	Invisibility Spell	175
21	A Sack of Potatoes	187
22	Chance of a Lifetime	199

23	Astrid Sees All	207
24	Going Uptown	215
25	Aviva B.	219
26	The Moon and Thurman Munson	225
27	What Happened at the Funeral	231
28	The Rooster Man	239
29	The Famous Astrid	245
30	Visitation	255
	Acknowledgments	259

1

GOING UNDERGROUND

I am sitting, alone, in the apartment on Avenue A that Carmen and I first rented one year ago. The cats are here, and her typewriter is here, and some of her clothes, but she is not, and I wonder if I'm to blame for that.

I wouldn't be in New York—I wouldn't be "Astrid"—if not for her. For at least two years, maybe three, Carmen has played a part in every decision I've made. What she would think, what she would do in my place, would this attract her or repel her . . . I considered these questions when choosing what to wear, who to date, where to work, where to live, everything. She wasn't the most beautiful or most glamorous person I knew, but that was why I emulated her: she found ways to be fascinating without relying on those easy tactics. She had the seen-it-all attitude of a native New Yorker, and I wanted to see it all.

I moved to Manhattan right after college graduation—to the Upper West Side, because Carmen lived on West Eighty-Ninth Street with a friend from Dalton, Sarita Feinman. I imagined Carmen would teach me the secret codes of the New Yorker, the two of us out on the town, people-watching in Central Park, and lounging around drinking beer the way we had in college.

I found a room in a run-down tenement apartment on Eighty-Seventh and Amsterdam—only two blocks from Carmen, so I jumped at it, even though it was small, dark, dirty, full of roaches, overpriced, and came with four roommates. Robin Greene, an assistant editor at a romance publisher, held the lease, which gave her the power to choose who would occupy which room and to kick out girls who didn't have the right attitude. She preferred wholesome young women like Mary Frank, a devoutly Catholic law student, and Krissi, who had moved from Kansas in search of a job at *People* and a rich Wall Street husband. A flamboyant actress named Marin Berlin had sneaked in somehow when Robin's guard was down. Marin was my favorite, but she was hardly ever home. She'd just landed a part in an off-off-Broadway play, a drag melodrama called *Medea on Mars*.

I called Carmen, who seemed delighted to hear from me. She immediately trotted me across town to her parents' swank apartment on Sutton Place. Her mother was a former actress, and her father was the famous avant-garde composer Leonard Dietz. Carmen knew Len and Betsy would like me, and they did. Parents always liked me. Back then (a mere year and a half ago), I looked like a girl who couldn't get into trouble if she tried.

I found a job at Bellow Books for minimum wage. It was a start, but four shifts a week at $3.25 an hour didn't come close to paying my $350-a-month rent. I lived on bagels, frozen French bread pizzas, pasta, and peanut butter. Once in a while, Carmen and I went out for beers at the Dublin House and bitched about our jobs. I complained about having to work the bag check at the bookstore, pestering customers to hand over their shopping bags lest they stash stolen copies of *Ham on Rye* in them. She complained about working as an assistant to her mother's former acting teacher, Bertha Sykes, who was writing her memoirs. Bertha blamed Len for Betsy's abandonment of her career, and still resented him some twenty-five years later. Carmen toiled in Bertha's plush Park Avenue apartment: making Bertha's tea, nursing Bertha's hangovers, enduring Bertha's insults, and cleaning up after Bertha's miniature Yorkie, Mimi, who left a yellow puddle or a neat pile of dog shit in the entry hall almost every morning.

But I only saw Carmen when she wanted to see me. Her boyfriend, Atti, lived downtown, and she spent most of her free time with him.

I wouldn't hear from her for days, and then suddenly she'd surface, like an orca, to see her parents or Sarita or, if I was lucky, me. She was friendly; she tolerated me; but I didn't seem to interest her anymore.

One night I answered the phone and heard Leonard Dietz's snappy voice. "Hello, darling, can I speak to Carmen for a sec?"

"Carmen?" I stalled for time, caught off guard. Her father had never called me before. I wasn't even sure how he'd gotten my number.

"Yes, you know that delightful daughter of mine? She told us she was spending the evening with you tonight."

I was pretty sure Carmen was downtown with Atti, and quickly realized she was using me as an alibi. "Right! She is. She's with me. She just nipped out to get us some ice cream. She'll be back in a few minutes."

"Ice cream? Okay. Well, ask her to call me when she has a minute, would you?"

"I will. Is it important?"

"Not an emergency, I'd just like to speak with her."

"Okay. I'll tell her."

"'Bye, dear."

She didn't ask me if I minded. She just did it. And I didn't mind. I was flattered. But it reinforced my sense that I had to earn her friendship. She expected to get something out of being friends with me—an alibi for her secret affair, or at the very least a good story.

I wanted to be more than useful. I wanted to be real friends. So I kept an eye out for ways to make myself interesting to her.

That first summer in New York, the bookstore and my tiny room felt like cages; I was stuck inside them watching the rest of the city live wild and free. It seemed to me that money was the key to freedom, but the only legal source of good money—besides a trust fund—was a corporate job. Another cage.

Every other week, when I got my meager paycheck, I performed a little ritual. First, I strolled through Zabar's—past the grumbling old people who waved their deli numbers like protest signs—just to smell the coffee and the cheeses I couldn't afford to buy. On my way out I tapped the nose of a baguette for good luck. Then I went next door to the takeout café, ordered a cup of frozen yogurt—chocolate-vanilla swirl—and perched at the counter by the window to eat it and watch people hurry up and down the gray expanse of Broadway. Except for the obviously insane, most of them looked disappointingly ordinary.

One day in September, I was sitting at Zabar's counter eating my chocolate-vanilla swirl when a man sat down next to me. Not the usual old man mashing pastrami with his gums; not a lady bumping her wheeled shopping basket into my legs; no. A man with an aura of adventure. He wore a white oxford shirt under a rumpled navy blazer and a steel watch on a sun-gilded wrist, and smelled lightly of bay rum. Dark hair fringed over his collar, which was unbuttoned. He turned and faced me: a square chin, a hawkish nose, eyes black as tar pits. I self-consciously spooned more yogurt into my mouth.

"Is it good?" he asked.

I swallowed the cold goop. "What?"

"That stuff you are eating."

The yogurt had a funny metallic taste that was strangely addictive. "Yeah, it's pretty good."

"I've never tried frozen yogurt before." He sipped espresso from a miniature white cup, his elbow resting on a folded-up copy of the *Times*.

"Never?"

"Never." He had a slight accent, vaguely European . . . not English or Irish. Continental. "I prefer a chocolate croissant. May I get you one?" He rose to his feet. "I'd like to. Please."

"Oh, no, no thanks." I tapped my plastic spoon on my Styrofoam cup. "I couldn't eat a chocolate croissant now."

"What about a coffee then? I'll buy you an espresso."

"Well . . ." I liked espresso, but it was so expensive.

"Wait here. I'll be quick."

He went to the counter. His khaki pants were cinched by an artfully beat-up leather belt that looked as if it had been around the world. His shoes were expensive loafers that needed a shine. How old was he? I couldn't guess. Everyone between twenty-eight and fifty looked basically the same to me. He was at least thirty. Maybe older than that. Forty?

He returned and placed a tiny cup before me. "Voilà."

"Thank you. That was very nice of you." I reached for a packet of sugar.

"You are very welcome." He watched me sip.

"Mm. Good." I nodded self-consciously. Since he had so generously bought me this extravagant coffee, I felt I had to make a show of enjoying it.

"What's your name?"

"Phoebe."

He waited.

"Hayes."

"Phoebe Hayes, would you like to have dinner with me sometime?"

My mouth dried up. "Dinner?"

"Yes, that's all. Just dinner. Or a drink, how about that?"

"Well, um, shouldn't I know your name first?"

"I'm sorry! It's Ivan. Forgive me. I just . . ." He trailed off, shaking his head at himself as if my charm had overwhelmed his manners. "What do you do, Phoebe? Are you a student?"

"No, I graduated last May. I work at the bookstore, right there on the corner." I nodded toward the other end of the block. "Bellow Books."

"A good bookstore. I go there often."

"You do?" I hadn't seen him. "What about you?"

"I'm a physician." He glanced at his watch. "In fact, I should be going. I have an appointment." He stood and reached into his jacket pocket. "Will you call me?" He gave me a card.

IVAN BERGEN, MD

INTERNAL MEDICINE, INFECTIOUS DISEASE

There was an address on West Fifty-Sixth Street and a phone number, and at the bottom:

MÉDECINS SANS FRONTIÈRES

A doctor, like my father. Only Dad didn't dress with this insouciant elegance. And on a workday he would have carried his stethoscope with him somewhere—around his neck, or in his jacket pocket.

But I wasn't thinking about my father then, because he was still alive.

"Call me later this afternoon. If you don't, I'll come back here looking for you." Ivan grinned to show that he didn't mean to sound threatening. He just wanted to see me very badly.

"All right."

He left, his jacket flapping like a cape, and hailed a taxi. I stared out the window, long after the taxi had disappeared, with the strong feeling that my life had just changed. I couldn't wait to call Carmen and tell her all about it.

When she finally called me back, very late that night, she asked me what I planned to wear on my date with this exciting older man.

"I don't know," I wailed. "I don't have anything decent."

"I'll come over tomorrow and help you figure it out."

Just like that, I became interesting to her.

Then, on December first, my sister, Laurel, called to tell me that Dad was sick.

He'd been sick for several months, but none of us knew it. Over the summer my mother had mentioned that he was run-down and working too hard, but when I asked him about it he said, "Nothing a little exercise won't cure." He used to say that to me when I complained of feeling tired: "A little exercise will pep you up." I moved to New York just before he got sick, so I didn't witness the shadows deepening under his eyes, the pallor of his skin, the way his cheekbones sharpened.

"He has AML," Laurel told me over the phone. She was premed and liked to show off this link between her and Dad, the jargon they shared.

"What's that?"

"Leukemia. The worst kind."

He'd ignored his own symptoms for four months: classic doctor behavior. Now it was too late. The disease had progressed beyond treatment. "There's not much you can do for it anyway. I mean, even if he'd had chemo and all that . . ." Laurel tried to steady her voice as a doctor would, factual and unemotional, but I caught the quaver in it and understood what she didn't want to say: he was going to die, and soon.

I took the first train to Baltimore. It was strange that Mom hadn't called me herself, but when I got home I saw why: her tongue was so swollen she couldn't speak. She couldn't even close her mouth. It had happened at the doctor's office, when the oncologist presented Dad's grim prognosis. She had a psychosomatic reaction. She was embarrassed about it and had shut herself in her room.

Laurel and I drove to the hospital to see Dad. When I kissed him his breath smelled sharply of ammonia, and the sight of his ashen, bony face shocked me. How could he not have known he was sick? How did no one notice?

But he was still Dad. "Phoebe!" He gripped my arm as I leaned down to kiss his papery cheek. "Now that you're here we can celebrate at last."

He meant the Orioles' recent victory over the Phillies in the World Series. I'd watched it at the Dublin House with Carmen, who'd talked through the whole game and had barely paid attention. Until I'd left for college, I'd watched the Orioles games and every World Series with Dad. We loved the O's, they were our home team, but Dad was a Yankees fan at heart. Phil Rizzuto—small and scrappy, superstitious, bug-phobic, a bunter and a great shortstop—was his favorite player. After he retired, "the Scooter," as he was known, became a radio and TV announcer for the Yankees, famous for spouting non sequiturs and jokes and stories about his golfing buddies and his beloved wife, Cora. Dad considered him a kind of accidental Zen philosopher, à la Yogi Berra. He listened to the Scooter call the Yankees games whenever he managed to tune into the New York station on the radio, and loved quoting Scooter classics like "That ball is out of here! No, it's not. Yes, it is. No, it's not. What happened?"

In August 1979, a few weeks before I left for college, the Yankees catcher Thurman Munson was killed in a plane crash. The team played the Orioles in New York the next night, and they held a solemn tribute to Munson before the game. I sat with Dad in the den, watching on TV as the Scooter came onto the field to say a favorite prayer for his friend Thurman.

Angel of God, Thurman's guardian dear,
To whom his love commits him here there or everywhere,
Ever this night and day be at his side,
To light and guard, to rule and guide.

I thought it was corny, but when I saw the tears well up in Dad's eyes, I started crying too.

"It's just something to keep you really from going bananas," the Scooter said. *"Because if you let this, if you keep thinking about what happened, and you can't understand it, that's what really drives you to despair."*

Now, in the hospital, I tried to be cheerful. "Hey there, Telly Savalas," I said. Dad had lost a lot of hair, but this was more of an inside joke. One of our favorite Scooter moments was when he spotted Telly Savalas in the stands at Yankee Stadium and complained of the blinding glare coming off Telly's bald head.

Dad came back with a Scooter line, as I knew he would. *" 'But that's the thing lately. They say being bald is very sexy.' "*

My cheerful mask crumbled, but he kept his up. He asked me if I'd heard any good music in New York, and joked about poor Mom and her tongue. "You know your mother; she always overreacts. Remember how she used to break out in hives if you were late coming home from school?"

Laurel and I tried to stop crying but we couldn't. When we were upset as little girls, Dad used to say, "Let's go to the window and see if we see anyone as unhappy as we are." And he would lead us to the window, where we'd watch people pass by in the street until we cheered up.

Now, in the hospital room, he said it again. He couldn't get out of bed, but Laurel and I went to the window and looked down at St. Paul Street. "Tell me what you see," Dad said.

"An old man hunched over with holes in his pants," Laurel said.

"A young woman in a white doctor coat walking very fast," I said.

"A woman yelling at a toddler who's not walking fast enough," Laurel said.

It didn't seem like anybody was happy. But I couldn't tell if they were as unhappy as we were.

We stayed with him until visiting hours ended, then brought home a pizza to eat with Mom. She refused to come out of her room. Laurel and I went to my room and cried until we were dehydrated. No one ate the pizza.

Mom's tongue shrank back to normal by morning. The rest of the week was a hospital blur. Dad had developed pneumonia in one of his lungs. "Get my stethoscope, Phoebe," he said. "I'll show you how you can tell which lung is infected."

His stethoscope was rolled up in the pocket of his sport coat, which hung on the back of the door of his room.

"Put it on."

I put the earpieces in my ears and he guided the chest piece to his right side. "Now listen." He whispered, "One, two, three . . . One, two, three . . . Do you hear anything?"

"No."

"Try the left side."

I moved the chest piece to the left. Once again he murmured, "One, two, three . . . One, two, three . . ." a breathy waltz. This time I heard the whispers through the stethoscope.

"That's the infected side," he said. "The consolidation in my lung carries the vibration of my voice. In a clear, normal lung, there's no infected gunk to vibrate, so you can't hear the whisper."

Laurel walked in, back from the cafeteria with three cups of tea. "Laurel already knows all this, don't you, Laurel."

"Egophony when auscultating the lungs," she recited.

"They don't teach that in med school anymore," Dad said. "Hardly ever."

After about an hour Dad weakened, so we went home to let him rest. As I was leaving his bedside, Dad said, *"'Son of a gun, I thought that ball was out of here.'"*

I finished the quip. *"'Why don't I just shut up?'"*

He died a few days later. We had a funeral. Lots of people came. At the cemetery, a strange feeling overwhelmed me, like an allergic reaction: my throat closed, my vision bleached out, my lungs failed to draw air, my brain's circuits stopped firing. My immune system was fighting off an infection of grief.

For a whole day I couldn't remember that Dad was dead. It was as if accepting his death would kill me, too. I lost my mind; I can admit it. If you don't go at least a little crazy when your favorite person dies, something is wrong with you.

But my reaction scared Mom. She wanted me to go to the hospital and stay there for a long time.

I couldn't do that. I had to get back to New York. I had reasons. A week after the funeral I started packing my things.

"What do you think you're doing?" Mom took the clothes out of my suitcase and put them back in my dresser. "You can't leave now."

"Why not?"

She pressed my folded nightgown to her chest. "You're not strong enough."

I was an adult, twenty-two years old, capable of taking care of myself. I'd already proven that by living on my own for five months in New York. I didn't need her to watch me.

"You mean *you're* not strong enough."

"Don't pull that trick, Phoebe. Making your problems about me."

"I'm perfectly fine and there's no reason for me to stay here. I've got things to do in New York."

It was practically the middle of December, and I was desperate to get back in time for New Year's Eve. I needed money—a lot of money. It wasn't just the high cost of living in New York, though that was a struggle. Things had gone sour with Ivan, and he'd given me a thousand dollars when I was in a jam. I had not been in a position to turn down the money, but I hated owing Ivan anything. I carried the debt in my body—a heaviness in the pit of my belly, as if I'd swallowed a paperweight. I couldn't get rid of that heavy feeling.

That was why I had to go back. I had a two-part plan: First, earn a thousand dollars. Second, burst into Ivan's office and throw the money in his face. Then maybe I'd feel light again.

I was broke—beyond broke—but I had a miraculous job waiting

for me: telling fortunes at a party at Plutonium, a downtown nightclub. *The* downtown nightclub. Three hundred bucks for one night's work. All I needed was a few more gigs like that and voilà, a thousand dollars. Downtown New York was full of buried treasure, and I was going on a hunt.

Mom rubbed her tired eyes. "Don't run away like this. Your father just died. You're fragile. You need time."

"I'm not running away. I'm returning to my real life."

She closed my suitcase and put it back in the closet. "I'm sorry, Phoebe. But after what happened at the funeral . . . You're staying here."

I could have yelled and kicked and screamed, but I knew that wouldn't sway her. The problem was, without her help I couldn't really go back. When Dad had gotten sick, I'd left my job at Bellow Books without giving notice. It didn't pay enough to live on anyway. I was three months behind on my rent, and Robin was threatening to kick me out if I didn't pay up immediately. I had nothing to pay her with, unless I asked my mother for a loan, which she'd never give me now. The fact that I needed her help paying the rent only strengthened her case.

"I'll stay until Christmas," I conceded, irrationally hoping that I'd find a huge chunk of cash in my stocking.

"I want to keep an eye on you for a few months at least. Till you're stronger. New York isn't going anywhere."

A few months! No.

New York by New Year's Eve. I refused to let this chance slip away. My life—by which I meant the life I wanted, a life I considered worth living—depended on it.

The house was full of sympathy flowers, ugly pastel arrangements that gradually withered and browned. No one had the heart or energy to throw them away, so I amused myself by slowly picking them apart, one by one, petal by petal, carpeting the floor with their crisp remains. In my room, I practiced telling fortunes using my special divination method: movie ticket stubs. I'd saved the ticket stubs from every movie I'd ever seen, keeping them in a shoebox decorated with stars and moons and mystical eyes. Throughout my childhood, whenever I had a question—*Does Darryl Morgan like me? Is Winnie talking about me behind my back? Will I get into Yale? Have I met the person I will marry yet?*—I asked the box. I shook it, reached inside, and picked out a ticket stub. The name of the movie on the stub gave me my answer.

Some answers required interpretation, of course. When I asked if Darryl Morgan (the object of a torturous, unrequited high school crush) liked me, I pulled *All the President's Men*. Darryl was friends with Lisa Buñuel, the student-body president. I decided that meant yes.

In blue moods, I asked the box questions like, "What is the purpose of my life?" I'd ask the same question over and over, pulling out stubs and tossing them back until I got an answer that made sense. *Ode to Billy Joe. Car Wash. The Aristocats.* I suppose if you tried hard enough—if you squinted—you could come up with a philosophy of life from those titles, but I never managed it. Still, I believed in the magic shoebox. It was my personal *I Ching*, my tea leaves, my tarot deck.

"Does Ivan think about me?" I asked the box.

Zelig.

Maybe if I rephrased the question. "Did he ever care about me?"

Stardust Memories. Two Woody Allens in a row.

I occupied myself this way, mutilating flowers and telling imaginary fortunes, for two miserable weeks. Christmas came and no cash appeared in my stocking, only a candy cane, barrettes, and lip gloss. Just when I'd been ready to leave one cage, I'd landed in another.

But there was one more package under the tree, a mysterious square box wrapped in brown paper, addressed to me.

"What's this?"

"It came in the mail yesterday," Mom said. "I forgot to give it to you, so I put it under the tree."

I opened the box. Inside, nestled in tissue paper, was a blue silk turban. The card said, *I saw this and thought:* Phoebe needs this turban. *For your fortune-teller costume. See you on New Year's Eve. Love, C.*

I put on the turban and checked my reflection in the mirror. With all my hair covered, my pale face had a disembodied, ghostly quality. I looked strange and mysterious. Unfamiliar. I liked it.

I pulled the phone into my room and called Carmen to thank her. I half expected her not to be home—she so rarely was—but Sarita answered and put her on.

"Hey," she said. "When are you getting your ass back up here?"

"If my mother has her way, never."

"Is she keeping you chained to your bed? She can't hold you prisoner. And what about Plutonium? Partying with famous people on New Year's Eve! You can't miss that. It's once in a lifetime."

"I've got no place to live. Robin has already rented my room to some girl from Connecticut." She'd called a few days earlier to let me know that she was going to pile my stuff on the sidewalk if I didn't come pick it up soon.

"I always said that Robin was a bitch."

"Yeah. Anyway . . ." I waited for Carmen to invite me to stay with her and Sarita. They didn't have much space, but I could sleep on the couch.

She was quiet.

"Thanks for the turban! That's why I called."

"Do you like it?"

"I love it. I'm wearing it right now."

"Good. It was worth it then."

"What was worth it?"

"All the trouble I'm in."

"What trouble?"

She was quiet again.

"Carmen?"

"I stole the turban. From Bertha."

"You stole it?" I pulled the turban off as if it might burst into flames on my head.

"She has a closet full of them. I didn't think she'd miss it."

"But . . . she *did* miss it?"

"She fired me."

"I thought that was impossible." Bertha adored Betsy Dietz. Carmen had always assumed that Bertha wouldn't want to upset Betsy by firing her daughter, even if her daughter's attitude was on the slack side.

"Apparently it's possible."

"Shit. Well, you hated that job anyway."

"It gets worse. Bertha told Mom that she'd fired me. For stealing! It sounds so harsh. And of course Mom squealed to Dad. I tried to explain I was only borrowing the turban for a friend, but they won't listen to me. Dad says he can't trust me anymore." She sighed. "So now they're saying I have to go back to the Humph in January, first thing."

"What?" She'd told me a little about her stint in the Humphrey-Worth Center, a psychiatric hospital in Westchester County. She'd pleaded with her parents to send her to Silver Hill instead because Edie Sedgwick had done time there in 1962, but they were in no mood to indulge her whims.

"I know. I'm not even using! I have nothing to rehab myself *for*. It's ridiculous. But Dad doesn't believe me. Everybody's overreacting."

Whenever Carmen did anything wrong, made any slight miscalculation or lapse in judgment, her parents accused her of falling back under Atti's spell and shooting up again. She *was* seeing Atti; secretly, behind their backs, of course. And lying about it, saying she was with me. But she wasn't using heroin anymore.

"Carmen. I love the turban but it wasn't worth it."

"Don't say that. It's for the party!"

"What are you going to do?"

"I was thinking," she said. "I need to get out of here. And *you* need to get out of *there*. . . ."

"Wherever you go, I want to go with you."

"We could hide out in the East Village, at Atti's. We'll just leave it all behind. No one will find us there unless we want to be found. It's the Land of the Lost."

Lost. I wanted to get lost.

"Are you in?"

"I'm in."

We planned it together. I'd sneak out late that night and catch the train to New York. Carmen would meet me at Penn Station and take me downtown to Atti's. We'd go to Plutonium on New Year's Eve; I'd tell fortunes and get the money I'd been promised. We were sure our Fates awaited us at the party, ready to change the course of our lives.

"The train gets in at five a.m.," I said.

"I'll be there."

Late that night, after Mom and Laurel had gone to bed, I scribbled a note: *I'm sorry, but I had to go back to New York. Don't worry about me, I'll be fine. PROMISE. I'll call you soon. Love, Phoebe.*

I slipped out of the house with one suitcase, my box of movie ticket stubs, the turban, and the baseball bat signed by Phil Rizzuto that Dad left me in his will. Then I hurried through the night to catch the train to New York. This time, I was going underground, with Carmen as my guide.

AN APARTMENT

We arrived at Astor Place by subway, two fugitives, and walked through the cold to Atti's. It was dawn. Colored Christmas lights blinked quietly in tenement windows while the neighborhood slept it off. In the southwest corner of Tompkins Square Park a rooster perched on the head of a statue, silhouetted against the whitening sky. I had been up all night on the train from Baltimore.

Atti lived on Seventh and C. His apartment door stood open, but he wasn't home. We crashed on the mattress, still bundled in our coats and hats, and slept until three in the afternoon, when Carmen rolled over and wrapped her arms around my waist, murmuring, "Atti . . ."

"It's me." I brushed her hair out of her face and she hugged me tighter, then nipped my ear with her teeth. She sat up and looked around. Still no Atti.

I tried to see Atti's apartment as charmingly bohemian, but it was difficult. One room, no heat, no hot water, electricity siphoned from the light fixture in the hall. Two gated windows overlooking a trash-strewn vacant lot and beyond that, the neon beacon of a liquor store sign. He'd furnished it with junk he'd found on the curb: a stained and sheetless mattress piled with blankets; a child's wooden table and chair; a plastic lamp shaped like a pair of lips; a paint-by-numbers picture of a huge-eyed girl in capri pants putting a record on a turntable. A combat boot with a hole in the sole lay next to a pair of worn blue Keds. Candy wrappers, beer bottles, and fast food containers littered the floor, everything coated with a film of grime except the two guitars, one acoustic and one electric, propped in a corner against a beat-up Marshall amp.

"Zowie, it stinks in here." Carmen lifted the window in spite of the cold. An open can of pineapple chunks rotted on the sill. She touched the radiator and shivered. "Let's get out of here."

We headed to Avenue A, snatching up a copy of the *East Village Underground* on the way. Flyers clung to walls and lampposts on every block, advertising bands and stoop sales and guitar lessons and the fact that a girl named Susannah Byers, who gazed at us from her high school yearbook picture with feathered hair like Farrah Fawcett's, was missing.

Inside Odessa it was so warm the front window dripped with steam. We settled in a booth and ordered coffee and pierogies and eggs; then we opened the paper and scanned the classifieds, circling promising jobs and apartments. By the time we returned to Atti's it was dark out and he was home. He greeted me with a hug and kissed Carmen on her forehead, each cheek, her chin, and then her mouth, a sign of the cross. Then he shut the window and slid his bony body under the pile of blankets. He was so thin I thought of a character from one of my favorite children's books: Flat Stanley, who was flattened like a sheet of cookie dough by a falling bulletin board. Flat Stanley could slide under locked doors and visit faraway friends by being folded up and mailed in an envelope. He could pretend to be a painting on a museum wall. He was two-dimensional.

"Atti, what happened to the heat?" Carmen asked.

He shrugged. "I don't know, the water went off? It's okay. My downstairs neighbor has an electric heater. He lets me crash on his floor." Carmen crossed her arms and waited to hear more. "His name is Dean. He's got a hot plate too. He gives me hot soup."

"In exchange for what?"

"Carmen, stop it. Do you want to stay here or don't you?"

The door opened and a young man poked his head into the room. "Hey Atti—you got company? I thought I heard voices."

"You must be Dean," Carmen said.

"In the flesharooni." Dean sat on Atti's floor, scratching dirt off his knee through a hole in his pants.

"Atti, does he have to be here?"

"What's wrong with him? Dean's cool."

To show us how cool he was, Dean stretched his mouth wide with his fingers and said, "Eeeeeeeeeeeeee."

"You got anything to eat?" Atti asked.

"No," Dean said. "But I'm itchin' for some yardbird."

"What's yardbird?" I asked.

"Chickenarooni."

"Dean thinks he's Jack Kerouac," Atti said.

"Naw, man. Charlie Parker. He lived around the corner from here, you know."

"Everybody knows that," Carmen said.

"I didn't," I said.

Dean went out to the Dominican place on the corner and brought back Styrofoam containers of chicken and rice and plantains and a six of Bud. We ate the chickenarooni and drank the beerarooni sitting on the floorarooni, listening to *Berlin* on Atti's boom boxarooni.

"Whaddya say, Atti? Hit the park? Find the Oz-Man?"

"Yeah."

"He's got that great stuff, what's it called," Dean said. "Pomegranate Seed? Blows your hair off your scalp. Girls coming with?"

It was almost midnight, and freezing out. "We're going to sleep," Carmen said.

"Be back soon." Atti kissed Carmen. The guys went out to score, leaving me and Carmen to huddle together on the bed, listening to bottles and car windows shatter outside, angry and lovesick drunks bellowing in the street, and mice skittering in the walls. *I'm free,* I thought happily. *I'm with Carmen and I'm free.*

The apartment was a meat locker, but we didn't go to Dean's place with the heater. "I don't trust him," Carmen said. "That phony beatnik talk, the way he smiles wide with his mouth while his eyes shift around. I feel safer here."

"The door doesn't lock." I played with the flimsy hook-and-eye latch that barely kept Atti's door closed. "Not in any meaningful way."

"If someone really wants to come in, a lock won't keep them out." She curled up and pulled the covers to her chin. "They won't be back." Not before morning, she meant. We had the place to ourselves and could sleep in peace, or try to, until they stumbled home and collapsed.

In the morning, I woke from a fitful sleep, cold, dirty, and unrefreshed. There was no sign of Atti.

"He's a vampire," Carmen said. "You'll see him at night." She sat up and rubbed her eyes. "I'm sorry about this place, Phoebe. I haven't been here in a while. I didn't realize how bad things had gotten." She kicked the *Underground* with the toe of her sock. "Do you want to stay here?"

"Well . . . do you?"

She shook her head. "We'll get some breakfast and then go chase down these apartment leads."

I followed her downstairs. She opened Dean's door without knocking. He was asleep in his bed, and Atti was passed out in the dry bathtub, wearing his jeans and no shirt. His skin was gray and drops of blood seeped out of one nostril. "Is he okay?" I asked.

Carmen called his name and rubbed his bony sternum with her knuckles.

"Ow." He stirred, opened his eyes, grunted, and curled into a fetal position.

"Why did you do that?" I asked her. "Why did you rub your knuckles on his chest?"

"Because it hurts. Sometimes a little shake isn't enough to wake him up. It hurts but it doesn't cause any damage, you know what I mean?"

She checked his pupils, his fingernails, his tongue and lips. She pressed two fingers to the pulse point on his wrist, watching his chest rise and fall and listening to his slow, even breath. "He's just nodding." She smoothed his hair, then pulled a towel off a rack over the tub and covered him with it.

We went to Odessa again and gorged on blintzes and coffee. I studied the listings Carmen had circled. Most of them were sublets—sometimes you could nab one without paying a deposit or signing a lease. "We have to find a place soon," Carmen said. "Before we get the squat stink on us. How much money do you have?"

"About seventy-five dollars."

"Total?" Carmen frowned.

"I'll be getting three hundred dollars on New Year's Eve—"

"Yeah, but we need money now. My grandmother sent me some Christmas money. We can use that for the first month."

We looked at six apartments in the neighborhood. The first, most promising one was already taken. The second had no windows and a hole in the ceiling, through which we could see the upstairs neighbor's rug. The third was also already rented, but the landlord had another apartment available for three times what we could afford. The fourth came with a roommate not mentioned in the ad, a leering old man in his seventies. At the fifth apartment we found a dead rat in the closet, along with a nest of screaming rat babies.

To get to the last place on the list, a basement apartment on Tenth Street, we crossed through the park. I'd seen a little of the neighborhood as we tramped through the cold: Gem Spa, St. Mark's in-the-Bowery, Love Saves the Day. We drooled over cannolis and cakes like glazed jewels in the window of De Robertis bakery. We stopped at Café Orlin for cappuccinos to warm us up. Now, the sunlight fading, we entered the park near the statue of Samuel Sullivan Cox, "The Letter Carrier's Friend." Just beyond the statue some homeless people and hippies had set up camp. A guy with dirty brown dreads beat a bongo and sang out, *"Hey girls come here, hey girls come here, hey girls you got a dollar for me? Come play the bongos, a dollar a bongo. . . ."*

"Keep walking." Carmen led me north past a small stone pavilion with a waterless drinking fountain. On top stood a statue of a goddess offering us a pitcher and a cup, surrounded by the words CHARITY - TEMPERANCE - FAITH - HOPE. People slept on benches or huddled together smoking. We passed another fountain, a lion's head suspended over an ice-filled basin. Above him, carved in relief on a marble slab, a boy and a girl stared off into a leafy paradise, looking like an illustration from an art deco children's book.

"THEY WERE
EARTH'S
PUREST
CHILDREN—
YOUNG AND
FAIR"

A plaque on one side explained:

IN MEMORY OF
THOSE WHO LOST
THEIR LIVES IN THE DISASTER TO
THE STEAMER GENERAL SLOCUM
JUNE XV
MCMIV

And on the other:

DEDICATED
BY
THE SYMPATHY SOCIETY
OF GERMAN LADIES
THE YEAR OF OUR LORD
MCMVI

I stopped to rub the dress of the marble girl. "It's getting dark," Carmen said. "Come on."

The last apartment was perfect, except that a couple of nice girls like us had just rented it that morning.

Back at Atti's, the boys were up, drinking coffee, eating Froot Loops out of the box, and smoking a joint. "Chicks missed a great time last night," Dean said. "Gasper stole a bottle of Jack Daniel's right off the bar at the Blue & Gold. Ukrainian fuck who owns the place tried to snatch it back, Gasper bashes him on the head with it. Then Gasper starts tearing the place up, throwing chairs, throwing glasses—"

"One of the glasses hit an Angel on the shoulder—"

"Yeah, that was unfortunate. There were about five Angels in the bar and they started brawling."

"I'm so sorry we missed it," Carmen said.

"We sneaked out the back," Atti said.

"Yeah, we ran over to the Verk and watched from the window. Took four cops to pin Gasper down. Hells Angels ran off like rats to their hidey hole. Cops don't dare chase them back to Third Street. The Angels is armed to their rotten gold teeth."

Carmen explained that Gasper was an English punk friend of theirs.

"Sadly, Oswald got caught in the sweeparooni," Dean added.

Carmen told me that Oswald was the most important man in their lives: their dealer.

"Gasper just came by and said they sprung him this morning, but Oz is still locked up." Atti shook his head. "That could be it for old Oz."

"He's got a record as long as John Holmes's dick." Dean crossed himself.

For dinner, we devoured a pizza and washed it down with beer. It started raining, freezing rain that tapped on the windows with tiny icy claws. Atti didn't want to go out. By then the cold had sunk into our bones, so we went downstairs to bask in the glow of Dean's electric heater. He played a Joy Division tape while we passed around a bottle of vodka. Atti sat with his knees drawn up, shivering under a blanket. Carmen felt his forehead. "I think you have a fever."

"No, I don't."

"Phoebe, come here. Does he have a fever?"

His forehead felt damp and hot. "I think so."

"I don't. Leave me alone."

"You girls gonna get me into Plutonium on New Year's?" Dean said.

"I don't think we can." Carmen shot me a look of warning.

"Eh, you'll get me in. After all I'm doing for you, letting you stay with me for free, a roof over your heads on a cold rainy night—"

"We're staying with Atti, not you," Carmen said.

"—stuffing your hungry little faces with the finest pizza the East Village has to offer—"

"Carmen bought the pizza," I said.

"I supplied the vodka, right? And the tunes? And we snagged a few vikes off Oswald before the five-0 set him on a new life path." He shook a small pill bottle at me. "Phoebe? Vicodin? Takes the edge off."

I looked to Carmen for guidance. She shrugged and took a Vicodin, so I took one too, washing it down with vodka. Soon I felt loose and warm, sleepy but not tired. Carmen and I danced and sang, *"Love will tear us apart again."* Dean scratched his face and watched us. Atti, legs jiggling, focused on an invisible movie projected on the wall. Carmen wanted something bouncier and put on the B-52s, singing along, *"I'll give you fish, I'll give you candy."* Dean and I ran through the rain to the liquor store for another bottle of vodka, pointing out the cheapest brand to the clerk behind the bulletproof plexiglass. Back at Dean's, Carmen was dancing alone to Tom Tom Club. Atti had gone upstairs to his place, she said; we'd go up soon too.

Hours later I woke in the dark, curled up against the cold. A girl outside was screaming, *"BILLY! BILLY! Fuck you, Billy, I'm coming to get you . . . BILLY! . . ."*

I tried to figure out where I was. What was I doing in this frigid room, on this thin mattress? I rolled over onto Carmen's arm, and I remembered: *Dad died.* I quickly shooed that thought away. We were here for Plutonium. The New Year's Eve party. The money to throw in Ivan's face. Carmen and I were going to reinvent ourselves.

Some time went by, I don't know how much, but I woke again to a gray dawn. I got up to pee, stumbling into the bathroom. Atti was crouched on the floor, vomiting into the tub.

"Oh, shit." I ran back to the mattress and jumped under the covers as if I'd seen a monster. Carmen woke up.

"What? What happened?"

Retching sounds answered her from the bathroom. "Fuck." She sat up and pulled on her favorite army jacket, the one with MITCH stitched over the pocket in pink. Then she hurried to help Atti. From my hiding place under the blanket I heard him throwing up and Carmen saying, *"Shhh . . . sshhhh . . ."*

I peeked out from under the covers, tilting my head upside down to look through the window. In the sky, low clouds refracted the lights of the city, turning everything sulfur-orange.

"Shhh," Carmen murmured. *"It's okay. You'll feel better soon. . . ."*

I didn't think Atti would feel better soon. I didn't know much about junkies, but I knew a sick person when I saw one.

I tiptoed back to the bathroom. She'd rolled him over to keep him from choking on the vomit. She cleaned him up, wiping his face with a washcloth, and then went through her checklist of pupils, breath, lips, tongue, pulse.

I hated to see sickness, but I watched because it was her, because I wanted to know about everything she did. Because she was keeping him from dying, and I couldn't bear another death.

Eventually, we went back to sleep, and I slept until late morning. Carmen snored lightly beside me. I had a headache and longed for a bath, but Atti was passed out on the bathroom floor, and there wasn't any hot water anyway. I bundled up and walked to Ray's Candy for some coffees to go. The *Underground* came out every Wednesday, the latest edition waiting in a fresh stack just inside the door. I picked one up. I didn't want to stay at Atti's another night.

Carmen was just stirring when I returned. I gave her a coffee and opened the paper to the classifieds. "Maybe there's something new this week."

She sipped her coffee and watched me scanning the "For Rent" ads, circling ones that sounded good but that I knew we couldn't afford. "Wait a minute," she said. If Oswald was in as much trouble as Dean thought, he'd be going to prison for a long time. And if he was in prison . . . what would happen to his apartment?

Dean confirmed that Oswald had been denied bail and was almost certain to be convicted on drug charges and who knew what else and given a long sentence, considering he'd been caught holding and this was his fifth arrest. He had a pretty sweet place, too, on A between Ninth and Tenth. "Park view," Dean said. "Lap o' luxury." The landlord was an old Polish lady who'd probably be thrilled to rent Oswald's place out from under him to a couple of decent girls.

"Hurry over there," Dean said. "Before some parasite gets the same idea."

Mrs. Lisiewicz scrutinized us in her cabbage-reeking hallway. "You're friends of Oswald?"

"No," Carmen assured her. "We don't know him. We've never met him. We just heard his apartment might be available, from friends."

"What friends?"

I let Carmen do the talking. She hesitated, and I could tell she didn't think the name Attila Pilkvist would impress Mrs. Lisiewicz, so she said, "Do you know Dean Rutherford?"

"I don't think so."

"Oh. Well, he's a lawyer, he's the one who put Oswald in jail! He told us about the apartment."

Mrs. Lisiewicz squinted. "A lawyer?"

"Not the kind who sues landlords," Carmen said. "He puts hooligans in jail. And criminals. He takes hooligans and criminals off the streets. That's all he does."

"He hates hooligans," I said.

"All right." She disappeared into her apartment, which was on the first floor, and returned with a ring of keys. "Let's go look."

Mrs. Lisiewicz unlocked the door to a third-floor apartment and two Siamese cats flung themselves at her feet. She soothed them in Polish, going to the cupboard for a can of food. "You like cats?"

"Sure," I said.

"I feed them for Oswald while he's away. They're yours now."

"You mean we can have the apartment?"

"If you want it. Four fifty a month."

The kitchen opened onto a living room with windows facing Avenue A and the park. Next to the kitchen sink, the bathtub was covered with a board that doubled as a countertop. There was a toilet in a nook the size of a closet, and a bedroom in the back, overlooking a weedy cement yard. Someone must have come to take most of Oswald's stuff, because there wasn't much in there besides the furniture: couch, kitchen table and chairs, a double bed, a dresser, and a small black-and-white TV. The dresser was empty except for the bottom drawer, which held a stash of neatly paired men's gym socks. The kitchen cabinets contained glasses, cups, mismatched dishes, cans of cat food, a bag of rice, and a box of sugar. In the fridge: a rotten lime, a can of Café Bustelo, and a bottle of Gatorade.

I loved it. Carmen was a genius. She knew how to navigate this world. Thanks to her I'd gotten the job at Plutonium, and now an apartment. I didn't see how I'd survive without her.

The cats were devouring their food from a dish on the floor. "What are their names?" I asked.

"Julio and Diego."

I crouched and traced a finger along the charcoal line of Diego's spine. He cast a sidelong glance at me but kept eating.

Carmen gestured to me and we conferred in the bedroom. We agreed we'd never find a cheaper place that was livable, and it seemed pretty safe as long as Oswald didn't get out of jail anytime soon. We told Mrs. L that we'd take it. Carmen gave her a hundred-dollar deposit and she gave us the keys. We could move in immediately.

I had a place to live. I now felt secure enough to call my mother.

"Mom?"

"Honey! Where are you?"

"I just called to tell you I'm fine—"

“Where are you???”

“I’m at a pay phone—”

“WHERE EXACTLY ARE YOU RIGHT NOW?”

“Everything is okay. I swear. I just wanted to tell you not to worry.”

“Phoebe, if you don’t tell me where you are this minute—”

If she knew where I was, it would only upset her, I reasoned. The crime, the drugs . . . I kept her in the dark for her own good.

“Say hi to Laurel for me. I have a nice place to stay and I’m perfectly fine.”

“PHOEBE!”

“Please don’t worry.”

“PHOEBE!”

“Happy New Year! Love you!” *Click.*

I hung up and thought, *My new life begins now.*

3

THE TALE OF ATTILA AND CALEDONIA

I first noticed Carmen one night at the Grad Center Bar. I was drinking beer while my roommate, Tara, played *Space Invaders*. Tara was obsessed with *Space Invaders*. It was freshman year, September 1979, first week of classes, and Tara and I knew hardly anyone besides each other.

A girl walked in, all energy—thick auburn hair cut in a blunt wedge around a triangular face, and knowing, playful gray eyes—trailing an entourage. She must have brought her entire West Quad floor with her. At the sight of her I sat up and sucked in my breath with a whoosh, tiny but noticeable.

"Do you know her?" Tara asked.

I didn't—at least I didn't think so—and yet I had the feeling of recognizing someone. I felt that I knew her, though that wasn't possible. She shouted, "Wine for all my friends!" and started ordering people to push the little tables together to make one big one. The next thing I knew, the bartender set down two glasses of wine in front of me and Tara. "I guess we're her friends," Tara said.

We weren't—not yet. But I wanted to be.

There were plenty of normal suburban kids hauling books around the Brown campus, but I was too blinded by the glamorous ones to notice them. The daughter of a famous jazz singer buzzed around College Hill in a red Porsche convertible. The niece of the deposed shah of Iran wanted to be a filmmaker. The son of a senator was dating the daughter of a governor. The daughter of a famous writer played guitar in a punk band.

The biggest distraction was John F. Kennedy Jr., son of Jackie O. and a lionized dead president, famous child mourner, and, as Carmen would say, *Zowie*. He was so hot, looking at him burned out the retinas of the entire freshman class. From the first week of school, his presence set a tone of gossipy hysteria. Who would be his friends? Who would he go out with? What would it mean to date him? How would it change your life? Just a few dates could give you a glimpse of a rarefied world. If you were impossibly lucky, you—yes *you*, intense semiotics geek; *you*, self-serious modern dancer; *you*, humorless econ major; or even *you*, premed grind—could become American royalty.

He was in my psych class, but I was too shy to talk to him. Once he flashed me a vacant, unseeing smile as we trudged out of a lecture hall, but that was it. He didn't need new friends; he already had plenty among the preppy hordes matriculating from Andover and St. Paul's.

There was a girl in my dorm named Lacey Risch, a Manhattanite who spent warm afternoons skateboarding around the quad in tiny shorts. She was leggy and dark and thin as a model, her wavy hair striped with gold highlights. John asked her out the first week of school, and she said no.

Rumors flew. People said that a movie star had fallen in love with her over the summer, and she turned him down too. What was going on behind that chiseled, unsmiling face of hers? Did she have something against John-John? Did she hate attention? Was she a lesbian? If she wouldn't go out with him, who *would* she go out with?

No one knew. Lacey Risch was very mysterious. I concluded that growing up in New York had made her so blasé that no one impressed her.

* * *

A couple of weeks later I went to an open mike reading at a campus coffeehouse. I brought along a short story I'd written over the summer and, in a rare fit of boldness, signed up to read. I listened to the first two readers, gathering my nerve. *Forget it,* I thought. *I'm not doing this.* But the emcee called me to the stage, and I had no dignified way out. With shaking hands and voice I read my story.

It was about a ninth grader named Annie who has a crush on her French teacher, a film buff. Inspired by her love for the teacher, Annie starts saving all her movie ticket stubs in a shoebox. She's close to her father, who makes a point of teaching her what he calls "the finer things in life": little tricks like whistling, eating noodles with chopsticks, slurping oysters, and keeping a box score while watching a baseball game.

One day, Annie spots her beloved teacher going into a movie theater with a girl from her school, a senior. They're holding hands. Annie is upset, telling herself that they must have been on a field trip, yet not really believing it. Her father, sensing that something is bothering her, suggests she turn her ticket stub collection into a kind of oracle. "Ask it a question, pull out a stub, and see if it gives you an answer," he advises. Annie asks her shoebox why the teacher and the senior went to the movies together. She pulls out a ticket for *The Love Bug*. At first she finds this answer confusing, since *The Love Bug* is about Herbie, a Volkswagen Beetle with a mind of its own, which has nothing to do with her question. But she decides to take the title at face value and concludes that her teacher and the senior are in love. She lost a little bit of her innocence that day.

I left the stage to polite applause, overcome with embarrassment, my face hot and my heart pounding in my ears so loudly I barely heard the next few readers.

Then the final reader stepped onstage: the wine-for-all-my-friends girl. She wore a flowered dress under an army surplus jacket with MITCH stitched over one breast pocket in pink thread. Her name was not Mitch but Carmen Dietz, and like so many of the kids I admired at school, she was from New York City. She read a story about a girl named Caledonia and her boyfriend, Attila. They lived in the East Village, young bohemians in love. They shoplifted, they drank beer on their tenement roof, they wore eccentric hats, they got high in an abandoned van they found near the East River. They were sad and wounded in their different ways, but they'd never admit it, hiding their pain with outlaw bravado.

Carmen finished reading and was greeted with rowdy cheers as she stepped off the stage. I crumpled up my story, vowing to throw it away when I got home. It was childish compared to Carmen's. Her story wasn't about a crush—it was about a love affair. But I didn't know how to write about that kind of love, because I hadn't experienced it yet. As far as I was concerned, I hadn't experienced anything at all, and I was determined to change that deficiency.

That October, a junior who'd sold me his mini-fridge invited me to a party at his off-campus apartment. Upperclassman, off-campus: catnip to me and Tara, both of us hoping for an entree into the golden world that swirled around us yet seemed to find us invisible. Tara was an earnest brunette from Yardley, Pennsylvania, where she'd been star of the field hockey team, president and valedictorian of her large public high school, as well as a smash as Nancy in *Oliver!* It was not too late—yet—to avoid getting stuck with the people who were just like the people we'd grown up with. We already knew that crowd. We were looking to shake off our pasts and re-create ourselves, to test our charms and see how far they'd carry us.

We arrived at the party too early and sat around the apartment drinking beer and feeling awkward. Christian, the host, offered us a joint. We smoked it. A little while later I realized the room had somehow become very dark and noisy and crowded while I wasn't looking. Tara was dancing with Christian. Lacey Risch sat on a windowsill talking to a guy with a popped collar and blow-dried blond hair. She'd been fairly friendly in the dorm, so I went over to say hello. She didn't seem to recognize me. I apologized for interrupting their conversation. The blow-dried guy said, "Hey," without taking his eyes off Lacey. I reddened and skulked away in shame. For something to do, I stood in the bathroom line. The girl ahead of me in line was Carmen. She was wearing her Mitch jacket over a Betsey Johnson dress. I'd noticed she wore that jacket a lot.

"You know about her and the movie star, right?" Carmen said. She indicated Lacey, who was leaning out the window, blowing a stream of cigarette smoke out of the side of her mouth.

"Do you know who it was?"

"Uh-huh." She named an actor famous for portraying sensitive antiheroes. "She claims he came in one day while she was working at Cake Masters last summer. Ordered a black-and-white cookie, stared at her while she fumbled with the wax paper and the little white bag, tried to pay for it with a hundred-dollar bill, then, when she said she didn't have change for that, emptied all the change in his pockets on the counter and paid her in nickels, dimes, and lint."

"*He* did that?"

"Finally he asked her out. He's, what, forty-two? And married. I think. She said no. He came in every day after that. Always a black-and-white cookie. Asked her out once a week, begging her to say yes before he got fat from all the cookies, until she finally left for college."

"And she never said yes?" I didn't think I'd have the willpower to turn down a movie star every week. Didn't Lacey want to find out what he'd be like on a date?

"Never."

Apparently in New York, a summer job behind a bakery counter wasn't drudgery, it was a chance to meet movie stars and make them fall in love with you. Opportunities abounded on every corner, in every pizza place and grocery store. All you had to do was stand there long enough and a fairy tale would swoop by and make you its star.

"What about John-John? Why won't she go out with him?"

Carmen shook her head. "Who knows? Maybe she's scared."

She didn't seem scared to me. And anyway, what was there to be scared of?

"He's going out with a girl in my dorm now," Carmen said. "Or at least he took her to a play once."

"Which girl?"

"Celeste Gwynn. Big green eyes, curly hair, outdoorsy type from Vermont?"

"Oh yeah." Celeste Gwynn also had long legs and freckles and beautiful rosy cheeks.

A guy came out of the bathroom, and we moved forward in the line. "You know, I save all my movie ticket stubs too," Carmen said to me. "Also theater and concert tickets. But I never thought of telling fortunes with them."

She remembered my story. I reddened. I didn't know whether to be embarrassed or pleased.

"I'm serious, that's a brilliant idea," she said. "I'm going to do that from now on."

At last she reached the head of the line. She invited me to come into the bathroom with her. I was afraid saying no would be rude. She peed. I tried to pee but couldn't.

From then on, we were friends. I looked for her when I stopped in the Blue Room for coffee between classes, and if she was there she'd beckon me to her table whether she was sitting alone or with friends. One day, over cigarettes and Tab, I asked her about Attila. Was he based on a real person?

"He gave me this jacket," she said, touching the pink MITCH over her heart. "Not only that, Attila Pilkvist is his real name."

His father, Terry, a Midwesterner, and his Hungarian mother, Borbála, had somehow ended up in Massachusetts. Borbála had insisted on calling their firstborn Attila, a name still popular in Hungary. Terry associated it with brutality and begged Borbála to call their son something less barbaric—Tim, perhaps, or Scott. Borbála would not change her mind. Terry refused to use the name Attila and called the baby Kyle, just to annoy her. Soon after that they got divorced.

Carmen had met him the year before, around Christmas. She and her friend Sarita went to a bar somewhere in the West Village, and Atti played a few of his songs. His straight brown hair shagged over light almond eyes and high, fine cheekbones. The girls in the room pressed closer to listen as he strummed his guitar.

"I live across town on the East Side," he said. "Most days I sit in my room and stare out the window, writing down what I see. Here's some things I've seen lately. This song is called 'The Birds Gossip About Me.' "

The birds outside my window watch me
Eat chicken
Right in front of them
They call me a monster
They call out to the other birds
Monster
Monster
I'm afraid to go outside
Can't face the birds.

Carmen bought him a drink. Around two she realized Sarita had left, so she walked with Atti through the bitter cold all the way across town to his squat on Avenue C. His room looked down on a garden full of trash, and the moon shining through the metal window gates cast a pattern of diamonds on the floor. He kicked off his boots and stretched out on the mattress and she lay in his arms, staring at those diamonds of moonlight. He had a hole in the toe of his black sock.

That was it. She was lost forever.

At first, when he shot up, she was content to observe the smile melting across his face like butter on toast, and to wonder what sweet scenes he viewed behind his fluttering eyelids. But she hated being left behind, and after a while watching wasn't enough. Wherever he went, she wanted to go with him. She started by snorting a little, and before long Atti was helping her tie off her arm with two condoms knotted together, saying, "Are you sure? Are you really sure?" until she playfully slapped him and said, "Yes, do it."

Her parents kept trying to bring her back uptown, to keep her away from him. When they found track marks on her arms, they sent her to Humphrey-Worth to help her kick. She stopped using, but it didn't matter. Her soul had been sucked through that hole in his sock, and she couldn't go back.

Some of this history was familiar to me from Carmen's stories. When I think back to it now, to us talking in the Blue Room, the facts she told me get mixed up with the stories she read at the coffeehouse. I can't remember which parts were true, and which parts she made up. But I do remember how I loved her talk about abandoned blocks and glass-strewn streets and gardens of trash, and how I marveled at her.

I can escape myself, I thought back then. All I had to do was forget the rules and follow her.

THE GATSBY PARTY

When our freshman year ended, Carmen and I promised to write to each other over the summer. I hoped she would invite me to visit her in New York, but felt I couldn't ask. I wrote long, chatty letters about how bored I was in Baltimore, hinting that I was ready to hop on the train to New York at any moment. She answered my first letter with a short note complaining that her old Dalton friends had changed and were no longer fun. After that, I didn't hear from her until we got back to Providence in September.

She didn't say much about how she'd spent the summer, and I was afraid of boring her with my tales of life as a pizza counter girl. But soon we were as close as ever. When a break approached, I fervently hoped for an invitation to her parents' apartment, but it never came. She dropped out of touch whenever she went home, with no explanation. This ritual disappearance kept a distance between us that I began to suspect she wanted. But I refused to let that stop me. I was convinced I could bridge the rift she cultivated if I could hook her interest somehow. I assumed she saw me as conventional and boring, but I knew, based on nothing more than my own conviction, that beneath my wholesome exterior beat the heart of an adventuress. All I had to do was set the adventuress free and let Carmen see that here was her true friend.

We were never roommates; she lived with a girl named Hannelore freshman and sophomore year, until they had a fight that ended their friendship. Carmen moved out of their room and took a single, which she kept for the next two years. I took a single junior year too, and senior year I lived off-campus with Tara and one of her hockey teammates. We lived on Meeting Street, behind RISD, next to a houseful of art students.

In the fall of senior year, a boy in my Religious Themes in Cinema class asked me out to see *Fitzcarraldo*. He was a poli-sci major with stiff posture named Mark Coughlin, and in spite of our common interest in movies, I found him a little dull. He liked to read books about how stupid people are and quote factoids from them. Like: Let's say you're a doctor considering a new cancer treatment. If the drug salesman tells you that after five years ninety out of a hundred patients who had the treatment were still alive, you are likely to prescribe the drug to your patients. If you're told that five years after the treatment ten out of a hundred patients died, you're likely to caution your patients against it.

"The two statistics are exactly the same," Mark crowed. "Even doctors are idiots." He was always looking for proof that everyone was stupid except for him.

But Carmen encouraged me to give him a chance. I hadn't had a boyfriend in college yet, just a few unsatisfying frat-party flings. The guys I liked didn't notice me, and the guys who noticed me I didn't like. Carmen said I was too picky, so I took her advice and agreed to see Mark again. The date wasn't a disaster, so I kept seeing him out of romantic apathy.

Mark found everything about my body fascinating. The single black hair that curled off my right nipple; the pouchy shape of my breasts; the birthmark, like a large freckle, centered over my pubic bone; the pale-brown hair there; my plain milky smell . . . He liked it all. I wasn't his first girlfriend, but still he seemed amazed and excited that a girl would let him see her naked. He let me explore his body too, very frankly and without embarrassment. His body had a kind of correctness to it, perfect proportions, everything in its place, nothing extreme, except for a worrisome abundance of moles.

After a few weeks of this, early in my last semester and deep in the dull heart of a Providence winter, I came across Carmen and Mark having coffee in the Blue Room. Carmen waved me over and I sat down with them. She leaned toward Mark in a way that suggested intimacy and a secret. Soon I realized, the way you sense these things, that Carmen and Mark had slept together. Not recently, but at some point, and probably more than once. I was tempted to ask her about it, but she hadn't said anything before, when she was urging me to go out with him, which was strange. I got the message: whatever it was, she didn't want to tell me about it.

So I asked Mark. He told me that he'd dated Carmen's roommate, Hannelore, sophomore year, until Carmen seduced him.

"Seduced you?" I said. "What does that mean?"

"You don't know what *seduced* means?"

"I know what it means, but how did she do it?"

He shrugged. "You know, things happen."

"Did you feel bad about it? About Hannelore?"

"She was upset," Mark said. "But she had no right to be. She didn't own me." He swallowed, and I watched, with the faintest hint of disgust, the rise and fall of his Adam's apple. "She was madder at Carmen than at me. They had a huge fight."

Carmen was my friend, yet she withheld basic facts of her life from me. I thought the problem was with me, that in some way I was unworthy of her confidence. What was I doing wrong? I looked around at the behavior of my fellow students and came to the conclusion that Carmen sensed how much I wanted her to like me, and that repelled her. I opened my eyes and received the message blaring all over campus: vulnerability equals weakness, and weakness arouses contempt. I had only to hide my longing and my desire, and they would be fulfilled. Or at least they'd have a chance.

But hiding my feelings wasn't easy for me. My face gave everything away and my curiosity tormented me. At last I couldn't stop myself from confronting her.

"Why didn't you tell me you slept with Mark sophomore year?"

"Does it matter?"

"Not really, I guess, but you could have told me. He said you stole him from your roommate."

"*Stole* him. Ha. As if he had nothing to do with it. It wasn't exactly hard."

She was refusing to see my point. "But . . . if you were dating an ex of mine, I'd tell you. I'd tell you anything you wanted to know. We could compare notes."

"He's not my ex," she said. "It was just a fling. I felt like messing with Hannelore, that's all. She's so fucking frail. She's a vegetarian, but plants are her friends, so she can hardly eat anything, not even vegetables! She always has a headache, or an earache, or a stomachache, or this weird thing she calls a 'hair-ache.' Sometimes I just wanted to punch her. Plus, that name. Hannelore. Like a Nazi princess."

"But you lived with her for two years."

"God, I *know*." She offered me a Marlboro, which I took. "Don't you think Mark is kind of boring?" She couldn't remember what she'd ever seen in him.

That spring I started hearing about the Gatsby Party. A consortium of Beautiful People—the shah's niece, the jazz singer's daughter, a von Bülow, and other fancy rich kids—had rented Rosecliff, a historic Newport mansion overlooking the ocean, and were inviting all their friends. The theme was *The Great Gatsby*, and everyone had to wear twenties clothes. There would be a caterer and champagne and a Dixieland band and dancing and Japanese lanterns. It was rumored that Gang of Four was going to play a private concert, because the shah's niece was somehow friends with them from when she lived in London. She wouldn't confirm it. The party would be just like the ones Jay Gatsby threw in the novel, only better, because no vulgar hangers-on would be invited, only cool people. I desperately wanted to go. At the very least, I would get to see what they did on the other side of the golden gate they locked behind them.

The blond boy with the popped collar, who had stopped blow-drying his hair by then and whose name was Spence, had invited Carmen to the party with the understanding that she'd bring enough coke for him and his friends. Everyone knew she had drug connections, through Atti. Carmen didn't have the power to bring me along. You had to be officially invited by the host consortium, or asked as a date by someone who'd been officially invited.

One warm Saturday afternoon Carmen stopped by my apartment on her way to the library. I was sitting at the little desk in my room—chained to it, really, since I had two papers due Monday—with a two-liter bottle of Tab and a blank sheet of onionskin rolled into my typewriter, staring out the window. The RISD students who lived next door were cutting one another's hair in the little yard outside their building, accompanied by side two of *Abbey Road*. They'd been doing this all spring, whenever the weather was nice. Always cutting their hair—sometimes dyeing it—always *Abbey Road*, always side two, the side that starts with "Here Comes the Sun." Carmen came in and stood by my desk, watching them with me. *"Oh, that magic feeling,"* the Beatles sang, *"nowhere to go."*

"I wish I were an art student," I said.

"I know," she said. "But I'm sure there's a downside." She draped herself across my bed and I turned away from the window. "You still want to go to the Gatsby party?"

She knew perfectly well that I did. "What do I have to do? Sacrifice a kidney?"

"Nothing that drastic. Brendan McMurchie is going to ask you to go with him."

"He is?" I knew who Brendan was—a squash player from Bermuda, tall, sun bleached, with chlorine eyes. The kind of person you notice as they cross the green, whose name comes up when people are gossiping. But I'd never spoken to him.

"Spence mentioned that Brendan doesn't have a date, so I asked Spence to ask Brendan to ask you."

"You did?" I jumped up and danced around. "Thank you!" I grabbed both her hands and tried to pull her to her feet to dance around with me, but she stayed glued to the bed, so I let her pull me down next to her. "But . . . does he know who I am?"

"Of course. Well, I described you to Spence, and he said you sounded fine."

"It's weird that he doesn't have a date. Isn't there someone he wants to ask? Someone he likes, or someone he knows?"

Carmen shrugged. And then I remembered that I had a boyfriend.

"What about Mark?" I said.

"What about him?"

A few days later, I was in the post office checking my mailbox when Carmen led Brendan over to me. She introduced him and stepped aside. "Hey," he said. "You want to go to a party?"

I said yes, and we agreed that the four of us would drive to Newport together in Spence's car. I didn't hear from Brendan again until the night of the big bash, two weeks later, when he and Spence picked us up at Carmen's dorm in a red BMW.

The film society was holding a Fassbinder retrospective the same weekend, and Mark wanted me to go with him to see *Ali: Fear Eats the Soul*. I told him I was busy that night. "I'm going to a party," I said. "The Gatsby party."

"Great! I can see *Ali* another time."

"I can't bring you with me," I said gently. "I'm going with Brendan McMurchie."

His chest caved in, as if I'd knocked the air out of him. "As a date?"

"I don't know. I mean, not really." I knew that Carmen had asked Brendan to ask me. I hoped he had some interest in me, but had no idea if he really did.

"But he's a douchebag."

I shrugged.

He spent a minute regaining his composure. Then he said: "If you go to that party with that guy, it's over. We're finished."

I didn't quite believe him, but I was willing to risk it. I didn't really care about Mark, which, I now understood, gave me power over him. I thought I had to harden my heart to get what I wanted, to get anything at all. I became a very mean girl.

Carmen and I went thrifting in search of sparkly twenties dresses. As we were walking up Thayer Street we spotted Lacey Risch staring through the window of a frozen yogurt shop. Since freshman year she had become anorexic, wasting away to a sallow walking skeleton, her jaw puffy and distended by swollen salivary glands. When she smiled, the skin on her face seemed to crack with the effort.

"Is she going to Rosecliff?" I asked Carmen.

"She was invited. She said no."

The night before the party Mark came to my apartment to find out if I was still planning to go. I said yes and asked if he wanted me to model my dress for him. He fell on his knees and wrapped his arms around my waist. "Please don't go. I don't want to break up with you."

I wriggled out of his grip and lost my balance, tumbling onto the bed.

"Why are you doing this to us?" he said. "You don't know what you want. You can't trust your own judgment. You are influenced by your peers. Teenage girls who see that other teenage girls are having babies are more likely to get pregnant themselves. Your opinion about a person can be affected by what kind of coffee you drink!"

"What?"

"Hot or iced. In studies, people given iced coffee were more likely to see others as selfish and cold than those given hot." He began to cry. "There is no free will."

I tried to comfort him, but the longer he groveled, the more disgusted I felt. Did Mark really like me this much? If he did, wasn't it kind of gross of him to show it? I experienced the contempt for him that, I now understood, others had felt for me, back when I was eager to make friends. I cringed at the memory of Lacey Risch and popped-collar Spence snubbing me at parties freshman year. It stung to realize how pathetic I must have seemed to them. I didn't know Brendan, but secretly—so secretly I was afraid to admit it to myself—I wished that an exciting romance would bloom in Newport and we'd return to Providence at dawn, a Beautiful Couple.

And yet, all that silliness and meanness and delusion led to that spring night in Newport, the highlight of my college years.

Rosecliff shimmered under a three-quarter moon, a white palace, strangely familiar. As Spence's BMW circled the drive I realized that this was the actual house where *The Great Gatsby* had been filmed. It wasn't very original of the host consortium to throw a Gatsby party in the *Gatsby* house. I was disappointed in their lack of imagination, but too grateful to be there to say that out loud. I half expected Carmen to say it, but she only said, "Zowie."

We entered the ballroom to the tinkle of laughter and ice and crystal and music, while high overhead on the cake-frosted ceiling silver clouds floated in a pale painted sky. The shah's niece greeted Spence and Brendan with kisses, and had warm hellos for me and

Carmen. "The ladies' salon is upstairs. You've never seen anything like it. Come on, I'll take you." She led us up a curving sweetheart staircase.

"Save some for us," Spence called from the foyer. "And come back soon."

The ladies' salon was the size of three normal living rooms put together, with chandeliers, velvet slipper chairs, gilded mirrors, Japanese screens, Persian rugs, and two gigantic bathrooms, one at each end. Girls in flapper gowns lounged and smoked and chatted, or sat at the vanity tables, fluffing their hair.

Carmen and I followed the shah's niece—her name was Nava—into one of the bathrooms and shut the door. Carmen produced a vial of coke and we chopped it into lines and snorted it off a silver hand mirror we found on a marble-topped washstand. We rubbed our gums and wiped our noses and checked our lipstick. Nava slipped the vial into her tiny beaded purse.

I had done coke a couple of times before, at my summer restaurant job in Baltimore. That coke had tasted of talc and witch hazel, but this was different. My blood soaked up the drug like oxygen; my energy felt pure and clean, my head clear. The lavish setting, the costumey clothes, the familiar faces made strange by a new context . . . all this, fueled by a racing clarity, boosted my confidence.

Spence and Brendan waited at the foot of the stairs. Carmen slipped them a vial and they disappeared into the billiard room. We wouldn't see them again that night. Luckily, Carmen had brought a third vial.

We grabbed flutes of champagne and passed through the ballroom to the lawn, which glowed in the light from the house. The warm May air smelled like honeysuckle and roses. A couple, holding hands, darted behind a tree to kiss.

"We're in a movie!" I said. Carmen shushed me. I lowered my voice. "Don't you feel it? I'll set the scene: Here we are, students celebrating as the end of our college days draws near, blithely unaware of the pain and trauma that lies ahead of us, the terrible compromises of adulthood. . . .”

“Me-e-em-ries . . .” Carmen sang in a bad Barbra Streisand imitation, *“. . . of the way we were . . .”* She gave me a jokey little shove. The heel of my silver shoe caught in the grass and I stumbled, laughing and reaching for her wrist to balance myself or to pull her down with me if I fell. She steadied me.

A boisterous laugh came from the group mingling by the fountain, so we headed that way. It turned out to be John-John’s crowd. He’d brought his current girlfriend, a fun-loving California blonde named Kate. His frat buddies and their silk-haired girls surrounded them, protected them, a party within the party. Four years in proximity with him and I hadn’t spoken to him once. But I’d watched him. I’d watched him threading among the tables in the Ratty, his tray piled with broiled haddock and spinach pie, till he settled in a corner crowded with rowdy friends. I’d watched him sunbathe on the porch of his frat, stretched out shirtless on a lawn chair. Asleep at a carrel in the library, lazy curls shading his face. Talking to girls at parties: the pretty, nervous ones and also the ones who weren’t pretty, weren’t nervous, the confident, funny girls, loudmouths who directed plays and edited literary journals, whose lack of beauty gave them strength, permission not to please—which appeared to please him. Or at least amuse him. He had a checked-out air, as if the world pressed on him, too attentive, while all he wanted was not to offend.

“I dare you to dance with him,” Carmen said. “By the end of the night.”

“What do I get if I do it?”

“My eternal respect and admiration.”

I clinked my flute against hers.

In the ballroom, people had begun to dance. The band played old songs, the kind our parents liked and that we were only beginning to appreciate. "April in Paris." "Someone to Watch Over Me." "I Can't Get Started." Carmen and I twirled and dipped each other like children at a wedding. We took breaks to eat tiny quiches and crab balls, to refill our champagne flutes, to smoke cigarettes and snort more cocaine, bringing new friends with us to the ladies' salon each time. The ladies' salon was now coed, and everyone had dropped the pretense that this was 1922. Sequined headbands had been ripped from itchy heads and tossed to the floor, stockings peeled off, and high-heeled shoes kicked aside. It was 1983, no time to be confined by convention.

At midnight, Carmen taunted, "You haven't danced with him yet." But he hadn't ventured near the dance floor. I couldn't drag him there. "Maybe he'll dance on the lawn," Carmen said.

We went outside. John and his friends hadn't moved from the edge of the fountain, having claimed it as their territory. They were passing around a joint. I was barefoot by this time, my fringed dress split up the side as high as my hip, my body buzzing, my mind accelerating. I climbed up on the marble lip of the fountain and followed its circular path to where John stood, his back to me. He'd taken off his tux jacket—Kate was wearing it—and his tie hung loose at his neck. His broad back narrowed at the waist in a shape that made me think of a saddle. I rested my hands on his shoulders. Startled, he cast his sleepy eyes at me.

"Give me a piggyback ride," I said, leaping onto his back. My arms clung to his neck, my legs wrapped around his waist. He laughed, so his friends laughed too, even Kate with her sunshiny hair. We were all high by then on whatever we liked to get high on. Everything blurred and glittered and seemed very funny. John galloped me over the lawn to a wall bordering the cliff. "I'll toss you over!" he joked, jerking his shoulders as if to throw me off his back. I linked my ankles in front of his belt and he shifted my weight so it settled comfortably on his hips. We paused there, watching the moonlight dapple the water. Someone had once owned this house, I thought, and lived in it, had it all to themselves, the mansion, the fountain, the lawn, the cliff, the ocean, the moon.

"Seen enough?" he asked. No, never, never enough, but I said, "Yes, take me home please, Secretariat," and he turned and galloped me back to the fountain, letting me off on its lip, to applause from the gang. He gave me a smile, indulgent but clearly telegraphing, *That's enough now*. I got the message. Carmen and I ran back to the house, holding hands and laughing, thirsty for more champagne.

"That was better than a dance," Carmen said. "My eternal respect and admiration are yours."

The party broke up around two, but Spence and Brendan had left without us. Nava said we could squeeze into the back of her Mercedes, and so we chugged home to campus crammed together with John and Kate and their friends, Carmen on my lap, passing a bottle of champagne and singing "Love My Way." I had the strange sensation of nostalgia for all this—the night air, the car, everyone in it, especially Carmen—even as it happened. John held Kate in one arm and rested the other over my shoulder in a gesture of comradeship, keeping it there all the way back to Providence. He never asked my name.

Reading period began the next week. When I passed Mark on the green, he wouldn't speak to me. I was sorry I'd hurt him, but not really, because it had been worth it. I'd glimpsed the golden world, and returning to it was my only goal. Now I knew for sure that it existed, and I could go there, if only I could find the door. I didn't particularly care about being famous or rich, or even happy. But I needed to know what else was behind that door.

I ran into John once during finals, in the library. He smiled, nodded, and went on his way, just like before . . . but the vacancy in his eyes was gone. I hurried to the periodicals reading room, where I knew I'd find Carmen. She lounged in an armchair, feet up on a table, face buried in a copy of *Rolling Stone*. I squatted beside her chair and spoke softly into her ear. "He saw me. Just now. He saw me, and he knew me."

She shut the magazine, marking her place with her thumb. "Now you can die happy."

"Maybe we'll run into him in New York." I still hoped Carmen and I could get a place together when I moved.

"Anything could happen." She reopened the magazine. "That's what they say."

5

CHANTERELLE

In middle school I knew of a girl named Kiki who claimed she'd spent the summer as an Aerosmith groupie. Her mother was a belly dancer. Kiki could do a head slide, that *I Dream of Jeannie* thing where you move your head from side to side in isolation from the rest of your body. She was a grade ahead of me, and we weren't friends. She wouldn't have been friends with me. She smoked clove cigarettes and sipped Coke spiked with Southern Comfort out of a 7-Eleven cup. I practiced aerial cartwheels on the front lawn and translated picture books into French for fun. She lived in a world where fourteen-year-olds were groupies, and I lived in Bubble Wrap.

When I got to college and read *Lolita* I finally understood the difference between me and Kiki: she was a nymphet and I was not. I lacked the necessary traits, identified by Nabokov as an "elusive, shifty, soul-shattering, insidious charm," and instead was doomed to be one of the dull "wholesome" children Humbert Humbert despised. I am not saying that I wish I'd been a teenage Aerosmith groupie. But in the lives of neglected kids who "grew up too fast," as my mother liked to say, I saw—until recently—not pain, but glamour. To me, a girl who felt smothered, neglect looked like freedom.

I spent my first months in New York wondering when something was finally going to happen to me. I wanted something big—good, bad, I didn't care, as long as it shook me until my head spun. Something to make a good story out of my life—and something big enough to recapture Carmen's interest. Then I met Ivan. Here at last was my chance at the seedy glamour I'd always yearned for.

Carmen and I spent hours trying to cobble together a decent outfit for my first dinner date with Ivan. It wasn't easy, she complained, since I owned nothing but baggy college girl dresses and painter's pants. Then, at the last minute, he called and canceled—an emergency with a patient, he said—and changed the date to lunch a few days later. I was disappointed—lunch was not as romantic as dinner. "Maybe he's having second thoughts," I said.

"He's just busy," Carmen said. In retrospect, that cancellation was the first hint of trouble. Carmen later admitted it had roused her suspicions, but I was so excited and she didn't want to ruin it for me.

He took me to Chanterelle, in SoHo. I hadn't been to SoHo yet, hadn't heard of Chanterelle, but Carmen said it was small and chic and hard to get a reservation. "I'm very jealous. Remember everything you eat and everything he says and everyone you see and be prepared to describe it all to me later." Then she told me how to get to SoHo on the subway.

SoHo on a weekday: cobblestone streets and unmarked doors, strangely quiet yet humming with the energy of a hidden world. Chanterelle glistened on an isolated corner of Grand Street, minimal and muted except for the chandelier and the huge flower arrangements. I was so excited my skin tingled. Here at last were the people I'd imagined New Yorkers to be: slim, serene, and beautifully dressed in a tossed-off way, even the artists in their paint-stained jeans. At a corner table Laurie Anderson, spiky and dimpled, talked intensely to a man with a motorcycle helmet on the seat beside him. Grace Jones stalked by on her way to the ladies' room, tossing a red boa over her shoulder. I felt dowdy and suburban in my Indian print dress and Ann Taylor jacket, but Ivan looked me over in a way that suggested he could see through my clothes to the real me. So to speak.

He ordered white wine and we ate salad and fish while he talked about the two years he'd spent working in Sudan for Doctors Without Borders. He'd had his own driver and a cook, he said, and had become friends with a British aristocrat, a sort of leftover colonialist, who opened a social club for the doctors, with a bar, a tennis court, and a croquet lawn—made mostly of sand and dirt, of course. Jim—the British friend—knew how to get things no one believed they could have, like bourbon, and champagne, and X-ray machines, and Cipro. Once Ivan and Jim were driving back from Khartoum with a Jeep full of supplies and got hijacked by bandits. The bandits lined them up under a tulip tree, ready to shoot them and leave them to the vultures, when Ivan noticed that one of the men had a rash and a badly swollen hand—early symptoms of river blindness. Ivan warned him that he would go blind unless he got swift treatment, and said they happened to have some ivermectin in the Jeep. They didn't really have ivermectin, but Ivan gave him some antibiotics and some instructions, and the bandits were grateful and, after emptying the Jeep of all the supplies, they let him go.

"What about Jim?"

"They kept Jim."

"Oh my God. What happened to him?"

"I don't know."

Things were a little awkward after that. I kept thinking, *Okay, a British guy who was probably some kind of black marketeer got killed by bandits*. That was awful. But Ivan had gone to Sudan to help Sudanese people. He assumed the risks, I supposed, and accepted them. The waiter refilled our glasses and offered us more bread. Finally I said, "You must have treated a lot of sick people while you were there. Children, and babies?"

His face went blank.

"I'm sorry—"

"Why would I want to talk about that?"

"Because you were doing good in the world?"

The blank look masked his face for a long moment. The restaurant revolved around us, bustling with quiet, efficient activity, while we freeze-framed at our table. Then he softened and laid a dry hand on mine. "What kind of talk is this for a bright autumn day? We're in New York City, Sudan is oceans away. Let's be where we are."

"I've got things I don't like to talk about, too."

He flinched, and I wished I could slurp those words back into my mouth like a strand of spaghetti.

"Let's see . . . while I was fighting malaria in Sudan you must have been safely in school reading Hemingway."

"This time last year? Gide."

"Gide. In French?"

"No."

He leaned back and pulled a pack of Gitanes from his jacket, offering me one. I took it and leaned across the table to let him light it.

"When I was in college you were probably a very little girl. If you were even born yet."

"What year are we talking about?"

"Sixty-three? Do you remember nineteen sixty-three?"

"I remember nineteen sixty-four. I was three."

"You remember being three? That's remarkable. I can't remember much before the age of ten."

"I remember dancing to my babysitter's Beatles records," I said. "She had a stack of forty-fives as tall as I was. And I remember our dog, Snookie. And the Bark Button."

"The Bark Button?"

We had a miniature dachshund named Snookie (named after Dad's favorite New York jazz club), who barked whenever the doorbell rang. So I called the doorbell the Bark Button. I used to beg my father to lift me up so I could press the Bark Button and make Snookie "talk."

"That's your very first memory? The doorbell thing?"

"Uh-huh."

"I expected something more . . . elemental. Something about a lost doll or potty training."

"I remember getting spanked a couple of times. Once for crossing the street alone and once because I bit my mother on the ankle."

"That's better."

I tapped my Gitane in the ashtray and rolled it between my fingers, glad of something distracting to do. "What about you? What's your first memory?"

"Oh, I don't remember much about my childhood."

"I don't believe you."

"It's true. Some people are like that, you know. They grow up to be so different from the child they once were that it's as if their childhood happened to someone else. And they can't remember a thing about it. Clearly you're the other type, the type that remembers everything."

"Not everything." But I did remember my child self vividly, my delicate child feelings, my fierce opinions, how frustrating it was to have no power, how interesting to observe without understanding. How could he have forgotten?

We smoked and drank coffee while the restaurant emptied. The elixir of wine and sunshine had made me drowsy. He reached for my hand, placed it on the tablecloth, and traced the veins radiating from my wrist to the tips of my fingers. The waiter brought the check. Ivan put down his AmEx without glancing at the total, and the waiter whisked it away.

"I know a lovely little hotel near here. Let's go there and have a drink."

"Oh. I have to work tonight." I usually worked in the day, but I'd traded shifts with a coworker so I could meet Ivan for lunch.

"Work? I don't understand."

"At the bookstore. I have to be there by five." When he'd asked me to lunch, I hadn't thought about what would happen afterward.

He stubbed out his cigarette and rubbed his face, smoothing the irritation away. When he dropped his hand, the warm smile was back. The waiter set down a small silver tray with the check, his credit card, and two chocolates. Ivan said he had another appointment in the neighborhood, so he couldn't see me home. He hoped I didn't mind.

He ushered me outside and hailed a taxi. The air had cooled since lunch began, the old factory buildings casting long shadows on the empty street. "I'll call you soon," he said. He shut me into the Checker, tossed a twenty through the driver's window, and waved it off. I looked back as the cab pulled me uptown. He was walking away in the other direction, his hands shoved into his pockets, where, I assumed, he kept his key to the golden world.

6

DON GIOVANNI

Ivan didn't call. A week passed. Then another. It was October. I watched every game of the World Series, O's versus Phillies, either at home by myself or at the Dublin House with Carmen.

I should have skipped work that night and gone to the hotel, I lamented. My practicality had cost me Ivan's interest, and Carmen's. Instead of having my first-ever hotel tryst to dissect with her, I had to milk the mystery of why he wasn't calling for all it was worth, which was starting to bore her.

"Do you think I should call him?"

"No," Carmen said.

"Maybe he likes aggressive women."

"He doesn't."

"How do you know?"

"No one likes aggressive women."

The night the O's won the series, I was at the Dublin House. When I got home, I found a note on my bed in Robin's handwriting—someone had called! But the message wasn't from Ivan; my dad had called to celebrate the Orioles' victory. By then it was well after midnight, too late to call him back.

Meanwhile, I needed money. Every week I answered classified ads for entry-level jobs in publishing, marketing, advertising, and publicity, to no avail. I went to a temp agency, but they frowned at the dismal results of my typing test and dismissed me as unemployable. I applied at every restaurant with a HELP WANTED sign in the window, but they all required New York waitressing experience, and I only had Baltimore waitressing experience.

"You're supposed to lie," Carmen said, and I said, "I am lying," and she said, "Well, obviously you're not lying hard enough."

Robin complained that I owed her rent for September and October. "I have a three-months-and-you're-out policy."

I promised to pay her soon, but I had no idea where I'd get the money. I hated to ask my parents for a loan. I was trying to prove to them that I could make it in New York on my own. Something would come through, I knew it would.

Carmen took me to see *Danton*, set during the French Revolution's Reign of Terror. We were on a Gérard Depardieu kick.

"That was depressing," I said afterward. "And long."

"Robespierre was such a prick." Carmen hunched forward into her Gérard Depardieu impression. *"Peuple de France!"* she rasped, imitating Danton at his trial near the end of the movie, when he was losing his voice. "Only *you* have zee right to judge me."

"Peuple de France!" I echoed hoarsely.

"You sound like Marlon Brando in *The Godfather*."

Across the street the Metropolitan Opera House glowed like a crystal jewel box. "Let's go over there and see if we can find anyone as depressed as we are," I said.

"Yes, what *are* the bourgeois pigs up to?"

People milled around the fountain in Lincoln Plaza, under a fat October moon. "Nobody looks depressed," Carmen said.

"I'm not depressed anymore either." We walked along the lip of the fountain. I showed Carmen the little hops and leaps I used to do on the balance beam as a child. "I want to go to the opera sometime," I said. "How much do tickets cost?"

"A lot." Carmen started singing,

Oh Theodora,
don't spit on the floor-a,
use a cuspidor-a,
that's what it's for-a.

"Where'd you learn that?" I asked.

"It's from my opera."

"What do you mean, *your* opera?"

"*Carmen*, dummy!"

I reached into the fountain and splashed a little water at her. "Do you know this one?" I faced the opera house and belted out, *"Kill the wabbit, kill the wabbit, kill the wabbit!"* I played Elmer Fudd, serenading Carmen. *"Oh Brunhilde, you're so wuvwy."*

"Yes I know it, I can't help it," Carmen sang.

The doors of the opera house burst open and people streamed out, flooding the plaza with tuxes and diamonds and evening gowns and chatter. The lip of the fountain became our stage, with some of the operagoers cheering us on.

"Oh Brunhilde, be my wuv!"

A man in a long coat caught my eye. He winked, and I realized with a start that it was Ivan, escorting a tall woman whose golden hair was twisted into a poof high on top of her head.

I nudged Carmen. "It's him!"

"Where?"

He'd grown a goatee. The woman with him tugged a mink stole close around her shoulders while the hem of her dress swept the ground.

"With the blonde. Over there."

Ivan held my eyes for half a second. Then he pressed a hand to the small of the woman's back as the crowd carried them to the street.

Carmen took my hand and we bowed to the five people applauding us. The plaza emptied quickly, the crowd's energy draining away. We hopped off the ledge and started walking home.

"Do you think she's his girlfriend?"

"Who knows?"

"She can't be his girlfriend. If he has a girlfriend that gorgeous, what's he doing playing around with me?"

"Please." She bumped me with her hip. "You may not have a mink stole, but you have your charms."

We paused at Broadway and Seventy-Ninth, the neon harp of the Dublin House blinking TAP ROOM, TAP ROOM. "Beer?" Carmen nodded in the direction of the bar.

"Beer."

We ordered at the bar and settled into a booth.

"No wonder he hasn't called. She's tall and elegant and about a thousand times more beautiful than me."

"Would you stop?" Carmen blew beer foam at me.

"He goes to *Don Giovanni* at the Met while I stand outside singing Elmer Fudd. It's so embarrassing." I daubed the beer foam off my forehead with a cocktail napkin. "She's got to be his girlfriend, right?"

"Maybe she's his wife."

"His wife!" I hadn't thought of that. "That's impossible. He wasn't wearing a ring."

"So?"

Married: it had never occurred to me.

When I got home, after midnight, my roommates were asleep. The phone rang. I went into the hall to get it.

"I'd forgotten how cute you are," Ivan said, "until I saw you tonight." He wanted to see me again, to take me to dinner. I said yes. Then I called Carmen.

"Maybe I should have said no," I said. "What about the blond woman?"

"You don't know who she is," Carmen said. "That's his problem."

"If I don't go, I'll never find out what would have happened if I went," I said.

"That's right. You have to go so you can tell me all about it."

7

SHADOW

This time, instead of Chanterelle, he took me to Le French Shack, a down-at-the-heels bistro on West Fifty-Fifth Street, tucked among a few unremarkable Italian trattorias and a crêpe place. The restaurant was pseudo-fancy, with gold light fixtures, white linens, and tuxedoed waiters, but the rug was worn and the ceiling tiled with the kind of soundproofing squares you see in suburban basements. I lifted my napkin to reveal a wine stain on the tablecloth. But what did I know? Maybe the food was really good here. Maybe Le French Shack was the best-kept secret in New York.

I ordered steak and he ordered Dover sole. He peered at me over his reading glasses, taking in my Laura Ashley dress, which was too tight on top, flattening my breasts. Carmen said it looked like a reject costume from *Little House on the Prairie*. It was my best dress.

When he spoke, I noticed that his teeth were slightly yellow and his lips chapped. "Let me take you shopping."

I flushed. I desperately wanted beautiful new clothes, ones like the blonde at the opera had worn. Clothes that said, *My rightful place is at the center of this story*.

"I see you in rose-colored silk, high heels. . . ." He rubbed his thumb over my hand. At a nearby table, two middle-aged women stared at us and whispered. Their disapproval sent a jolt of pleasure through me. I was a nymphet at last, my ugly dress turning me into an object of fascination. I imagined people wondering what kind of girl would wear a dress like that, a child's dress almost, to a restaurant in New York. Maybe a spoiled crazy rich girl who didn't care what people thought. Maybe a teenage prostitute.

After dinner he said, "Let's have a drink," and led me up the street. He didn't say where we were going, but I assumed it would be a bar of some kind. Instead we turned onto West Fifty-Eighth Street and stopped in front of a sleek glass high-rise that looked like a corporate headquarters. "I'll go in first. You walk around the block and go in after me."

I was thrown off by this sudden instruction. Walk around the block? "Why?"

"Just do as I say." He softened, adding, "I need a few minutes to get the place ready for you."

"No, you don't, really, I don't mind if it's messy—"

"Walk once around the block and then come up to 27A." His goatee was an arrow pointing down. "I'll be there waiting for you." He strolled into the building, nodding at the doorman, and continued on to the elevator without a backward glance.

The wind cut through my coat as I began my trek around the block, quiet at this hour. I glanced back, and suddenly there was a man behind me. Where had he come from?

I kept walking and turned the corner, tilting my head slightly to catch the man turning the corner too. He wore a trench coat and a black knit cap, exactly what a spy or a detective or a hit man would wear. He was tall, which made him easy to spot. I walked up Sixth Avenue to Fifty-Ninth Street and turned right again. A few paces back, the man in the trench coat turned right too.

Okay, that was weird. If he turned south onto Fifth, he was definitely following me.

Instinct told me to duck into a phone booth and call someone, Robin maybe, because I knew Carmen wasn't home . . . or no, grab that passing yellow cab and speed away, go home, go anywhere but get away from this, whatever this was.

I didn't do it. Because if I went home I'd never find out what would happen if I stayed. If the man in the trench coat was really following me, and why. What Ivan's apartment looked like. What he was planning to do with me. Leaving now would be like walking out of a movie in the middle, and I never did that.

At Fifth Avenue I turned right. Behind me, the man turned right as well.

I had no way to reach Ivan, no phone number for his apartment, only for his office. Would he want me to shake this guy off before I went into his building? Or would he want me to show up no matter what?

When the man followed me onto Fifty-Eighth Street, I got scared. I had circled the block, and so had he. I wanted to duck into a safe haven, the nearest place I could find.

The nearest place was Ivan's high-rise building, apartment 27A.

I pushed through the revolving door and glanced back. The man had stopped. He was watching me through the glass.

"May I help you?" the doorman asked.

"Um, I'm going to 27A."

A nod. "Sign here please."

I signed my real name without thinking. The doorman dialed Ivan to let him know a Phoebe Hayes was on her way. I wanted to smack myself in the head. My real name. I should have made up something.

I rode the elevator to the twenty-seventh floor, thinking of aliases I could have used. Holly Golightly. Philippa Rizzuto. Iona Frisbee. Nancy Ann Cianci.

Ivan opened the door before I had a chance to knock. The apartment was a glossy studio, a wall of tinted windows looking out at other midtown high-rises. A shaggy white rug and some modern furniture—leather, steel, and glass—but not many personal objects. No souvenirs from Sudan, no framed photos, no plants.

"What is this place?"

"My apartment." He led me to a black leather daybed and prompted me to sit.

"But . . . do you live here?" I'd expected him to have a bigger apartment than a studio, and in any case it didn't look like anyone really lived here.

"Yes, sometimes. When I need a place to stay. Do you like Scotch?"

"Sure."

He put a heavy crystal tumbler in my hand, Scotch on the rocks. I thanked him. We sat at opposite ends of the leather couch. I stared out the smoke-colored window at the blurry lights. I sipped my drink. "Do you ever think that Scotch tastes like scotch tape?"

"No."

"I do." I took another sip. It sounds weird, but that's what I like about Scotch: the tape taste.

"I'm not in the habit of tasting tape." His eyes had been fixed on me, but now they roamed the room. "What about here?"

"What do you mean?"

"Would you like to live here?"

"Here?"

"Yes."

"Sure, I guess so."

I waited for him to explain further, but he didn't. It wasn't an apartment I would have chosen, if I could live anywhere I wanted. But it was about ten million times better than the roach motel on Eighty-Seventh Street. Was he really saying I could live there?

"Do you have any music?" I asked.

"Music? Yes, of course. What kind do you like?"

"All kinds, except for prog rock and jazz fusion."

"I don't know what those are." He fiddled with the stereo, settling on a classical station. Then he put down his glass and stood in front of a mirrored wall. "Come here."

I was confused. He was standing four feet away from me. "I am here."

"Come here." He pointed down at the rug.

"You want me to sit on the rug?"

"Come here."

I gulped my Scotch and set my glass on the floor. Then I crawled onto the rug and sat down cross-legged. He knelt beside me and kissed me. I understood that we were going to have sex, and I felt nervous and a little repelled, but also curious. It was as if whatever happened would not happen to me. It was all part of the movie.

His kissing gradually got rougher, his goatee scraping my cheeks. He put his hand on my back and positioned me on my knees, facing the mirror. He pushed the skirt of my dress up over my hips and pulled down my tights, rubbing his hand over my ass. I saw him in the mirror, staring at my ass with weird concentration. I worried that it looked fat, and told my brain to shut up. Kneeling behind me was a mad scientist with slick black hair and a pointy gray beard. I dropped my head, not wanting to look. He lifted my chin and held my face toward the mirror. When he let go, I dropped my head again. He lifted my chin impatiently.

He unbuttoned his shirt, took off his belt and pants. I watched him obediently, still on my hands and knees, like a doomed piglet.

"Get that thing off," he ordered. I pulled off my dress and kicked off my tights. He pushed me down again, parallel to the mirror and onto my back, pressed my legs apart, and pushed into me. I watched him while he fucked me: the beads of sweat on his forehead, the animal sound of his grunting, and the way his hair shaded his eyes, which fixed on my body but not my face. They widened until they looked like they might pop out of his head. I tried to notice what I felt—I knew I felt something, but I couldn't find it. I was floating on the ceiling, watching a dough-skinned girl lying on the floor underneath a hairy back.

Ivan saw me watching him. He turned my face toward the mirror and held it there.

"Look!" he gasped. "Look!" His eyes blurred again, and he was lost inside his own sensations. He watched himself thrust into me. He wouldn't let me turn away, so I closed my eyes. It was one thing to see everything through my own eyes like a camera . . . but to see the scene whole, in the mirror, as if someone else were filming it, was too real.

He pumped his hips harder and faster until he came with a violent jolt, yelped pitifully, and fell on top of me, a moist and heavy blanket. I lay beneath him, listening to his panting. I had an urge to apologize, to say, *I'm sorry I did this to you*. It surprised me that I could elicit such a strong response from a grown man. I knew that any woman could do it; even the image of a woman, or just part of her, or anything could, but still I marveled: *I reduced him to this*.

He rolled off me onto the rug, propping his arm on his bent knee and beaming. "Miss Phoebe! With rosy cheeks. You look like a Renoir."

"Thanks." I reached for my tights and pulled them on, trying to remember what Renoir nudes looked like. He watched me with wolfish satisfaction.

"Are you in a hurry to leave?"

"Well . . . no, I just thought I'd get dressed."

He stretched out beside me, put his arms around me, and kissed my cheek. "We must do this again sometime. We must do it again very soon, and again (kiss) and again (kiss) and again (kiss). Will you go out with me again? (kiss)."

"Sure."

"We'll go to a nicer restaurant next time. Have you been to the Russian Tea Room?"

"I've always wanted to go there." I'd seen it in a lot of movies: *Tootsie*, *The Turning Point*, *Manhattan* . . .

"Have you? Let me take you."

"Okay." I shivered slightly; it was chilly there on the rug. He picked my dress up off the floor and handed it to me.

"Here, you'd better put this on. I must get a robe to keep here for you, and a negligee. . . ."

I pulled my dress over my head while he put his own clothes on. My breasts strained against the fabric even more than before, as if they'd swelled in the last few minutes. "What should we do now?"

He rubbed my back with absentminded affection. "It's late. I'll take you downstairs and put you in a cab." He reached into his pocket, flipped through some bills, and pressed forty dollars into my hand. "That should be enough to get you home."

It wasn't enough to make me feel like a hooker—though I had no idea how much a hooker would be paid—but it was enough for five or six cabs and almost twice as much as I earned in a day at the bookstore.

"There's something you should know." I reached for my shoes. "Someone followed me tonight when I walked around the block. After you went inside."

"Followed you?" He rushed to the window and looked down, as if he might spot the culprit from the twenty-seventh floor.

"I walked around the block like you told me to. A man in a trench coat kind of popped up behind me and followed me until I got back to this building."

He grimaced, stroking his beard. "Come on, let's go." He helped me into my coat and led me, his arm around my back, to the elevator. We descended. He nodded at the doorman and told me to wait in the lobby while he hailed a cab. Out on the sidewalk, he surveyed the area until he was comfortable that no one was waiting or watching for him. He flagged down a taxi, then beckoned me to get in as he opened the door. I ran out of the lobby. He kissed me quickly on the forehead, shut me inside the cab, and hurried back to his glass high-rise.

I called Carmen as soon as I got home, but Sarita said she was out. Half an hour later, she called from a pay phone. She was at the Pyramid with Atti.

"What happened?" She had to shout over the noise in the club.

"A lot." It was too much to tell over the phone.

We met at the Dublin House after work the next day. We ordered beers and pumped quarters into the jukebox. I told her everything. Almost everything. I held back a few of the more embarrassing details, like the way he'd forced me to look in the mirror—even though I knew she'd like that. Somehow it felt too sordid to say out loud.

"He might let me live in his apartment."

"Is it nice?" She flipped through the songs on the jukebox, looking for something.

"In a way. It's kind of sterile."

"Maybe I could live there with you! Secretly."

"What about when he's there?"

"I'll hide." She punched in the numbers for three Patsy Cline songs. "What else?"

"He wants to take me to Bergdorf's and buy me clothes and then take me to the Russian Tea Room for dinner."

"No one goes to the Russian Tea Room for dinner. Only for lunch." She leaned against the jukebox, soaking in the opening bars of "I Fall to Pieces."

"Oh." I felt stupid, not knowing that.

"Maybe he's afraid he'll see someone he knows there at lunchtime."

"And he doesn't want to be seen with me?"

"Well, you said someone followed you. . . . I hate to say this, but all signs point to *he's married*."

I flipped through the jukebox.

"What are you looking for?"

"The Jam."

"I don't think this jukebox has the Jam."

"Every good jukebox has the Jam." I hit the *J*'s; no Jam. I punched in James Brown. I felt like a fool. "I don't *know* that he's married."

"True. We're just assuming, based on his weird behavior, that he's married. But we don't know it for a fact."

"I should stop seeing him."

"You can't! Not now. Not when the mystery is just getting good. I mean, a guy followed you. You have a right to find out what the hell that's all about."

"I guess."

"And even though the Russian Tea Room is Siberia at dinner, they still have those blinis with caviar."

"I'm crazy about caviar."

"We can't stop now, Phoebs. We have to find out what's behind all this before you quit. I'm dying to see how this story ends. Aren't you?"

8

EXAMINATION ROOM

He didn't take me to the Russian Tea Room. He asked me to come to his office, a maisonette on the ground floor of an apartment building on West Fifty-Sixth Street. He gave me a glass of brandy, hinted that he was going to Paris soon and wanted to take me with him, and then pushed me into an examining room and fucked me on the padded table, which was covered with that white paper doctors use for sanitary purposes. It crinkled noisily under me the whole time. When he was finished, he opened his eyes and seemed surprised to see me. "Okay?" he said.

I couldn't understand why I felt like crying, because I really didn't care about him or any of this or anything. Nevertheless, sobs like storm clouds brewed inside me. I choked them down. I refused to let him see them. I'd read somewhere that dolphins evolved to look happy and cute so that humans won't want to kill them and eat them. It might be true. An instinct for self-preservation told me to act like it was all okay. And it was all okay. I was using him, or trying to, but it wasn't going well.

When I left the office, I spotted a tall man in a black knit hat across the street. He paced back and forth in front of a building, half obscured by parked cars. I couldn't tell if it was the same man who'd followed me or not. I hailed a taxi I couldn't afford and went home.

I sat on my bed in the dark. Carmen was waiting to hear how things had gone at the Russian Tea Room. I didn't feel like calling her just then. I didn't feel like talking to anyone.

I stared out the filthy window. It was streaked with grime and pigeon shit. I thought, *Someday I'll clean it*. I knew I would never clean it. Across the air shaft, lights burned in the building next door, in bathrooms and kitchens and stairwells. A man sat at his kitchen table in his underwear, drinking milk and laughing over something he was reading in the paper.

The phone rang. I sat quiet and tense on my bed. I heard Mary Frank answer it. She said, "I think so. Just a minute and I'll see."

Her footsteps grew heavier as they neared my door. She knocked. "Phoebe? Are you in there?"

Robin's voice: "I heard her come in a few minutes ago."

Mary Frank knocked again. "Phoebe? It's your mother."

The last person I wanted to talk to was my mother. But if I put it off, she'd call again, and keep calling until she reached me, and if she didn't reach me by midnight she'd call in a SWAT team to break down the door. I might as well get it over with now. "I'll be right there."

I rose from my mattress, creaky as an old woman, and shuffled out to the living room. It took all my energy to infuse my voice with brightness and emotional health. "Hello?"

No one spoke. Someone was there; I could hear small noises in the background, clanks and tinklings.

"Mom? Hello?"

An intake of breath, and the person hung up.

Maybe something was wrong with my parents' phone. I called back.

"Hello?" My mother's clear voice.

"It's me. Is your phone working all right?"

There was a pause. I imagined her pulling the receiver away from her ear to look at it and see how it was working. "I think so. It rang, I answered, I heard your voice, you seemed to hear mine. . . ."

"So why did you hang up on me just now?"

Another pause. "I didn't."

"You didn't just call me a minute ago?"

"No."

That rattled me.

"Honey, what's going on?"

"Nothing! Sorry, it was a misunderstanding."

In the background, Dad said, "Is she okay?"

"What kind of misunderstanding? Is something wrong? Something's wrong. Your voice is getting squeaky."

Sometimes my voice gets squeaky when I'm nervous. I made an effort to speak in a lower register. "It must have been a wrong number. A woman called and Mary Frank thought it was you, that's all. So what are you up to?"

"Don't change the subject. What are *you* up to?"

I could practically see her suspicious squint over the phone. Once the gears of her anxiety are set in motion there's no shutting them down.

"I'm spending a quiet Tuesday night at home in my pajamas," I said. "So stop worrying."

"Your dad wants to talk to you."

The phone changed hands. "Hi Phoebs."

"Hi Dad."

"You doing okay up there?"

"Yes."

"We're coming to visit you soon. Who's playing at the Vanguard these days?"

"I don't know."

In the background, Mom's voice: "Honey, not this weekend . . ."

"We'll figure out something," Dad said. "Take care of yourself. Don't forget to have fun."

"I won't."

"Give me that." Mom wrested the phone away from him. "We

want to come up and see you, but your dad's been working too hard. He needs to rest."

"Okay." I didn't want my parents coming up to visit me. I couldn't face them. I had become a person they wouldn't recognize.

"Sleep well, honey."

I hung up the phone, then dragged it by its long cord into my room. Across the air shaft, the man in his underwear paced the floor, talking to himself and waving a chopstick. I dialed Carmen. I told her about the weird phone call.

"What about the Russian Tea Room?"

"We didn't go to the Russian Tea Room."

"Stay right there. I'm coming over."

Fifteen minutes later she appeared with a bag of Cheez Doodles, a bag of jellybeans, a pint of mint chocolate chip ice cream, and a bottle of whiskey. "I know you like all of these. I wasn't sure which one you'd want right now."

I took the ice cream. She took the Cheez Doodles. I stared out the window while we talked. Mr. Underwear across the air shaft turned out his kitchen light.

"I don't want to see him again," I said. "Next time he calls, I'm dumping him."

She agreed. "No reason to see him again. Now we know how this story ends."

Except the story didn't end there. It kept going.

9

THE DIETZES' PARTY

I was feeling low. My apartment was dark and dirty, I was behind on my rent, I hated my roommates, and I hadn't been able to dump Ivan yet because he hadn't called—and Carmen thought a party might cheer me up. Her parents happened to be throwing one. And she didn't want to go alone.

Len and Betsy Dietz held a bash for their music and theater friends every November, but this year's party was a bigger celebration than usual. Len had composed the score for a new ballet that had just opened to raves. Hundreds of guests crammed into the Dietzes' Sutton Place apartment, drawn by the electricity of success.

We took off our coats in the vestibule. I could see people glamorously puffing in the living room, but I didn't want to ruin my angelic reputation with Carmen's parents, so I left my cigs in my coat. After a quick hello to the Dietzes—Betsy surreptitiously sniffing Carmen's breath as she kissed her—Carmen led me to her room, where we spent the first hour of the party smoking a joint with her younger brother, Sid, a tenth-grade pothead in Converse high-tops and a Black Flag T-shirt.

"Nice hairband," Sid said to Carmen. "You look like Nancy Reagan."

"That's what I'm going for." Around her parents, Carmen camouflaged herself in wool skirts, pearls, turtlenecks, and black flats. She'd worn her tweed reefer to the party, leaving Mitch at home.

"You're not fooling anybody, you know," Sid said.

"Shouldn't you be at the piano doing your Oscar Levant imitation?"

"I can't face those people. Every time I poke my head out there someone says, 'Where's Rosa? Is Rosa here? Oh, so sad she couldn't make it.'"

"Tell me about it." Carmen rarely mentioned her older sister, Rosa, who had moved to L.A. to take a small part in a movie.

"Do you have a picture of her?" I asked.

"Out in the living room," Carmen said. "On top of the piano."

"We couldn't possibly come from the same family as Rosa," Sid said. "She's skinny and tall—tall for a Dietz, anyway—and looks like a ballerina."

"It's true," Carmen said. "She takes after Betsy's side of the family. Our California cousins."

On top of Carmen's dresser, next to an upside-down top hat, I found a framed photo of three little Dietzes posing together on a pony, lined up by height. I recognized Sid and Carmen's pointed chins and rascally grins, Sid squinting in the sun and Carmen shaded by a cowboy hat. The girl behind them—Rosa—let her hat hang down her back so that her smooth hair glistened in the sunlight. With her serene, heart-shaped face, she did look like she belonged in a more elegant family.

"How old were you here?"

"Let's see . . . three, nine, and eleven, I think."

I peered inside the top hat, which held a bunch of random bits of paper. "Is this your stub collection? Can I look at it?"

"Go ahead."

I took the hat off the dresser and riffled through the ticket stubs: *A Chorus Line*, *Annie*, *An Unmarried Woman*, five *Rocky Horror Picture Shows*, *Behind the Green Door* . . .

"*Behind the Green Door*? Isn't that a porn movie?"

"What can I say?" Carmen shrugged. "It was the seventies. Len and Betsy went out a lot back then."

"Rosa and Carmen did whatever they wanted until Carmen ruined it," Sid grumbled. "Because of *you* they watch *me* like I'm some kind of criminal mastermind."

"You *are* a criminal mastermind."

There was a sharp rap on the door and Betsy popped her head in. "Kids! Everybody's asking for you."

"We're coming." Carmen rose reluctantly from the bed.

" 'Where's Rosa? Where's Rosa?' " Sid sniped. " 'What's she working on now?' "

In spite of Carmen's reluctance, I was eager to meet the Dietzes' friends. The living room was crowded, but Len spotted us immediately and waved us over to the piano, where he was talking to a good-looking middle-aged couple. He threw an arm around Carmen's neck and kissed the side of her head. He introduced me to John and Amanda Rubin, but I'd already recognized John, a Broadway star who also did commercials for home insurance.

"What are you doing with yourself, Carmen?" Amanda asked. "Are you writing?"

Len gave Carmen's shoulders an affectionate shake. "She's been working for Bertha Sykes."

John laughed, and Amanda said, "Oh, you poor darling. That's really paying your dues."

"Is Adam here yet?" John scanned the room.

"I haven't seen him," Amanda said. "He'll want to hear all about what you're up to, Carmen."

"Carmen is such a talented writer," John said to me. "We went to see a play she wrote in high school. Remember that, Mandy?"

"How could I forget? *The Limbo Cafeteria*!"

"Starring Rosa as the Cheerleader," Len said.

"Rosa was lovely in that," Amanda said.

"She lights up the stage," John said.

"She's got that rare quality," Len said. "She . . . how can I put it? She *elevates* whatever material she's given."

Carmen's lips tightened.

"I hope you're working on something, Carmie," John said. "You know, you could have a play produced like *that*." He snapped his fingers.

"Carmen doesn't have time to write," Len said. "She's too busy playing downtown bohemian."

John shook his head. "Adam's the same way. I tell him, 'Don't go on any streets that have a letter for a name, you'll get yourself killed.' Does he listen to me?"

"All the proper streets are numbers," Amanda agreed. "Except in Greenwich Village, of course."

"What kind of an idiot goes walking around Avenue C at night?"

"Ah, well," Amanda said. "We all go through that phase."

"Is it a phase?" Len said. "I don't remember going through a phase like that."

"You know what?" Carmen said. "I need a ginger ale. What about you, Phoebe? Do you need a ginger ale?"

"Ginger ale. Yes." I let Carmen drag me away toward the bar. "Nice to meet you!"

She ordered us two whiskey and gingers. We slipped into the dining room to pick at the shrimp platter. Through the window, the East River flashed and rippled under the Fifty-Ninth Street Bridge. "They seem nice," I said about the Rubins.

"Ugh."

"Carmen, there you are." A stout woman in her sixties bustled toward us in a sequined caftan, toting a miniature terrier around like a purse. "Hold Mimi for a minute while I straighten my unmentionables," she growled, thrusting Mimi into Carmen's arms and proceeding to tug on something beneath her caftan. Once her unmentionables were settled, she retrieved her dog. "Thank you, darling. Now, get me a drink so I can throw it in your father's face. A Manhattan, nice and sticky."

"Bertha, this is my friend Phoebe," Carmen said.

"Charmed." Bertha barely glanced at me. "That drink . . . ?"

"Coming right up."

We bypassed the bar and went into the kitchen, where Carmen freshened up our whiskey and gingers and mixed her own Manhattan for Bertha. "See that light fixture up there?" She nodded at an unremarkable frosted glass shade, flush against the ceiling.

"Yeah?"

"See how the plaster around it looks kind of patchy, as if there'd been an explosion or something?"

"Now that you point it out . . ." The plaster around the light had a slightly different texture from the rest of the ceiling, as if a hole had been patched.

She dashed bitters into Bertha's tumbler. "There's a story behind it."

I waited to hear the story, but she kept jerking the little bottle over the glass. I hoped Bertha liked her Manhattan heavy on the bitters.

"You don't have to tell me if you don't want to."

She capped the bitters bottle and stirred the drink with her pinky. "I want to. The story is this: Many years ago, when I was about ten, I had some friends over for a slumber party. We were watching TV in the living room in our pajamas, eating popcorn and giggling and getting goofy over staying up till midnight. Rosa and Sid were asleep, and my mother wasn't here. That was the strange thing—I don't know where she was, but I think she and Len had had a fight. He was going through a hard time then. He'd written an opera that bombed, and we were having money troubles. I knew we were having money troubles because I heard my parents fighting late at night over all the unpaid bills."

"I didn't know he'd ever had a time like that," I said. He radiated the confidence of someone who'd known nothing but success.

"This is a couple of years before *Cottonmouth*. Anyway, I didn't know what was going on, my parents never told us anything, but Len was acting weird that night. He kept walking between us and the TV, back and forth from the hall closet to the kitchen, carrying things. He'd say, 'Don't mind me, girls,' and then walk in front of the TV with a stepladder. 'Dad, get out of the way! We can't see!' I yelled at him. He said, 'Sorry, sorry,' but then he did it again, this time carrying a rope. I didn't think about why he was making a big show of carrying a rope and a ladder in front of us, and I didn't care. I wanted him to leave us alone and let me be with my friends."

I studied the ragged plaster around the light fixture. "What was he doing?"

"The next thing I know there's a huge crash in the kitchen. We all run in here and there's Dad in a heap on the floor with a rope around his neck, covered in plaster. He'd pulled down half the ceiling trying to hang himself."

"I don't see how you could tie a rope around that light. There's nothing to hook it to."

"You can't. That's the new one, replacing the one Len pulled out of the ceiling. Betsy bought that specifically because you can't tie a rope around it."

"Oh."

"Once he got over the shock of the fall, he started sobbing."

"Oh my God. What did you do?"

Carmen sipped Bertha's Manhattan. "We all just stared at him. I didn't know what to do. Finally he got up and brushed himself off and tried to act like it was funny, like he'd done it to amuse us. 'Nothing to see here, ladies.'" She imitated him leaning back on his heels, thumbs in his belt, like Don Knotts in *The Shakiest Gun in the West*. "Then he said it was time for bed. Nobody argued. We ran into the living room, dove into our sleeping bags, and pretended to sleep for the rest of the night."

"He obviously wanted you to see what he was doing," I said. "Maybe he wanted you to stop him."

"How? I was ten."

From the living room a foghorn voice bellowed, "Carmen! My drink?"

Carmen took another slurp from Bertha's Manhattan. "Come on."

"Wait." I paused at the swinging door between the kitchen and the dining room. "Did he ever try anything like that again?"

"Not that I know of. Whatever the problem was, he got over it." She pushed through the door with her back. "Bets was mad at him for a long time though. Pretty hilarious, right?"

"Yeah." Anyway it seemed like her father was doing okay now. I didn't find the story all that funny, but it had a happy ending, or at least not a tragic one—a big hole patched up with visible scars. It was such a Carmen story.

As Carmen delivered Bertha's Manhattan, I overheard a woman complaining that she'd had a genius idea for a song while her boyfriend was going down on her.

"I mean, what do you do?" she said to her friend. "I don't want to spoil the moment, but I don't want to lose the lyrics either. I know if I don't write them down right away I'll never remember them, but I also know as long as I'm repeating these lyrics in my head I'll never come!"

"What were they?"

"What?"

"What were the lyrics?"

"I don't know!"

"You went for the orgasm?"

"I went for the orgasm."

"You'll find them again."

"No," she sighed. "I won't."

The woman was in her thirties and beautiful, with thick dark hair, black leather boots, a red wool dress, and lots of gold chains. "Who's she?" I asked Carmen.

"I don't know. Some lyricist."

"Is something wrong?"

"I hate these parties."

"Why? Your parents have such cool friends."

"Let's go to my room and smoke."

"I left my cigs in my coat."

In the vestibule, I dug through my coat pockets until I found my Camel Lights. I was digging for matches when the door opened and a young couple walked in. The guy was wiry and energetic, late twenties, with thinning hair. The woman wore dark glasses, jangly silver earrings, and a military coat studded with jeweled pins. She waited languidly while he helped her remove the coat. Underneath she wore a dress made of one long silver scarf wrapped around her body. Waves of black hair flowed around her melancholy face, pale except for a bright red pout.

"Carmen!" the guy said. "This is Zuzanna Ruiz-Alta."

"Zu." She offered a creamy, beringed hand, nails polished metallic blue. *"Ciao."*

Carmen perked up. "*Ciao*, yourself. What's up, Adam?"

Carmen and Adam exchanged a hello kiss. She introduced us: Adam Rubin, the musician son of John and Amanda.

"Come get a drink," she said.

"Our parents used to fantasize about me and Carm getting married," Adam told me.

"Not in a million years," Carmen said.

Adam made kissy noises at her.

Zu's silvery presence parted the crowd in the living room as we headed back to the bar. I overheard Adam telling Carmen that he'd picked up Zu at 8BC the night before. "She's fantastic—but a slippery one. Hard to pin down. She works the door at Plutonium and says she can get me in whenever I want. But she won't give me her phone number."

"Can I come to Plutonium with you? I'm dying to go there," Carmen said. Everyone was talking about Plutonium. It had opened in September, a new kind of nightclub, club as performance art. Every month, artists completely redecorated the space to fit a theme chosen by the owners. In September they opened with Surrealism; for October, Honky-Tonk. November's theme was Home—an ironic take on suburbia, family, and nostalgia, just in time for the holidays. Night after night mobs clamored in the street outside the club, desperate to get in. They tried everything: bribes, pulling strings, showing up naked . . . nothing worked. The only way to gain entry was to be deemed cool enough by the door Nazis. "To stand in line and not get in is to die," Carmen turned to tell me. It meant you were nobody.

Zu accepted a vodka on the rocks from the Columbia student the Dietzes had hired to bartend, lifting her sunglasses to survey the room with eyes thickly outlined in kohl. She looked disdainful and lost, a gleaming silver island in a sea of sweaters and tweed.

"Are you in the theater?" she asked me.

"No. I work in a bookstore."

"Oh." Bookstores didn't seem to interest her. I felt desperate not to bore her. I sensed that catching her interest was like winning a prize. Maybe a bit of black magic would work.

"I'm also a fortune-teller," I said.

She brightened. "You are? Do you read palms?"

"She reads ticket stubs," Carmen said.

"What?"

"We'll show you." Carmen led us all down the corridor to her bedroom.

Adam picked up an old teddy bear. "You've done wonders with this place."

Carmen snatched the bear back and tucked it under her arm. "You still have that Snoopy bedspread?" She picked up the top hat and shook it. "Behold the Oracle of the Ticket Stubs. Ask her anything. It's amazing!"

Zu sat on the bed. "Oh, hmm, well, let's see. . . . Can you just tell me, what does my future hold, like, in general?"

I closed my eyes and shook the hat, hoping to look mystical. I reached in, drew a stub, and opened my eyes. *Fame*. What a stroke of luck.

I showed Zu the ticket. She laughed and gave a delighted shake of her bracelets.

"Ask her something else," Adam said.

"All right." Zu looked away from him and straight into my eyes, as if we were alone together in a room. "When will I find my true love?"

I performed the same routine—closing my eyes, shaking the hat—and pulled out *Airplane!*

"Are you planning to take a trip?"

"Not soon. I can't afford to go anywhere at the moment."

"Well, you will meet your true love on an airplane." I showed her the ticket. "It may not be until later in your life. But it will be worth waiting for."

"Zu, let's fly to Miami next weekend," Adam said.

"What is your name again?" Zu asked me.

"Phoebe Hayes."

"Phoebe Hayes, listen. There's a big party at Plutonium on New Year's Eve—the theme is 'The Future,' you know, like, will we all be wearing jet packs? Will robots take over? Will we live on Mars? And all that. Everybody wants to know what the future will bring. Wouldn't it be great to have you at the party to tell us?"

"Yes," I said, my pulse quickening. "It would be great."

"That would be *so* great," Carmen said.

Zu took a pen from Carmen's nightstand. On the back of my hand she wrote down a name, *Toby Belzer*, and a phone number. "Tell him I sent you."

I called Toby the next day. To my amazement, he hired me over the phone on nothing but Zu's recommendation, promising me three hundred dollars for one night's work—telling fortunes at a party in a club most people would never be allowed to enter. "You can thank me by bringing me with you," Carmen said, as if I'd ever consider going without her.

10

ROSES

A shiny new path unfurled before me, and the city sparkled with fresh possibility. Yes, I now owed Robin three months' rent, but I planned to beg her for one more month; after the Plutonium party I'd be able to pay off some of my debt, with more, surely, to come. Screw Ivan. I didn't care about him anymore; I was on to bigger and better things.

I enjoyed this optimistic feeling for a few days. Then: a bad omen. My period was late.

My breasts ached and I had terrible heartburn. I went to the drugstore and spent an outrageous amount of money on a pregnancy test. In the bathroom I unwrapped the test, read the directions, and peed on the stick. It burned when I peed. Everything burned.

While waiting for the result, I thought about a toddler my mother and I once saw outside the grocery store. His mother pushed her shopping cart through the parking lot, leading him on a leash. I was horrified. "She's humiliating him," I said. My mother saw it differently. "He may be humiliated, but he's safe." Parents had to see life that way, putting safety above all else. That wasn't for me. Not yet.

I checked the test stick. The second pink line bloomed.

On Friday, Carmen's gynecologist confirmed that I was pregnant, with a mild case of cystitis. She gave me a prescription for antibiotics and scheduled the procedure for the following Wednesday. It would cost a thousand dollars. I had five days to find the money.

Ivan's answering service said he was out of the country until Monday. Carmen and I spent the weekend lying on the mattress in my room, plotting ways to get the money if Ivan didn't come through, while I slurped endless vanilla milkshakes and chewed Tums. We could ask my parents—never. We could ask her parents—no. We could go to Belmont and bet on a long shot. We could play the slot machines in Atlantic City. We could buy a lottery ticket.

I called Ivan's office on Monday morning and left a message. I tried again at lunchtime, saying it was urgent. The fourth time I called, his secretary impatiently told me that she'd given him all my messages. He'd call as soon as he could.

The next day I went to the office in person, hoping to catch him. His secretary insisted he wasn't in; he'd be out in meetings all day. "He's avoiding me," I said. She didn't deny it. I asked her for a slip of paper and a pen. I wrote, *I'm pregnant. –P*, folded up the note, asked for an envelope, sealed it, and left it for him.

I walked the thirty blocks home. It was a gray afternoon in late November, the bite of impending snow in the air and the city tinseled in Christmas lights. Tourists clogged the sidewalks, gaping at store windows. At the edge of the park, horses tethered to carriages snorted and jingled, stamping their feet, their eyes big and frantic.

Back at the apartment, Robin was home with a cold. A long white box leaned against the door of my room. "Someone sent you flowers," she said.

Inside: a dozen thorny red roses and an envelope marked FOR PHOEBE HAYES. In the envelope: a thousand dollars, cash. No note.

Zowie.

* * *

In the waiting room I sat next to a young guy, eighteen or nineteen, trying to put pink socks on a baby girl in a stroller. She kept taking the socks off. "Jasmine, STOP. You want powpow?" He gripped her feet in one hand while she squirmed. "I'm holding your feet hostage." He laughed, turning to me and Carmen. "She's trying real hard to get out of my grip." He shook the baby's legs. "You can't get out. You're never gonna get out." Jasmine struggled and kicked to get free. "You gotta do better than that, Jas," he singsonged. "You gotta do better than that. . . ." She started to whimper so he let go of her feet and rested one of his legs across her lap. Calm now, she tugged on his sock, trying to take it off over his shoe.

In the operating room the nurse, a large man with a gold hoop in one ear, cracked bad jokes to relax me. "What's the difference between an elephant and a matterbaby?"

"Um . . ." I wasn't really in the mood for jokes. "What's a matterbaby?"

"Nothing, but thanks for asking."

The doctor snickered. I had to think about it for a second before I got it.

The nurse stuck a needle into me. "Knock knock."

"Who's there?"

"Closure."

"Closure who?"

"Closure eyes and count backward from one hundred."

I felt a stinging *whoosh*, and my ears roared the way they do when you cover them with your palms. I tried to protest, "That's not funny," but I don't know if I managed to utter the words. From what seemed like far away, I heard the nurse say, "What is the one question you can never answer yes to?" When I didn't reply, he said, "'Are you asleep?'"

Squiggles of gold flashed under my eyelids. I saw the patterns and textures inside my skin: ropy muscles and tissues and fibers twisting in a dark-green sea.

When it was over, I stumbled groggily into the waiting room. Carmen put her arms around me and led me outside to a taxi. At home, she settled me onto my mattress with books and magazines and Tylenol and blankets. She'd brought a tiny portable TV so I could watch soap operas if I felt like it. She kept my curious roommates at bay, telling them I had the flu.

I slept until nightfall. I woke up briefly to find her sleeping at the foot of the bed, curled around my legs, toes stuck under one of my pillows. When I woke up again, she was pulling on her socks. "Are you hungry?" she asked. "I'll get some Chinese takeout." She went out and soon returned with cartons of shrimp lo mein and chicken almond ding and cans of ginger ale. At eleven o'clock, she asked me if I wanted her to stay or go. "Stay," I pleaded. She stayed.

A few days later, Laurel called to tell me that Dad was dying. I had to go home. I thought I'd return to New York right after the funeral, but that's not what happened.

The whole thing—Ivan, the abortion, Dad's death, all at once . . . it swamped me. I was knocked off-balance by a big wave of grief. My reaction to all this was a little extreme, I'll admit that. I understand why my mother was worried. But Baltimore was quicksand; the longer I stayed, the more stuck I would get. I knew that if I didn't return to New York by New Year's Eve, I'd never live there again. And besides, the money bothered me. The money, and the weight in the pit of my belly. I couldn't move on until I repaid that debt.

WHAT TIME IS IT?

We spent the second to last day of 1983 fixing up our apartment and preparing for New Year's Eve. We walked to a discount store on Broadway for sheets and towels and cleaning supplies, then scoured the thrift shops on Ninth Street for party clothes. I chose a silver minidress to wear with my blue Bertha turban, fishnet stockings, and short silver boots. Carmen bought a long black lace dress and a red fake-fur stole. We passed eleven posters asking for information about the missing girl with the Farrah Fawcett hair, Susannah Byers. I know because we counted them. I was growing so familiar with her face from seeing her picture all over the neighborhood, I began to feel like I knew her.

That night, while Carmen was at Atti's, I sat at the kitchen table with my shoebox to refine my fortune-telling system. I'd had an idea of pulling two or three ticket stubs during a reading instead of just one, and interpreting them like tarot cards. The stubs didn't have mythological symbols or pictures, but the movie titles conjured images in my mind, images that could speak to each other and that I could use to construct a vision, to find a message, to look for answers.

"What if my mind goes blank?" I asked Carmen on the way to the club. "What if some celebrity sits down to have her fortune told and I can't think of a single thing to say?"

"You know what to do," Carmen said. "Fake it."

Zu was working the door when we arrived. It turned out she was our neighbor; she lived on the fifth floor of our building with her roommate, Marie-Claude Phan, a fashion designer who owned CloudCuckooLand, the dress boutique on the ground floor. The evening before, at midnight, Carmen and I had seen Zu leaving for work in a neon-green hearse decorated with flowers and skulls, driven by a guy in biker gear who bellowed her name from the street. Now, dressed like a tsarina in blue velvet and a tall fur hat, she led us to Toby's office. We passed through a lobby lined with urinal fountains spouting rainbows of colored water, and down a hall of live window displays, created by artists and changed every month to illustrate a theme. As Zu had promised, "The Future" was the Plutonium theme for January 1984. The first window showcased a sexy alien romping on the surface of a barren planet—a naked girl in green body paint, antennae sprouting from her hair. She waved at Zu as she finished off a box of Good & Plenty and stashed it behind a giant rock.

The second window predicted a future underwater, a world of undersea caves inhabited by merpeople. A live King Neptune presided over a clam dinner with his children, who were dolls with fish tails attached to their legs.

The third window contained a postapocalyptic suburb soon after a nuclear attack: a ruined backyard scattered with abandoned toys and barbecue equipment, a zombie child forlornly swaying on a swing.

"Aw," Zu said. "Poor Jeffrey." Jeffrey, the actor who played the zombie child, sported a convincingly gory head wound.

We toured the rest of the club, a warren of lounges and bars and dance floors, a shark tank with real sharks restlessly circling, a pool, a waterfall, a huge sign with 1984 spelled out in blinking light bulbs, and a live owl who flew from room to room, perching randomly on people's shoulders. We climbed a flight of clanging metal stairs to

Toby's office: a couple of desks in a storeroom crammed with sets and props like astronaut suits, nurse uniforms, carousel horses, ant farms, Matchbox cars, stuffed deer heads, mannequins, cereal boxes, candelabras, and a deflated bouncy house. Toby, in his late twenties, with intense black eyes and a shaved head, wore a sleek gray suit over a NASA T-shirt. He was on the phone and seemed very distracted and busy. He told me I was on fortune-telling duty from ten until two, and then to come find him and he'd pay me.

Zu left us in the bar and returned to her post at the velvet rope, where the mobs gathered like storm clouds to plead for her attention. Her partner, Looie, wore a German SS uniform and threatened people with a riding crop, daring them to call him a door Nazi.

In the bar, near the shark tank, I draped a red velvet cloth over my table and set out my box of movie tickets, a crystal ball, and a sign Carmen had made that said WHAT DOES YOUR FUTURE HOLD? ASTRID SEES ALL. Carmen settled at the bar with a bright blue Drink of the Future, keeping me company as the first guests trickled in. A big fat guy with a putty-gray complexion, a raccoon coat, and a tiny fedora perched on his head asked, in a high lisping voice, who I was supposed to be. He had the air of a cowardly mobster, someone who'd be killed off early in a mafia movie. My first customer.

"I'm Astrid. Astrid the Star Girl." I pointed to the sign. "I see all."

"You got a real name, haven't you?"

"Yes," I said. "It's Astrid."

Carmen had promised that downtown I could flee the past and take on a new identity, so I'd chosen a name I'd loved since first reading *Pippi Longstocking* when I was seven: Astrid. In Old Norse it meant something like "divine strength," but in English it suggested stars because it sounded like you were slurring the word *asteroid*.

The fat man laughed and sat down in my customer chair,

dropping an old-fashioned doctor's bag on the table. "I'll get it out of you one of these days, dollbaby. How does this setup work?"

"You'll see soon. What's your name?"

"Bix Pender." He spelled it for me.

"You've got a real name, haven't you?"

"Sure I do, dollbaby. When we know each other better." He rolled up his sleeves. A throbbing constellation of red scars snaked up his arms.

"First you ask a question. Then you shake this magic box, thinking hard about the question. I'll choose three tickets and place them on the table. I'll interpret them and give you an answer."

"Huh. Okay. My question is: Are you a phony?"

"Seriously?"

"Seriously."

"Your wish is my command." I put the box in his pudgy little paws. He shook it and picked out three ticket stubs himself. I watched nervously. I *was* a phony. I didn't belong in that room.

Fake it, fake it, I told myself, but Bix's eyes bored right through me and I could tell that he knew.

The Spy Who Loved Me. That's Entertainment! All That Jazz.

I lined up the stubs in a neat row, pretending to think about them very hard.

"I don't know, dollbaby. You ask me, two out of three of those point to phony."

"It's all about interpretation. The most obvious meaning isn't always correct. Like in tarot—you know how the Death card doesn't have to mean 'death'? It can be good! It can mean change, or an ending. . . ."

"Sure, sure." He patted my hand fondly as he heaved himself to his feet. "Come find me in my office and I'll give you a party favor." He picked up the doctor's bag and snapped his head toward the ladies' room. "Be seeing ya."

The party was in full roar now, people pressing into the bar, clamoring for drinks. I waited for another customer, but no one took any notice of me. "They need to look around and see each other and talk and get a few drinks in them," Carmen said. "Let's take a tour."

We threaded our way past people smoking and sipping cocktails and chattering and pouting and shrieking with manic laughter. No one was dancing. Waiters in robot costumes served drinks and canapés. A Bardot blonde wore a dress made of gold balloons and a crow on her shoulder, who pecked at the balloons, popping them one by one in a slow striptease. A Somali model with knife-blade cheekbones prowled from room to room, shadowed by a busboy whose sole job was to carry her fur coat. Guests climbed a ladder inside a rocket-shaped playhouse and whooshed down a spiral sliding board. People ate cold seafood off the body of a girl on a table, naked except for a G-string. In the pool, two guys in women's bathing suits and Miss America sashes floated on a raft, while a girl in a bikini pretended to struggle in the jaws of a giant plastic shark.

My pulse jumped a little whenever I saw a famous face, which was constantly. They glowed in the dark, leaping out like scares in a spook house. Andy Warhol. Sting. Bianca Jagger. Matt Dillon. Grace Jones. Donny Osmond, looking much like the preteen singer I'd swooned over as a kid, except that his face seemed to have melted slightly, like a plastic doll left out in the sun. Ed Koch, the mayor, alone by the pool, jerking his limbs in an attempt at dancing.

"Zowie," Carmen said.

Back at the fortune-teller table, people were lined up waiting for me: the Somali model; Christopher Walken; a beauty in a see-through plastic dress with nothing underneath but a garter belt, stockings, and duct tape over her nipples; William Hurt; Debbie Harry. I was seized with nerves, like tiny fishhooks digging into my ribs. What could I tell these people? I knew nothing, and they knew everything.

Fake it, fake it . . .

The model sat down and held out both hands to me. No one quite understood my ticket oracle; they seemed to expect me to read their palms or look into the crystal ball, which I'd brought as a prop. I admired her long and graceful fingers, but she couldn't hold them still. Her eyes darted around the room. The busboy waited nearby with her fur coat. She reached for it, wiggling her fingers impatiently. He took one step toward her, put the coat into her arms, and then took precisely one step back, standing at attention like a soldier. She wrapped the smooth skin of her shoulders in fur, then returned her right hand to me.

"What is your name?" I asked.

"Bilan."

"And what would you like to know?"

She leaned forward and spoke in a low voice, barely audible under the dance music. "Is someone trying to kill me?"

Not what I was expecting, but okay. She glared furiously at the shoebox as she shook it. The busboy she had enlisted to carry her coat stood by, ready to be of service whenever she needed him. He looked like a teenager, but he took this duty seriously. She took herself seriously too. Her question was not a joke.

Multiple Maniacs. Apocalypse Now. The Chosen.

She gasped. The ticket stubs had spoken, and there was no denying their message.

"Yes," I said. "Someone is trying to kill you. But he—or she—will not succeed."

She narrowed her eyes, pleased to have her suspicions confirmed. "My boyfriend keeps telling me I am paranoid, but we know the truth, don't we, darling."

"Do you have a bodyguard?" I asked, glancing at the busboy. "A real one?"

"I am hiring one tomorrow. What else do you see?"

I tapped the stub for *The Chosen*. "You are very special, but people often misread you. They think you're arrogant and fickle, but you aren't. Your heart is true. You're misunderstood."

"Thank you." She nodded solemnly. "Thank you."

Christopher Walken had drifted away, so my next customer was the beauty in the see-through dress. Her head did not go with her body. She had short brown hair and round, matter-of-fact eyes under straight brows. Except for her mischievous mouth, she did not look like someone who would walk around practically naked. She said her name was Caroline and she wanted to know what her true path was. I asked her what she meant.

"Like, should I be an art historian, or join the Sotheby's training program, or take my mother's place on the board of the ballet? Or should I be an artist myself?" She touched the stiff, clear plastic of her dress. "Can partying be an art form?"

I put the box in her hands. "Shake this, and concentrate hard on your question."

Bedknobs and Broomsticks. Rocky. Take the Money and Run.

Hmm.

"What does it mean?"

I stalled for time. "What are these movies about? Angela Lansbury flies around on a magic bed and uses witchcraft to defeat the Nazis. Sylvester Stallone triumphs by losing a boxing match. Woody Allen is an inept criminal. Do you see the thread connecting these stories?"

"Not really."

"Art is magic. If you use it, you will triumph—but it will take a lot of work. Like Rocky running up the steps of the Philadelphia Museum of Art. Did you see *Rocky*?"

"Uh-huh."

"Remember that part where he runs up the steps?"

"Uh-huh."

"But if you take a shortcut—like trying to steal money instead of earning it—you'll come to a bad end."

She frowned. "I didn't say anything about stealing money."

"You should be an artist," I said. "You will have great success."

"Thank you." She reached for the stubs. "May I keep these?"

"No, I need them."

Before the next fortune-seeker could sit down I excused myself to go to the bathroom. This was the most wonderful room in the whole club: a large lounge with the usual row of stalls, sinks, and mirrors, plus a bar, a sitting area, and a woman in a corner selling condoms, candy, cigarettes, aspirin, toys, and other supplies. A beautiful man in a tight dress and Nico hair—long, straight, blond, with bangs—sat on the velvet couch smoking and chatting with a guy in silver lace pants. I checked under the stalls for an empty one. In the last stall I saw a pair of feet in wet sneakers, one foot grossly swollen. The owner of the feet was sitting on the floor, leaning against the wall. I couldn't see his upper body. One of my new neighbors had swollen feet like that, an old woman who roamed the halls of our building in her robe and slippers. I'd met her for the first time when she knocked on our door very, very early that morning.

Back at the bar, Carmen was flirting with a tall guy in a blue satin tux with no shirt underneath—nothing but suspenders and a faintly hairy chest. He had a grown-out English-schoolboy haircut, and his skin had a sheen I'd noticed on Zu and Bilan and a lot of the other people at this party—skin as shiny-bright as a shield, deflecting any troubles, I imagined, to keep their insides soft and safe. Carmen's eyes were gleaming, perhaps from too many Drinks of the Future. I couldn't get her attention.

Andy Warhol wedged a sparkly HAPPY 1984 tiara onto the tall guy's shaggy head. It looked good on him, with his girlish upturned nose and full lips. He whirled around, laughing, and talked to Andy, touching the tiara but not removing it. Carmen finally looked my way, and we telegraphed the same message to each other: *Andy's flirting with the tall guy*. It was not surprising. The tall guy had an easy, natural glamour, and he was very good-looking.

Then Andy noticed my table. He held the tall guy by the arm and led him over to me. "Oh look. A fortune-teller. *Astrid*. Nice name."

"Would you like me to tell your future?"

"No, thank you. I already know the future." He shuddered slightly. "Too grim."

"It might not be so bad."

"Oh, yes. Yes, it will. Every story has the same ending, doesn't it?" He crossed his arms over his chest and closed his eyes, playing a corpse.

"What about you?" I asked the tall guy. He took me in, my turban and my shoebox and my homemade sign, and his eyes softened. I wondered how I looked to him. I was seized by a sudden interest in his future.

"I'll try anything once." He folded his long body into the chair and rested his paint-flecked forearms on the table.

"You're an artist."

"Tell him he's going to be famous," Andy said. "Any day now."

"What's your name?" I asked.

"Jem Farrell."

"I'm bored," Andy said. "It's almost midnight. We have to see Danger Dick."

"You go ahead," Jem said. "I'll find you."

Andy faded into the crowd. My cheeks warmed. Jem had let Andy walk away to stay with me.

"You ever see Danger Dick? He's doing a big stunt at midnight. We shouldn't miss it."

I'd never heard of Danger Dick. Jem said he was a performance artist whose canvas was danger. He once cocooned himself in Bubble Wrap—lots of it—and threw himself off the roof of a six-story building to see if he'd bounce. (He didn't bounce, but he survived.) One Halloween he rigged up a kind of jet pack, ran up a ramp, and flew over a huge pile of pumpkins to a landing ramp on the other side. A punk Evel Knievel. On this night, to usher in the New Year, he was going to dangle off the roof of the building in a harness, wearing a suit made of fireworks. At midnight he'd light the suit and the fireworks would go off as he was slowly lowered to the ground, assuming he didn't blow up or burn to death.

"It'll be fun to watch," Jem said. "What time is it?"

"What time is it?" I repeated. "That's what my neighbor kept asking this morning."

I told him how Carmen and I had collapsed into bed after a night of carousing when someone pounded on our door.

"I look through the peephole and there's this scrawny old lady in a stained housedress and slippers. She's got wild gray hair and swollen purple feet and she's hugging an alarm clock like a teddy bear. I opened the door and she said, 'What time is it?'" I tried to imitate the old lady's croaky voice. "It was after three in the morning, and I told her so. She squinched up her face like this"—I squinched up my face—"like she'd just licked a lemon. Like my answer didn't make sense. And she said it again, 'What time is it?' I thought, *Maybe she needs the exact time,* so I looked at our kitchen clock and said, 'It's three-twenty-two. Okay?' But she shook her head and said, 'What time is it?'"

"I used to have a neighbor like that." Jem tapped his temple.

"I reached for her clock and said, 'Would you like me to set it for you?' but she yanked the clock away and stamped her foot and yelled, 'What time is it!' I didn't know what to do. I didn't want to shut the door in her face. So we had a kind of staring contest, a standoff there in the hallway. It was like we were in a trance."

"Then what happened?"

"The rooster crowed. You know that rooster in the park?"

"Yeah."

"I don't know why he crowed. It wasn't dawn, not yet. Anyway, that kind of broke the spell. She said, 'Hello. What time is it,' and I said, 'I don't know what time it is. I'm sorry.' She seemed to accept that. She turned away and started inching up the stairs muttering, *'What time is it, what time is it.'* "

"So that's your neighbor," Jem said.

"One of them."

"Every building's got one of those ladies."

Someone yelled, "Ten minutes to midnight!"

"Hey, Miss Astrid Star Girl," Jem said. "Are you trying to avoid telling my fortune?"

"No I'm not. You haven't asked a question yet."

"All right. Let's ask Andy's question. Will I be a famous artist?"

"Shake up the box and we'll see."

Shampoo. Fast Times at Ridgemont High. Baby It's You.

"You will be famous, and you will have a lot of fun."

"Excellent. Now let's go watch Danger Dick blow himself up."

Danger Dick dangled off the roof of the club, suspended in a harness, a helmet on his head and fireworks attached to his body. He waved to the bleating crowd, and the countdown began. Dick nodded at Toby, who stood on the roof brandishing a barbecue lighter. Toby lit a fuse that sprouted from Dick's butt like a tail. It sizzled and sparked, spreading from fuse to fuse until he was a human sparkler, a ball of fire. We counted down, waiting for him to blow. When he did, it was spectacular. Rockets shot off his body in all directions, whistling and exploding into color. We screamed and ducked and laughed. Toby lowered him to the ground, where two guys in fireproof suits sprayed him with fire extinguishers.

"Welcome, nineteen eighty-four!" Toby shouted. "Ladies and gentlemen, Danger Dick!" Danger Dick bowed and waved through the smoke wafting off his clothes. He was singed, but not badly.

It was a new year. Jem kissed me quickly on the lips. He turned and kissed the girl standing behind him. He kissed the guy next to her. He kissed his way back into the club. I went inside to look for Carmen, and when I found her she was kissing Jem.

"My turn," I said. Jem stepped away to kiss the bartender, and I kissed Carmen. "Happy New Year."

"Happy New Year," Carmen said. "Everything's new. A new world!"

"The golden world!"

Jem put champagne flutes in our hands. "From now on we'll do whatever we like and nothing else," Carmen said.

"Whatever we like and nothing else!" We clinked glasses and drank.

I returned to my table and told fortunes for another hour or so. Tatum O'Neal pulled the stubs for *Paper Moon*, *Bad News Bears*, and *Coal Miner's Daughter*, which made us laugh and laugh. "They should make a film called *The Movie Star's Daughter*," she said. If she asked a question, I forgot what it was.

When my shift ended I went to the office, but Toby wasn't there. I finally found him in the rocket ship playhouse, making out with the green-body-paint alien girl. "Oh. Hey," he said, coming up for air. "Good job." The green alien girl leaned against him while he reached into his pants pocket and extracted a fat wad of cash. He counted out three hundred dollars, then fifty more. "Here you go. Happy New Year."

"Thanks."

"Did you have a good time?"

"Yes."

"You want to do it again?"

"Yes!"

"Fabulous. You can be the house fortune-teller. I can't pay you, but you can charge by the customer, whatever you want. Five dollars a head sounds about right."

"Okay. Great!"

"See you back here tomorrow night then." He turned toward the green alien girl, who flicked her eyelashes over his cheek in a butterfly kiss. I was dismissed.

Carmen and I went to celebrate in the ladies' room, which had devolved into chaos. A man was lying naked on the velvet couch, posing for photos. Bix was holding court in one of the stalls. He sat on the toilet lid, peering through a pair of blue granny glasses, his doctor's bag overflowing with pill bottles and cash. Three people were crammed into the next stall, having some kind of noisy sex. I detected the acrid Fourth of July smell of fireworks smoke.

"Ranger Rick is in that stall," I said.

"Danger *Dick*," Carmen corrected.

Bix slipped an amber vial into my hand. "Happy New Year, dollbaby. I take care of my friends."

Carmen and I found a stall and shut ourselves inside. We spread out two lines on a compact mirror she carried. The powder burned my sinuses.

"I think there's something else in this," she said. "Something else besides coke."

I peed, and then we snorted some more. A trapdoor at the top of my head opened, exposing my brains to the air. I felt light, as if I were walking a foot off the ground.

We went to the bar for more drinks. I sucked the life out of one cigarette after another. The DJ played Talking Heads and we danced. Everybody was dancing now; nobody was pouting and looking blasé. I had to pee again; back to the bathroom we went.

All the stalls were full. Under the door of the last one I caught a whiff of ammonia and the swollen foot I'd seen a couple of hours earlier. Carmen recognized it and cried out, "Atti!" and pushed against the door. It was locked. She kicked it until it opened. Atti lay crumpled on the floor, nodding. His ashen skin stretched over his bones, and blood seeped from his bloated foot through one of his sneakers.

"Fuck." Carmen shook him by the shoulder. He lifted his head, a sliver of yellow eyeball just visible through a slash of lid. "Heyyyy . . ."

"What are you doing here?"

"I have a girlfriend, you know. She's funny. I like her because she's funny."

Carmen pressed the bridge of her nose. "God, Atti. Fuck." Atti smiled and nodded and let his head float back to the floor.

"Hey—Carmen," Bix called from two stalls down. "Drugs are whatever, but Toby don't like ambulances."

Carmen looked to me—*What should we do?*

"I . . . I can't . . ."

I couldn't look at him. I couldn't touch him. He reminded me of something I didn't want to remember.

My head buzzed with static, and I went a little blind, my eyes strobing light. Thoughts could not form in my brain. Words could not form in my throat. I was flooded with a familiar feeling of being underwater, unable to breathe, unable to reach the surface.

From far away I heard Bix say, "Long as he's not with you, he's not your problem."

I tore out of the bathroom, gulping air, leaving Carmen behind to take care of Atti and hating myself, useless coward that I was.

By the time I got home my head was clearer. I counted my money and thought about how much Carmen and I would need for the next few weeks. I took fifty dollars and locked it in an old briefcase I'd bought to hold my Ivan stash. Only $950 to go.

CAFÉ LETHE

"How do people get money?" Carmen asked. "It truly is a mystery to me."

It was a mystery to me too. Money seemed to flow effortlessly to some people, and to resist others—like us. It was early February, and I had worked steadily at Plutonium for a month, but somehow I had not saved a thousand dollars as quickly as I'd hoped. At five dollars a reading, the most I ever made in a night was $125. Some of that had to go to living expenses like rent, and I kept raiding my Ivan stash to buy dresses (Astrid needed to look good, after all), dinners in restaurants, and coke.

Carmen squatted in front of a shard of mirror we'd found on the street, peeling away the corner of her eyelid to line the rim. We picked up lots of cool things on the street. I'd rescued a toy accordion, the kind they sold in Chinatown, still in its box, like new. Carmen had found a manual typewriter. "Are you going to start writing again?" I asked.

"I don't know. I took it because it was there."

I watched her from the couch while I fooled around with my toy accordion, pressing keys and squeezing and making noise. The cats hid under the bed at the first squawk.

"Atti always says, 'What do you need money for? We've got everything we want,'" Carmen said. "But all he wants is a leather jacket, cool sneakers, and a lot of dope."

Atti had refused to go to the hospital on New Year's Eve. He refused to go on New Year's Day. He refused to go the day after that, but finally, on January third, the pain in his foot got so bad he let Carmen take him to St. Vincent's. He had a kidney infection and severe neurotrophic ulcers on his foot. He was home now, doing a little better, but his foot was bandaged and the streets were snowy and wet and it was hard for him to get around, so Carmen brought him food twice a day. She had just come home from her new waitressing job at Café Lethe and was baking some potatoes to bring over to him for supper.

"Come with me," she said.

"I can't."

"You have time. Come on."

I picked out a few notes of "Frère Jacques" on the accordion. I claimed I couldn't visit Atti because I had to go to work at Plutonium. What if Carmen changed his bandages and I saw his oozing sores? Just the thought of it made me feel panicky. Like I couldn't breathe. And I didn't want Carmen to see me weaken or break down. I didn't want anyone to see that.

Through the wall came a sudden blast of David Lee Roth wailing "Running with the Devil." Gergo, the photographer next door, loved his stereo. We could hear everything Gergo did: we heard his feet hit the floor when he got out of bed, we heard him piss in the toilet when he left the bathroom door open (when he closed the bathroom door we heard the squeal of its hinges), we heard him talking on the phone, usually screaming at someone in Greek. I guess he could hear us too, if he listened.

"I have to keep my mind clear." I raised my voice so she could hear me over the music. "To see the future. For my clients." Carmen's care for Atti was admirable and steadfast. I was ashamed of my weakness, but my fear was stronger.

Carmen scoffed. "Tomorrow, then." The next day was Monday, my night off.

"Okay. Tomorrow." I'd find some other excuse by then.

I went to the window. Snow was falling, large flakes lacing the bare trees in the park and sparkling on the curb like crushed glass. Across the street, a junkie hunched by the park fence with his eyes closed, hands kneading the air. He eased himself down to the ground slowly, slowly, inch by inch, a narcotic tai chi routine. Snow frosted his hair and his eyelashes. He didn't bother to brush it away.

Carmen joined me at the window. "Looks like laundry soap."

"Ivory Snow," I said. "Ninety-nine point forty-four percent pure."

"Pure what? And what is the .56 percent impurity made of—poison?"

"Isn't purity one of those absolute things, like death? You're either dead or not dead."

"Pregnant or not pregnant."

"Pure or impure."

"Did you know that Marilyn Chambers was the girl on the Ivory Snow box?"

"Who?"

"Marilyn Chambers," Carmen said. "*Behind the Green Door*."

"Did you really see that movie?"

"Sure. Sarita and I cut school and sneaked into a matinee in Times Square."

"No, you didn't."

"Okay, I found the ticket stub in my mother's purse."

"Betsy? Not really?"

"I kept it in case I ever needed something to blackmail her with. But when the time came, it wasn't enough."

The junkie crouched on the sidewalk, staring at his hands. "Do you know him?" I asked Carmen.

She squinted through the falling flakes. "I don't think so." The apartment warmed with the fragrance of baking potatoes. Carmen went to the oven to check on them. I sat on the couch and picked up

Dad's baseball bat, touching the Scooter's autograph with my finger. The Yankees were about to start spring training, with opening day still a couple of long months away.

There was a knock on the door. I got up, bracing myself for the old lady with the clock or for Javier, who lived one floor above us in a cluttered studio with no bathroom—he and the clock lady shared the toilet in the hall. He was a skinny, idle busybody in his sixties who liked to hang out in the vestibule reading the magazines that wouldn't fit in other people's mailboxes. Zu and Marie-Claude subscribed to *Vogue*, Italian *Vogue*, French *Vogue*, *W*, *Interview*, *Details*, and *Paper*. Ten years ago, Javier said, the *Times* had declared this building, this very building we were living in now, the worst building in New York: broken windows, trash everywhere, junkies lining up to cop. He'd been a junkie himself back then, but he'd kicked it. He showed me his copy of the article, which he kept folded up in his pocket. There, in yellowed newsprint dated April 10, 1974, was a photo of our building with the caption "The worst building in New York City."

"And now look at it." Javier waved Zu's copy of *Details* over the grimy stairwell as if it were the Helmsley Palace and he its fairy godmother. "Girls like you live here. Girls like you and girls like them."

It wasn't Javier or the clock lady at the door but Doug, who lived below us with his wife, Kelly Ann. They'd just had a baby. Doug was an anemic hippie carpenter, and Kelly Ann was an anemic hippie vegan baker. The baby was skinny as a chicken.

"Hey," Doug said. "Sorry to bother you." He sniffed the warm air coming from our stove. "Smells good."

"Baked potatoes."

He nodded at his feet. "I've got a little problem." He'd been building shelves for some rich dude, he said, one of the yuppies who lived in the Christodora House—everybody hated those Christodora yuppies, except Carmen; she wanted to live there—and the rich dude had left town ("Gone to fucking Thailand, who knows how long") without paying Doug. He needed to borrow a little money to buy milk for the baby.

I hesitated. I was trying to save. But the baby . . . There was something pathetic about their skinny baby, and the way he frowned as he rode through the cold streets strapped to his mother's back, taking in everything he saw. I worried about him. So I went into the closet, unlocked my briefcase, took ten dollars from my stash, and gave it to Doug.

"Thanks a lot. I'll pay it back as soon as I can."

"Don't worry."

After he left, Carmen sniffed. "I don't like his ponytail."

"The baby needs milk," I said. "How could I say no to that?"

"He smells like patchouli."

I thought I heard a noise in the bathroom. A dripping noise.

"I don't like her braids either," Carmen added. Kelly Ann wore her hair in lots of mousy braids all over her head. "They're phonies."

"The baby's real."

She opened the oven door and squeezed a potato with a potholder. "It's your money."

"They're poor."

The potatoes needed a few more minutes. She closed the oven door. "*We're* poor."

"I don't feel poor," I said.

"You don't?"

Uptown I'd felt poor. Downtown, I just needed money. Two different things.

The dripping came louder and faster. Carmen yanked open the bathroom door. It was raining from the ceiling.

She grabbed the mop to soak up the water. It rained harder. I got the bucket. Water poured down. We screamed. A stream flowed through the kitchen and into the living room. Carmen threw a roll of paper towels at it.

I ran upstairs. Javier stood in the hall, shirtless, flexing his ropy biceps and bellowing gusts of stinking liquor-breath into the stairwell. In the bathroom behind him, the toilet lay on its side next to a hole in the floor with water gushing out of it. Javier inflated his skinny torso, roared victoriously, and placed a foot on the defeated toilet, a lion exulting over its prey. I shrieked and fled back downstairs.

"Javier ripped the whole toilet right out of the floor!" I cried. "How? He's sixty-five years old. He's got skinny little-girl arms."

"Booze gives him power," Carmen said. "He told me that."

I went to find Mrs. Lisiewicz. She cursed in Polish and said she would turn off the water and get someone to fix it in the morning. "*Glupek* Javier," she muttered. "He lives here twenty-three years! One of these days I'll kick him out."

Back in the apartment, the floor was sopping. The place was a wreck. The radiators were cold. Carmen and I piled our coats on top of the comforter and climbed into bed, snuggling together for warmth.

"I still don't feel poor," I said. She nipped the tip of my nose. "Ow." It hurt in a good way.

I got my hair cut by a Japanese guy named Akira, who only charged twenty-five dollars. He shaved it off on one side and let it fall to my chin on the other. Then he bleached it white. If I didn't put on makeup I looked washed-out and ghostly. Carmen said I looked like an alien. Zu suggested if I wore silver and white, and only silver and white, no one would doubt I was psychic.

The next afternoon, around two, I went to have breakfast and hang out with Carmen while she worked at Café Lethe, near the corner of Fourth and A. I sat at the counter with Bix and Wesley Temple, who edited the *Underground*. Wes was lean and brown-skinned, handsome, disheveled, and tweedy, his long rockabilly sideburns prematurely touched with gray. Bix schmoozed everyone, patting them on the back and joking around, presiding over the counter as if he were the godfather of the East Village. He *was* famous, in a way. He acted in indie films, and was best-known for playing a bookie in *Weird Garden*, the art-house hit of 1983.

Carmen poured me a cup of coffee and hustled away to clear tables, no time to talk. Bix added a dash of bourbon to his coffee and offered me his flask.

I waved it away. "I just woke up."

"Wes?"

Wes was engrossed in that day's *Post*. "Put that thing away."

Bix assessed my new hair. "It suits you, dollbaby."

Wes tapped a photo in the *Post* of Prince Charles and Princess Diana skiing in Liechtenstein. "Remember when they got married? Only a couple of years ago. Now they look bored."

"I remember," I said. "I was waitressing in a bar in Baltimore that summer. I had the lunch shift that day, and when I got to work in the morning the wedding was playing on TV. The ceremony was over by then, but the networks repeated the highlights all day long, and the cook refused to turn it off. She was a short lady in her sixties who wore her hair in a hairnet."

"Was her name Gladys?" Bix asked.

"No, it was Rhonda."

"She sounds like a Gladys."

"I remember thinking, *That could be me*, you know, in theory, because Diana and I are the same age. I said to Rhonda, 'Maybe *I* could be marrying the Prince of Wales, enveloped in a white fog of a dress and waving at people from a golden coach, instead of stirring industrial-grade mustard into a plastic vat of oil to pour over rotting spinach leaves.' And Rhonda looked at me in my waitress outfit with a dirty rag in my hand and said, 'Don't blame me for the spinach, hon. The boss forces me to economize.'"

"Maybe Charles will get tired of Di and send her to the guillotine," Bix said. "Like Henry the Eighth."

"I love Henry the Eighth," I said. "When I was little I had paper dolls of him and his wives." The six wives and their executions had held an almost erotic fascination for me, but I couldn't have said why.

"Did you cut off their heads?" Bix asked.

"I just dressed them and undressed them."

Someone banged on the café's plate-glass window. There was Atti waving from the sidewalk, his leather jacket unzipped despite the February cold and his bandaged foot propped on a skateboard. Carmen looked up from clearing a table and frowned.

"Mr. Pilkvist." Bix waved him in. "Come in off the street." Atti hobbled in and propped himself on a counter stool.

"What the hell happened to you?" Wes asked.

"My girlfriend bit off one of my toes."

Carmen popped up behind the counter.

"Carmen! My love."

"Atti, what are you doing here?"

"I'm bored! And I'm hungry. Can you give me a bagel or something?"

She sighed and reached for a poppy-seed bagel. "I was going to bring over pierogies later."

"Toasted," he added. "With lots of butter."

We were quiet while Carmen sliced the bagel and put it into the toaster, while she poured a cup of coffee and slid it over the counter to Atti, while he lightened the coffee with milk and let his spoon tingaling against the side of the cup. He was cadaverously thin, the whites of his eyes veined with red. I forced myself to breathe steadily, to keep breathing.

"You been writing, Atti?" Wes asked. "Or playing somewhere?"

"Trying. Hope to have a new song or two to play at the Ear next week."

Carmen kept her eyes on her knife as she slathered butter on the bagel.

"The thing to do is turn everything that happens to you into something beautiful," Wes said. "Even the horrors."

"Horrors, yeah, I got plenty of those to work with."

Carmen's knife scraped across the bagel.

"There's some bad shit going around, Attila," Biz said. "They found a girl dead in the park the other day."

"One of the Amelias?" Wes asked. "Not the one with the Farrah Fawcett hair?"

"I don't know," Bix said. "She didn't have Farrah Fawcett hair when they found her."

"Who are the Amelias?" I asked.

"That's what Wes calls the girls on those 'Missing' flyers you see all over the place," Bix said.

"After Amelia Earhart," Wes said. "The most famous missing person in history."

"This century, anyway," Carmen said.

"That's the first Amelia they've found," Wes said. "That I've heard about. When I see a new flyer I stare at it for a long time, and then I look for the girl as I walk around the neighborhood. But I haven't spotted one yet."

"They probably look nothing like those high school yearbook pictures their parents give to the police," Bix said.

"How many girls have gone missing?" I asked.

"I count five so far," Wes said.

"So where are the other ones?"

"Maybe they went home," Carmen said. "To Ohio and West Virginia."

When Carmen's shift ended, I helped her take Atti back to his squat. He stood on the skateboard and let us tow him along. As we skirted the park, the rooster leered at us from his lookout on Samuel Sullivan Cox's head.

"Whose rooster is that?" I asked.

"I don't know," Carmen said. "He's always been there."

The skin around my ribs started tingling, little fishhooks of anxiety gnawing at me. "What does he eat—rats?"

Atti twitched his fingers at me and hissed, "He eats human souls."

"Shut up, Atti," Carmen said.

As we got closer to Atti's building, I said, "Okay, see you guys later, I have to get ready for work."

"Phoebe—"

We let go of Atti's hands and he rolled ahead of us to his front door. I stopped on the sidewalk, drawing short breaths with effort. The air suddenly felt thick as water.

"You coming?" Carmen asked.

"I just can't," I said.

She frowned, and I felt her judgment: a coward. Weak. I tried to defend myself.

"How can you stand it? The sores and the vomit and his neediness . . . Why do you put up with him?"

She glanced at Atti a few yards away. He sat down on the skateboard to wait for us.

"You ever see that movie *Fat City*? About two boxers, Stacy Keach and Jeff Bridges?"

"I think so, on TV once maybe, late at night . . ." I started to breathe easier, talking about movies instead of Atti.

"Remember that barfly character, Oma? And she has this lover, I think his name is Earl. Stacy Keach lives with her for a while when Earl is in jail. But she's an annoying drunk, she drives Stacy Keach crazy, and finally he leaves her. One night when he's feeling down he goes back to her place and Earl opens the door. He's out of jail. Oma is drunk and shouting curses at Stacy Keach, and Earl says, 'Don't listen to her, she's drunk,' and Stacy says, 'I know.' And Earl says, 'The thing you gotta know about Oma is she's a juicehead.' He just accepts that about her. 'She's a juicehead, so don't pay her no mind.' She's a juicehead, and he loves her, and that's all."

Atti picked up a bottle cap and flicked it at us. It landed in the gutter.

"That's your definition of love?"

"Do you know another one?"

"What about loving someone because they're good to you? Because they're worthy?"

"What about it? If they're worthy, I guess you're lucky. But that's not love."

She loved who she loved. Once she loved you, you couldn't shake her. But you couldn't earn your way into her heart, either. So if she loved you, it made you a kind of royalty.

"Hey girls!" Atti called. "Hurry up. My foot's about to fall off."

"Sorry, Carmen." I ran home, leaving her to help Atti on her own. The club didn't open for hours, but I couldn't wait to get there and hide in the darkness, at least for a little while.

13

SO BORED OF HAVING MY PICTURE TAKEN

Toby's sister, Shan, had set up a new space for me in a corner of the ladies' lounge, with a red velvet curtain, a little Moroccan table, a crystal ball, and a stuffed panther as my familiar. I could close the curtain if my customer wanted privacy. I arrived at ten and sat at the table in my turban, smoking and shooting the breeze with Ruby until the club heated up—not till after midnight, usually. Ruby manned the concession stand. She was Hungarian and didn't speak English well. I told her fortune to pass the time, even though she said she didn't believe in it. She believed in auras, and told me mine was blue, which meant I was coolheaded in a crisis. I wished that were true. She supplied me with Teaberry gum whenever I wanted some, but I couldn't convince her to comp me cigarettes.

I wandered out to the shark bar. A kind of burlesque show was taking place on the small curtained stage at the back. Two women dressed in kimonos and white geisha makeup tried to walk with bowling balls strapped to their feet. They kept falling down, to the amusement of the five men watching.

A gang of artists rolled into the bar with a rowdy hoot, five or so scruffy guys, three wild-haired women, a few sleek dealer types, and some young and pretty art groupies. They were riled up, ordering vodka and champagne and toasting each other. One of them was Jem, in jeans and a T-shirt, a pack of Marlboros rolled up in one sleeve.

"Where are you coming from?" I asked.

"Group show at International," he said. I knew he meant International With Monument, a gallery on Seventh Street—and this gave me a little thrill of pleasure. I was beginning, at last, to know things. He had three paintings in the show, he told me, cityscapes of the Lower East Side: brick walls, apartment windows, graffiti, iron gates, empty lots, bums. Realism, but highly stylized and dreamy.

"I'd like to see them sometime," I said.

"You can. They're at International."

"I will then."

"Where's Carmen?" he asked.

"She's taking care of her boyfriend. He's sick."

A sleek woman in her thirties came over to congratulate Jem. Compared to the artists, she looked restrained and adult. She would have faded into the background in her black skirt suit, but the large gold cuff around her neck acted as a sort of reverse halo, floating under her head rather than over it and making her bobbed chestnut hair gleam in the dark. She said the *Times* reviewer had asked about Jem's paintings, calling them the standouts of the show. She took his chin in her hand and gave it a little shake. "Get ready. You're about to become a feeding frenzy." She stepped away to order a martini.

"Who's that?" I asked.

"Esphyr Collins. Collins Gallery?"

"Are you going to have a solo show?"

"I hope so." His eyes kept drifting toward Esphyr, keeping track of where she was and who she was talking to.

"Hey, dollbaby." Bix tipped his tiny hat at us. "You've got customers waiting."

"I'll be in my office," I said to Jem.

A mod Cleopatra waited at my table. She had black hair with very short bangs, a gold band around her forehead, and a short gold dress decorated with green snakes.

"Somebody burned my sleeve." She held out her butterfly sleeve to display a perfect round cigarette hole. "Are you the fortune-teller?"

"Uh-huh."

"Goody. Tell my fortune."

"It's five dollars."

She pouted. "I don't carry money. Can't you just do it for free?"

I looked into her eyes, black under silver-shadowed lids, and realized that she was Aviva B., NYU student turned It Girl. Her picture was in *Details* a lot, and on Page Six, documenting her attendance at celebrity birthday parties and nightclubs and openings with her best friend, a blond boy named Jacky St. Jennifer.

"Okay. Think about your question and shake up the box."

"Shake shake shake! Am I ever going to be a movie star?"

I closed my eyes, and to my surprise, I had a vision, clear as a TV show. I saw Aviva sleeping in a narrow bed, illuminated by the green glow of a digital alarm clock. Another girl, wearing a nightgown, stood over her, watching her sleep.

I reported this vision to Aviva.

"Oh my God! That happened! You're amazing!"

She told me that her freshman roommate had been crazy, "like, literally insane." She used to sleepwalk with a Swiss Army knife in her hand, and sometimes Aviva would wake up to find the roommate staring at her while she slept. Aviva's parents feared for her safety, so they bought her a studio apartment near Washington Square Park. It was so much better than living in a dorm, especially since she hardly bothered with classes anymore, except for her acting class.

"Did you really see that in a vision?"

In the back of my mind I wondered if I'd read it somewhere, that maybe Aviva had told a reporter this story of how she got her apartment. Other than the largesse of her parents she had no real source of income, but people offered her clothes and food and drinks for free wherever she went. She expected it.

"What about my question? Am I going to be a movie star?"

I pulled out three ticket stubs: *Flashdance. Network. The Day of the Dolphin.*

"Oh my God! I am! I am! That's so amazing. Can I do another one?"

I wouldn't necessarily have interpreted the stubs that way, but I wanted her to be happy. "Sure. Ask another question."

A flash startled me—a photographer taking our picture. Aviva turned and posed for him, leaning back in her chair, tossing her head, kicking her legs in the air and laughing. She moved her body fluidly from one pose to another, *click click click*.

The photographer moved on, and Aviva turned her attention back to me. She bounced in her seat.

"You have a lot of energy," I said.

"I do! I don't even do coke! I don't drink or take any drugs."

"How do you stay up all night without drugs?"

"I have energy!"

"You have to sit still or I can't tell your future."

She froze like a statue, making King Tut angles with her hands and neck. Then she broke the pose and laughed.

"Did you have another question?"

"Yes! Hmmm . . . what should I ask . . . hmm . . . How about: Is my father cheating on my mother?"

That surprised me; hardly anybody asked questions about other people. She squeezed her eyes shut and concentrated while she shook the box.

Shoot the Moon. Caddyshack. The 400 Blows.

"Do you really want to know the answer?" I hated to deliver bad news, but I also wanted to interpret the stubs as accurately as possible.

"Give it to me straight, Astrid baby."

"Then yes. I'm afraid he's cheating on her."

My reasoning: *Shoot the Moon* is about a disintegrating marriage,

Caddyshack has the word *cad* in the title, and, even though I'd seen *The 400 Blows* twice and knew perfectly well that it was about a French boy's difficult childhood, in this context the title suddenly sounded like porn.

"Wow. Okay. That sucks. But why did I ask, right? I mean, something must have made me wonder what was going on."

Andy Warhol walked in with one of the artists from Jem's gang, a handsome Asian James Dean type. The guy took off his T-shirt and posed against the red wall next to the sinks while Andy took pictures of him with a large, boxy camera. Aviva brightened.

"Andy's shooting Polaroids! I'm going to ask him to take my picture."

She was distracted by the entrance of a fashion designer and his entourage, including a pouting blond boy in a plaid dress. "Jacky!" She hopped up to greet him. "Jacky is here finally! Jacky, let's get our picture taken together!"

"Do it without me," Jacky said. "I'm so bored of having my picture taken."

It was a slow night. I sat on the couch and did a bump from a vial I'd bought from Bix. Then I wandered around the club, wondering where Jem had gone. I passed a live goat with a unicorn horn pasted to its head and a man in a stewardess uniform with the letters T-W-A-T on the cap. A very thin girl in a dress made of chain mail danced by herself beside the pool. She looked like a ballerina—long strawberry blond hair, a turned-up nose, and sharply arched feet—and her dancing was precise and skilled. "Dance vis me," she ordered in a German accent. Her pupils were dilated and I wondered if she was tripping. I swayed self-consciously beside her. She grabbed me by both shoulders and tried to push me into the pool. "Into ze Jell-O!" she shouted. I spun away and accidentally knocked her into the pool instead.

"I'm sorry! Are you okay?"

She did a somersault in the water and splashed up for air. "Yes, I love it!" She lapped at the water and made a face. "But zis Jell-O tastes terrible."

"It's not Jell-O." I offered her a hand but she slapped it away, laughing. She tried to climb out of the pool herself, but her metal dress, which must have been heavy, clanked. She ducked under water and slipped out of it. It sank to the bottom of the pool. An inflatable duck floated by; she caught it and tried to twist its neck.

"Are you sure you're okay?" I asked, but she ignored me, engrossed in her battle with the duck. Carmen appeared beside me, with Jem close behind.

"Why is a naked girl wrestling with a plastic duck?" she asked.

"That's Katinka," Jem said.

"Is she tripping?" I asked. "She thought the pool was made of Jell-O."

"She's Swiss," Jem said, as if that explained it.

"How do you know her?" Carmen asked.

He shrugged. "From around."

Katinka was punching the duck in the head now. "Let's go to the Gold Lounge," Carmen said. "She's freaking me out."

We found Zu in the Gold Lounge and settled around her on a couch. "You ran away from me today, Phoebe," Carmen said, but she didn't seem mad. Everybody was in a friendly mood. I admired Zu's earrings, two screaming faces with ruby-red eyes dangling over her collarbone. She'd made them, she said. She'd make some for me if I liked. She talked and talked and I agreed with everything she said and we both chain-smoked until we ran out of cigarettes. When I got up to bum some from Carmen she was shimmying on top of the bar, shaking her blue panties in Jem's face. She slipped and fell and everyone screamed but Jem caught her. He held her in his arms while she kicked her feet and laughed.

Zu and I went to find Bix. We did more coke and drank more vodka. We bought Camel Lights from Ruby and sat on the couch to smoke them. I was telling Zu the story of my life. She couldn't possibly have cared, but I couldn't stop talking. She'd mentioned her father, an astronomer in Chile, and so I told her about my father, that he'd been a doctor and my mother had been a nurse, which was how they'd met. Before that he'd gone to med school in New York, at Columbia, back in the fifties. He loved to tell stories about his wild friend Danny Washburn: the time they sneaked into Carnegie Hall through a backstage door because they just had to see Billie Holiday. The time Danny dragged him to Snookie's to hear Dizzy Gillespie play at 2 a.m. the night before an exam. The crowded parties they threw in their apartment, red wine, whiskey, bebop, smoke, poetry, dancing, and lots of talk. Danny flunked out of med school, but he ended up opening a jazz club, which was what he'd always dreamed of doing anyway. That Danny, Dad liked to say. He really knew how to live.

Dad and Danny were my age then. Danny would have loved Plutonium.

"I want to be one of those people who knows how to live!" Zu declared.

"So do I! But you are," I told her. "You so *are*." I dragged on my cigarette.

"I would like to meet your dad," Zu said.

I blew out a long plume of smoke and watched it swirl and shift. I looked for him in the smoke the way you look for shapes in a cloud.

"I would like to meet *your* dad," I said.

"Oh, he's in Chile, he's so far away."

The club was closing and I couldn't find Carmen. Zu had left on the back of someone's motorcycle. The geisha girls had removed the bowling balls from their feet. One girl stood on her head, her kimono falling open. The other geisha smashed raw eggs on the first girl's crotch and laughed while the yolk drooled down her belly. The first girl scissored her legs. She had a really solid headstand. Nothing knocked her over.

No Carmen, no Jem. Somehow I knew for sure they had left together. Maybe I really was psychic.

It was three thirty in the morning. I walked home on salt-dusted streets too frigid and desolate for muggers, hurrying from corner to corner, my bones rattling in the cold. In a vacant lot on the Bowery, three men warmed their hands over a trash barrel fire. "Go home, girl!" they shouted at me. "Get your little ass home!"

I hustled over to Second Avenue, the bars closed and dark, the street deserted. I cut down Fifth to First Avenue. At the light on the corner of Sixth Street I felt a presence behind me, about half a block away. A tall figure moving slowly in my direction. I couldn't make out much more than that. I speed-walked across First Avenue, against the light, and headed north. The man—I could tell it was a man now—cut across the intersection diagonally, closing in on me. A cab zoomed past him, honking.

I glanced back quickly. All I saw, in the bright light of First Avenue, was a black knit cap, a dark coat, and a white face.

I walked faster.

I turned right on Ninth Street. A third of the way down the block, I checked for him. The man turned the corner, steady and relentless as a shark.

This was beginning to feel eerily familiar. *You did too much coke,* I told myself. *You're paranoid.* But those thoughts did nothing to comfort me. I might have done too much coke. I might have been paranoid. Nevertheless, the man behind me quickened his pace.

I started to run, down Ninth Street to A. I ran the half block to my building and burst through the outer door. I patted my pockets for my keys, watching for the man. Found the keys. Fumbled open the door. Ran upstairs. Unlocked my door. Scurried inside the apartment. Locked the door behind me.

"Carmen?"

No Carmen. The apartment was dark. The cats stretched and meowed. I went to the window. The man stood across the street, watching our building. I stepped back from the window, glad I hadn't turned on the light. We stood frozen like that for a few minutes, in a standoff. Then he disappeared into the park, leaving a trail of footprints in the snow, and leaving me to wonder if my past had come looking for me.

JUNKIE HEAVEN

By 5 a.m. I guessed that Carmen wasn't coming home. I added fifteen dollars to my Ivan stash and changed into pajamas. The bed was rumpled, the floor carpeted with clothes. I'm a slob, but Carmen was worse. I started picking up dresses and hanging them in the closet, lining up shoes against the wall, folding shirts and pants and putting them in drawers, tossing dirty underwear in the paper grocery bag we used for laundry. She wouldn't have wanted me to clean up after her but I did it anyway. I pulled open the bottom dresser drawer to put away a scarf and noticed, under Carmen's blue Fair Isle, a white corner of paper. I lifted the sweater and found a thin stack of pages.

JUNKIE HEAVEN
BY CARMEN DIETZ

SETTING: *New York City, the East Village, early 1980s*

CHARACTERS:

ARI—*A handsome junkie musician*

CHARLOTTE—*Ari's girlfriend, a writer*

PENNY—*Charlotte's roommate, a would-be psychic*

NEIL—*Ari's gonzo friend*

Penny?

I hated the name Penny.

She'd never mentioned that she was writing a play. I'd thought we kept no secrets from each other. *Surely,* I thought, *she simply forgot to tell me about it*, and, full of rectitude, I sat on the floor and read the whole thing. It wasn't long—she'd only written the first act.

Ari and Charlotte were a lot like Attila and Caledonia in Carmen's college stories, funny and attractive and doomed. Neil was based on Dean, and Penny, Charlotte's comic foil, was involved with a married man named Vlad. Penny was naïve—ditzy, even. Okay, stupid. One scene in particular gnawed at me.

PENNY: *Do you think Vlad loves me?*

CHARLOTTE: *You've only gone out with him twice.*

PENNY: *I know . . . but he's so noble. He works for the Red Cross. He helps hurricane victims.*

CHARLOTTE: *I know, you told me.*

PENNY: *And he's so glamorous. He's got that Eastern European accent, like Dracula. Dracula is sexy, don't you think?*

CHARLOTTE *presses her lips together in a struggle to keep silent.*

PENNY: *Guess where we're going tonight? The Russian Tea Room.*

CHARLOTTE: *For dinner? No one goes to the Russian Tea Room for dinner.*

PENNY: *They don't?*

CHARLOTTE: *No, they don't. Everyone goes there for lunch. Only tourists go to the Russian Tea Room for dinner.*

PENNY: *But Vlad isn't a tourist. . . .*

CHARLOTTE: *Tourists and men who don't want to be seen with their mistresses.*

PENNY *blinks, slow to comprehend.*

CHARLOTTE: *Penny, wake up! Don't you see that he's using you?*

PENNY: *He's not! He's not using me! He loves me.*

CHARLOTTE *shakes her head ruefully.*

Obviously she was exaggerating. I'd never said anything about Dracula being sexy, and I never would. I told myself it was only fiction. But it stung. I pictured her imagining Penny, then thinking of me and asking herself, *What's something stupid that Phoebe would say?*

And then I wondered: *What other secrets did she keep from me?*

I put the play back in the drawer. Then I asked my shoebox oracle if I should tell Carmen that I'd read it. I shook the box self-consciously, as if Carmen were watching, as if I were the ridiculous Penny. I plucked out one ticket stub: *The Other Side of Midnight.* It was the first R-rated movie I'd ever seen, when I was sixteen, about a beautiful French woman who ruthlessly uses men to get what she wants. My friend Winnie's older sister took us to see it. My parents would not have approved.

I meditated on the title of the movie, and its message, and the circumstances under which I'd seen it.

Layers of secrets. If the play was Carmen's secret, then knowing about it would be mine.

Outside, someone screamed. I ran to the window. Another screech . . . but it was only the rooster.

The night grayed into morning. It was snowing again, snow blurring the branches of the trees, snow slowly erasing the footprints of the tall man who had followed me home.

Now, through the veil of snow, a smaller man appeared at the edge of the park, just inside the fence. I focused until his outline sharpened: narrow eyes and bent nose, a plaid tie and plaid sport coat that didn't match.

Dad.

He was alive.

I knew it. He hadn't died.

He gripped the iron stakes of the fence, shaking them like the bars of a jail cell, as if he wanted to leave but couldn't. He waved to me. He saw me in the window and beckoned, *Come in, come in, come in. . . .*

My feet had magnets in them; they tugged toward the iron fence. *Climb up on the windowsill,* my feet said. *And step out. That's the fastest way to the park . . .*

I tugged open the window. Cold air washed over me. I lifted my bare foot and rested it on the sill. Diego jumped up and rubbed against my shin. I caught him before he could tumble out.

Dad waved again, his figure fading and transparent. Where were his glasses? Where was his stethoscope?

When Laurel and I had croup, or a cold, he used to press his stethoscope to our small backs, murmuring, "Take a deep breath . . . again . . . again. . . ."

This wasn't him. More like an afterimage of him.

A ghost does not need glasses.

A stethoscope is useless in the land of no breath and no heartbeat.

I pushed the window closed.

The rooster crowed again. The snow stopped. The clouds burned away and the sun bloomed in the east, far beyond the park. I looked for Dad once more, but he vanished in the light.

15

INTERNATIONAL WITH MONUMENT

I woke up at noon to find Carmen asleep on the couch, two hours late for work. "Shit." She jumped to her feet and started pawing through the dresser in search of her jeans. "Will you call the café and tell them I'll be there in ten minutes?"

While she dressed I hunted for the phone. We were always leaving it inside boxes or cabinets and could never find it when we needed it.

"Jem and I tried to find you before we left," she called from the bedroom.

"I looked all over for you."

"We went to Florent for onion soup. Have you been there?" Assuming correctly that I had not been there, she explained that Florent was an all-night French diner on a greasy cobblestone block in the meatpacking district, deserted except for some meat warehouses and hookers from the West Side piers. "It was crowded, and Jem knew everybody. A guy came in with an accordion and the whole restaurant sang 'Auprès de Ma Blonde.'"

"'Qu'il fait bon, fait bon, fait bon,'" I sang. I wanted to go to Florent. "Here's the phone." I'd found it inside an empty planter.

"Forget it." Carmen emerged from the bedroom buttoning Mitch over a thick Irish sweater. "If you start dialing now I'll be at Lethe in time to answer the call myself. I'll save an onion bagel for you."

She hurried out. The day was clear and peppermint bright. The snow in the park had been trodden to mud, and it was hard to picture a ghost among the freaks playing bongos. Maybe I'd dreamed it.

I sat at the kitchen table and wrote my mother a postcard.

Dear Mom,

I saw Dad's ghost last night! He looked pretty good. He wasn't wearing his glasses. He waved to me. He didn't speak, but if he had I'm sure he would have told me to say hi to you.

Ha-ha. No. I crossed it out. Too bad, because the picture on that postcard was an innocuous photo of the Chrysler Building, and now I couldn't use it. The only other postcard I had showed Billie Holiday, head tilted back, mouth open, eyes closed. I assumed she was singing, but it looked like she was crying out in pain. I'd bought it at Gem Spa on St. Marks. It was one of the few cards there that didn't show punks or neighborhood landmarks, which might have given away my location.

Dear Mom,

Just a note to let you know that I'm doing well. I'm safe. I'm healthy. I have a job. I have a place to live. I would tell you where I am but I'm afraid you'll try to come and get me or something and honestly I'm fine and I DON'T NEED ANY HELP. I'm actually doing REALLY GREAT, and I don't want you to worry because THERE'S NOTHING TO WORRY ABOUT. Okay? I'll write to you again soon. Say hi to Laurel for me.

Love, P

P.S. If you'd just stop worrying, we could be a lot closer.

Billie Holiday was from Baltimore, and Dad had loved her music. Thinking about it now, I remembered that Mom disapproved of her, because she was an addict, which set a bad example. So maybe it wasn't such a great choice.

The next day I rode the subway up to the main Manhattan post office in midtown so the postmark wouldn't give my location away. Downtown people joked that they got nosebleeds when they crossed north of Fourteenth Street. I didn't get a nosebleed at the post office (all my nosebleeds happened below Fourteenth), but I felt lightheaded, as if the air were thinner up on Thirty-Second Street. I didn't feel like myself again until I got back downtown.

On my way to Café Lethe I saw a new "Missing" flyer posted outside Ray's Candy. This girl, Darlene Abidin, was seventeen and had last been seen three days earlier, walking home from Stuyvesant High School. In the photo she held a terrier; she and the dog were wearing matching red bows. A girl came out of Ray's and I found myself checking to see if it was Darlene Abidin, but of course it wasn't. Still, I kept scanning girls' faces as I walked down the street.

I turned up Seventh and stopped in at International With Monument. The gallery was famous for its lively openings, parties spilling onto the sidewalk and into the street. Most people never made it inside to see the art.

The front window announced the title of the show in black sans serif letters: FROM THE GUT: NEW WORK. It was a group show, very mixed: streaky photos, noisy videos playing on a monitor in the corner, neo-expressionist paintings in loud, screaming colors—a blast of anger. Jem's oil paintings stood out for their muted stillness; no neon yellows or blood reds, but browns and blacks and beiges, grays, whites, and brick reds.

First and First was an urban landscape: a graffiti-covered handball court surrounded by a chain-link fence, a block of brick tenements in the background. *Papi* was a portrait of a young man on a fire escape bouncing a chubby baby in his lap. My favorite: a view through a window, from the outside, into a tenement bedroom: bed neatly made, books piled on a nightstand, sharpened pencils in a Café Bustelo can, a spray of bodega daisies wilting in a jelly glass. In the painting, a miniature copy of *Papi* hung over the bed. This picture was called *Secret Sanctuary*. Around the window frame Jem had neatly printed tiny words: *- Chronicler - of the LES - Since 1981.* If you looked closely, you could read the titles on the spines of the books: *The Night Sky. Baseball Stats 1940–1980. Cooking on a Hot Plate. Wild Cats of Africa. The Big Sleep.*

Jem himself was at Lethe when I got there, leaning over the counter talking to Carmen, who had crouched down to sweep shards of glass into a dustpan.

"I broke a glass," Bix explained. "While making a dramatic point." He waved an arm across the counter in slow motion to demonstrate how a glass might become the casualty of such a gesture.

Carmen rose to empty the dustpan. I took the stool next to Jem. "I saw your paintings," I said. "I like them."

"Thanks. When are you going to see them, Carmen?"

"I'll get around to it one of these days." A coded smile passed between them.

"Can I buy one?" Bix said. "How much are they going for?"

"I like *Secret Sanctuary* the best," I said. "Are you living in that apartment now?"

"Maybe."

Carmen set a toasted onion bagel in front of me. "Saved one for you, as promised."

"Do you sleep with *Baseball Stats* next to your bed?"

"I'm a Yankees fan from way back," Jem said.

"Orioles." I tapped my heart. "But I love the Yanks too."

"You can't like both," Bix said. "They're sworn enemies."

"Who says I can't?"

Jem shook his head. "A girl who likes two teams at once can't be trusted." He grinned to show he was teasing. "I got work to do. See you all later."

"Me too." Bix slid off his stool. "One sec, Jem, I'll walk out with you."

Carmen filled my coffee cup and started wrapping up an egg sandwich to go. "For Atti?" I asked.

"You promised to come with me this time, remember?"

I couldn't think of an excuse not to, and besides, I didn't feel like being alone. We left when her shift ended.

"Are you going to see Jem again tonight?"

"What do you mean?"

"I mean, do you have plans with him?"

"No. Why would we?"

Maybe they were just friends, and the dinner they'd shared at Florent in the middle of the night was an anomaly that would never happen again. Maybe they really had tried to find me before they left.

Atti shivered in his bed under three blankets, in spite of the electric heater Carmen had bought for him. She felt his forehead, then unwrapped the warm egg sandwich and insisted that he eat it, at least a few bites.

The apartment was cleaner than ours now. The Marshall amp and the electric guitar were gone; Atti must have sold them. Carmen boiled water on a hot plate for tea and washed a bunch of grapes, putting them in a bowl and setting it on the floor beside his mattress. She took a thermometer from a shelf over the sink and slipped it under his tongue. His face was thin, all eyes and a slash of mouth, his bandaged foot hidden under blankets.

When the water boiled, I made a cup of tea for him. Carmen read the thermometer, frowning. She brought him some aspirin and said, "Let me see your foot."

This was the part I hated most, the unveiling of the deep, oozing sores. I brought the tea and set it by the bed. "Would you like some, Carmen?"

"No thanks." She started unwrapping the bandages. I felt pressure in my lungs, the can't-breathe feeling rising. I went into the bathroom and shut the door. I sat on the edge of the tub and tried not to listen.

She loved him. Anyone could see that. But she could love Atti and Jem at the same time. Why not? Like loving both the Yankees and the Orioles. Jem had said a girl who likes two teams at once can't be trusted. That was his opinion. I didn't agree, and I still don't.

"Phoebe, it's safe to come out now."

I flushed the toilet to make my bathroom visit seem legit. Atti was sitting up and had a little color in his cheeks.

"I wasn't hiding."

"Sure you weren't."

Atti sipped his tea. "Do you want to play cards?" Carmen asked. "How about Crazy Eights?"

"I'll play," Atti said. "But I must warn you, playing Crazy Eights fills me with rage."

Carmen laughed. I got the cards.

"I'm not joking," Atti said.

Carmen dealt. "Do you ever think about writing anymore?" I asked her.

She discarded an eight of spades over a heart. "Writing? What do you mean?"

I'd promised myself I wouldn't let her know that I'd found her play. But I couldn't stop thinking about it, wondering why she kept it a secret. I couldn't resist pressing her a little to see what she'd say.

"You know, like you did in college. Do you ever think about writing stories again?"

"No." She frowned at the ace of spades on top of the pile, and drew one card after another until she had another spade to play. "Damn it."

Atti played the jack. "I loved those stories you used to write about us."

"They weren't about *us*," Carmen said. "They were made-up characters."

"One of them had my name," Atti said. "You used to read them to me at night sometimes, remember?"

"I used your name because it's so irresistibly excellent," Carmen said. "It was still fiction. You never had a hat with antlers on it, did you?"

"No, but I had that hat with bug eyes on it."

"Totally different."

"Len and Betsy would probably love it if you wrote a play," I said. "Something with a great part for her, so she could make a triumphant return to the stage."

"I'm not so sure she wants that." Carmen tossed her cards down in frustration, abandoning the game. "Atti, have you finished your tea? I'll make you a little soup."

"You're quitting? Before my fit of rage?" Atti said. "Does this mean I won?"

I shuffled the cards and put them away. She heated up some chicken noodle soup and delivered a bowl to Atti.

"Eat this. And don't go out."

"Yes, ma'am."

"And if Dean comes in with some fantastic idea, don't listen to him. And don't swallow anything he gives you."

"I won't."

She kissed him, and we left.

"How did you learn to do that?" I asked.

"Do what?"

"Nurse a sick person. Bandage his foot and all that."

"I don't know. When you have to do something, you figure it out."

"I guess." We walked in silence for a few paces.

Maybe she put up with Atti because she could use the details about him in her play. Maybe she put up with me for the same reason. I thought about Ivan, how I'd put myself at his mercy just to see what would happen, to follow the story. When I'd wanted the story to end, I'd declared it over, but by then it had taken on a life of its own and was out of my control. For the first time I thought: *Perhaps even now, this very night, unbeknownst to me, my actions are having consequences somewhere in the world. Perhaps the story of Ivan lurks somewhere nearby, waiting to catch me off guard.*

We reached the east side of the park and walked west along Seventh Street. It was dark by now. I kept an eye out for suspicious-looking tall men.

"Phoebe, is everything okay?"

"Sure."

"You seem distracted."

"I'm a little freaked out, I guess," I said. "When I left the club last night, someone followed me home."

"You walked? Alone?" She punished me with a karate chop to the shoulder instead of a lecture. "Do you think it was the same guy as before, from uptown?"

"I couldn't tell. They were both tall. But a lot of men are tall."

"Not enough, if you ask me."

"Ha-ha."

We turned right onto Avenue A. A breeze blew puffs of snow off the trees.

"Something else happened last night," I said. "I saw my father."

"Where?"

"Right here. In the park."

We stopped. I pointed out the spot. She held my hand. Neither one of us had gloves.

"I believe you," she said.

"Thank you." And for that brief moment I felt, *She's mine again.*

16

PURPLE FOOTPRINTS

One morning in March, very early, Carmen and I were awakened by wailing sirens. We hurried to the window. Police cars, an ambulance, flashing red lights, and a small crowd of derelicts had assembled near the marble water fountain, the one that said, CHARITY- FAITH - TEMPERANCE - HOPE. I sensed Carmen holding her breath.

"I have a bad feeling," she said.

Two EMTs rolled a gurney down the path out of the park, ferrying a body covered with a blanket. As they loaded it into the ambulance, the blanket shifted, and a bandaged foot peeped out.

Carmen yelped and ran downstairs in her pajamas. I grabbed our coats, slipped my feet into boots, and followed. The sun rose, daylight drawing a curtain across the sky. By the time I reached her, she stood at the gaping door of the ambulance, talking to a police officer. He unveiled the face of the body on the gurney. "Save you a trip to the morgue."

Atti.

It was his eyes that did it, their frozen look.

The ambulance pulled away, cherry top flashing but no siren now, because no urgency was required. We stood abandoned on the sidewalk in shock, staring after the ambulance as it grew smaller and smaller and finally vanished. Carmen shivered. I draped her coat over her shoulders. "Bad batch," she murmured.

The ambulance was gone. The police cars drove away. The derelicts dispersed. All traces of catastrophe had disappeared. But the evidence lingered in my body, as if an electric current had fried my nerves, my skin, my hair, and the static continued to prickle and numb me.

I tried to lead Carmen back inside, but she resisted. She twitched from foot to foot, her legs jittery. She'd never be able to sit still or lie down or sleep, not for a long time. So we walked around the park, trying to shake off the memory of his eyes. We walked in silence, slowly, down A, rounding Seventh, over to B. Her breathing was ragged, a kind of dry sob. To distract her, and myself, I started talking.

"This is probably not helpful," I said, "but did I ever tell you about Snookie?"

"Your dachshund. The Bark Button?"

"This is a different Snookie story." I paused to help her slip her arms into her coat sleeves. "I was about nine, I guess. I went to a sleepover at this girl Donna's house. It was summer, really hot. She lived two blocks away, so I walked over there with my patchwork hippie girl sleeping bag and a little duffel with my nightgown and a toothbrush in it."

"I had one of those patchwork sleeping bags," Carmen said.

"We played Stiff as a Board, Light as a Feather. You know that game?"

"Something with fingers?"

"Right. You get someone to lie on the floor and pretend to be dead. We picked Donna, since she was the tallest and heaviest girl there."

"The fat girl."

"More big than fat. The type who plays volleyball. She lay down on the floor, giggling, and closed her eyes and crossed her arms over her chest like she was dead. The rest of us surrounded her and touched her with two fingers from each hand. We tried to lift her, but she was too heavy."

I stopped to gauge Carmen's interest in the story. She frowned and kept her eyes on the sidewalk, but she said, "Keep going."

"We chanted, 'Stiff as a board, light as a feather; stiff as a board, light as a feather,' ten times."

"I remember this game now . . ."

"When we tried to lift her this time, she floated high into the air." I demonstrated, raising my hands slowly. "It was so cool. After that, everybody wanted to do it. We stayed up half the night chanting, 'Stiff as a board . . .' "

"I thought you said this was a story about Snookie."

"It is. I'm setting it up."

We rounded the corner of Tenth and B. The story would probably last us another lap around the park. It seemed to take her mind off Atti for a few minutes, to give her a little relief.

"I woke up early the next morning, cranky and hot and tired from sleeping on the floor of Donna's basement. Everybody was hot and cranky and tired, and the party wasn't fun anymore, so I took my sleeping bag and walked home. It was Sunday, and Dad was away at a conference or something, and I figured Mom and Laurel were still sleeping, so I let myself in the back door. The house was quiet. It was too hot for cereal. It was so hot, the only thing I could stand the thought of eating was a Popsicle, so I slipped down to the basement to get one."

"Why did you keep Popsicles in the basement?"

"That's where the extra freezer was. We bought Popsicles in bulk."

"Okay." The ignorance of the lifelong apartment dweller.

"It was one of those long, low freezers that looks like a coffin. I lifted the lid and looked for the Popsicle box . . . and there was Snookie."

"In the freezer?"

I nodded and caught my breath, still upset at the memory. "He was lying in a clear plastic bag, all stiff and frozen." I left out the worst part—about his eyes, glassy as marbles, staring at me—in deference to Atti.

"Zowie. What the hell."

"I ran upstairs to my parents' room, screaming, 'Snookie's in the freezer!' Mom was in bed. I threw myself on top of her, and Laurel came in all sleepy, asking what was wrong. Mom told us that Snookie had died late the night before. He had a seizure on the kitchen floor and died. She used to be a nurse, so she knew for sure he was really dead and not just unconscious."

"Okay, but—the freezer?"

"It was late on a Saturday night, during a heat wave, and she was afraid the body would start to decompose before she could take it to the vet. So she put it in a plastic bag and put him in the freezer, thinking he'd last there till Monday. She didn't mean for me to find him like that."

"A dog Popsicle," Carmen said.

"She meant well," I said. "But I couldn't let it go. I couldn't stop crying. Mom said, 'He was very old,' which was true. But I kept yelling at her, 'You shouldn't have put him in the FREEZER, with the MEAT! Maybe you killed him! Maybe he was still alive and you suffocated him! You never loved him!' And things like that."

"What about your sister, did she yell at your mother too?"

"No, she just sobbed and hiccuped. She was in shock."

"I knew you were a little bitch."

I smiled. She liked the story. We rounded the corner onto Avenue B again. "It's true. Even while I screamed at her and blamed her and beat on her bed with my little fists, I knew I was wrong. It was like part of me had risen to the ceiling to watch the scene from above, and that part of me saw that I was being unfair—too old for tantrums, but having one anyway. I was perfectly capable of understanding what my mother had done, but I refused to do it."

"I was the same way at that age," Carmen said. "Remember that story about my dad and the kitchen ceiling? I understood what was going on then, too, better than I let on. But I didn't *want* to."

"Funny how both of our stories involve slumber parties."

"Slumber parties are the source of all childhood trauma."

The rooster watched us from the fence, flapping his wings as if he were going to take off, but he didn't. "Why doesn't he just fly away?" I said.

"Where would he go?"

We walked in silence, the wind biting through our coats, until we rounded Avenue A again.

"You know what's weird?" Carmen said.

"What."

"You see a dead person and your first thought is of a dog who died fourteen years ago."

"What's so weird about that?"

"Think about it."

I decided not to. But I knew what she was saying.

She kept her head down. We'd just turned onto Seventh Street, where the sidewalk was marked by a trail of purple footprints heading east.

"My father is not dead," I said.

She placed each foot on a purple print. "These are bigger than my feet."

"I saw him," I said. "I told you."

"Follow the purple brick road," Carmen sang. *"Follow the, follow the, follow the, follow the . . ."*

Maybe Atti will come back too, I was thinking. *He always liked hanging out in the park*. I decided not to say it out loud, not yet anyway, because I could tell she didn't want to hear it. We followed the purple trail along Seventh, and kept going, across Avenue B, across C, south on D, east on Sixth, along a pedestrian walkway over the FDR Drive, to the East River, where the footprints ended at the river's edge, as if the purple person had jumped.

17

WAKE

Atti had a lot of friends. Seemed like the whole East Village crowded into the bar for his wake, a week after he was found dead. Dean had spread the word: everyone meet at Downtown Beirut.

A glass of whiskey materialized in Carmen's hand as soon as we arrived, and her glass was never empty for long. She could have had anything she asked for, and many things she didn't ask for. "He was a saint," people said to her. "Too good for this shitty world."

She couldn't seem to get drunk, but I was getting drunk fast. We hadn't eaten all day. I kept an eye out for people going into the bathroom in twos or threes. When a trio popped out of the bathroom swiping at their noses I stopped them and pointed at Carmen, the grieving de facto widow, asking if they could help her out. Sure, of course, they said, and handed over what they had left. Carmen and I shut ourselves in the bathroom and snorted whatever anyone gave us. In the glare of the blue light bulb we read the graffiti scratched into the walls: band names, phone numbers, anti-Reagan screeds, the usual kill-the-yuppies sentiments. Someone had slapped up a sticker saying HELLO MY NAME IS KAFKA; someone else had drawn a cartoon of a man with a snarling dog latched onto his penis.

"Atti hated this place," Carmen said. Junkies couldn't find their veins in the blue light. It kept them from hogging the bathroom.

Taut as guitar strings, we popped back out to the bar. Someone played "People Who Died" on the jukebox, over and over. Carmen started pogoing. I put my hands on her shoulders and jumped up and down, mirroring her. People circled us, watching, bopping their heads. The song ended, then began again. We kept dancing. I saw Jem gliding toward us through the darkness, his head visible above the crowd. He broke through the circle and put a hand on each of our shoulders, pogoing along with us, until Carmen threw her arms around his neck. Then they danced together and I danced around them.

I'd thought maybe the Jem thing was over. She hadn't gone out with him since the night they'd gone to Florent. He did go to Café Lethe a lot, but everybody did. Now she was hanging from his neck at her boyfriend's wake. She was already into him.

Dean jumped up on the bar and called for attention. "Hey, everybody! Genie, can we turn off the jukebox for a minute?"

Genie, one of the bartenders, turned the music down.

"Thanksarooni. And thanks to all of you who skipped your disco naps to come out and toast our fallen comrade, the great bard of the streets, Attila Pilkvist."

"To Atti!" someone shouted. Bottles and glasses were raised and clinked.

"If anyone wants to say a few words, come on up."

"I got something to say." A large, bald, heavily tattooed biker jumped up on the table, shoving Dean off, to laughs. "Gasper!" someone yelled. "Ga-a-a-as-perrrr!"

Gasper downed a shot of whiskey and pounded on his chest. "The last time I saw Atti, he looked like shite. Fuckin' rotten. It pissed me off, you want to know the truth. I loved the guy. I said, 'Fuck you, Atti. You wanna die, go ahead and die. I'm not going to say anything at your fucking funeral, you wanker.' And old Atti says, 'When you die I'll piss on your grave.'"

The crowd cheered, raucous and drunk.

"Can ghosts piss? Hell. Atti's songs were poetry, so I wrote him a poem, and here it is." Gasper dropped his pants and bent over.

Everyone cheered and booed and clapped. Someone shoved Gasper off the table before he had a chance to pull up his pants. There was a scuffle. Genie came out from behind the bar to break it up. Then she turned up the jukebox. "People Who Died" was still playing.

"Jesus, you call that a eulogy?" Jem said.

Carmen said, "I think I'm going to cry." She was already crying, short, hysterical, hiccuping sobs.

"You're too wired, girl." Jem put an arm around her. "Come with me." He led her into the bathroom. They were gone for a while. I sat down at the bar and looked at the room. Without Carmen, I didn't have anything to do. I'd been taking care of her; now Jem was taking care of her. The faces and bodies blurred until they were squirming, jiggling shapes, a bunch of bugs crawling over an apple core. Genie gave me a glass of ginger ale. "People Who Died" ended at last, segueing into "Give Me Back My Man." *"I'll give you fish, I'll give you candy. . . ."* When Carmen and Jem came out of the bathroom, Carmen's pupils were dilated.

"I wish I could stay," Jem said, "but I've got places to be and people to see. Keep your chin up, baby. Be seein' ya." He kissed Carmen on the cheek and rolled out of the bar.

"What did he give you?"

"Vicodin, I think. Or Valium? It started with a *V*."

"Let's take over the jukebox," I said. Genie gave me a handful of quarters. I fed them into the machine while Carmen picked out Atti's favorite songs. She played the Clash and the Sex Pistols and Dead Kennedys and the Pogues. The entire bar sang along to "A Pair of Brown Eyes," and then "Dirty Old Town."

Soon after that, the whiskey caught up with Carmen at last. Her neck couldn't hold up her head. I found our coats trampled under a table. I handed her army jacket to her. "Mitch!" She brushed off some dirt and hugged it. "Poor Mitch." We put our coats on and walked home.

Doug stopped me on our way up the stairs. "Hey, I was looking for you." He took Carmen's other side and helped me steer her into our apartment. I settled her on the bed and led Doug back to the door, bracing myself. I knew what he wanted.

"Could you spare a couple of bucks? I hate to bother you again, but the baby . . ."

This was the third time he'd asked. I would not have parted with any of my precious savings if it weren't for the baby. Poor skinny baby, what could I do, let him starve? I reached into my pocket and pulled out a fiver.

"Thanks. I'm supposed to get paid next week. I'll pay you back, I promise."

"It's okay." I shut the door and went to help Carmen get undressed. She was so out of it she didn't even make a comment about Doug being a ponytailed freeloader.

"Atti was the only person I could count on." She cried while I tugged off her jeans. "The only person who loved me for my whole real self." She pulled off her T-shirt and flung it to the floor. I covered her with the blanket and crawled in with her. She was already half asleep. In spite of the tears she looked pretty, like the pastries in De Robertis's window, glazed white domes with a cherry on top of each.

"Carmen?"

"Hmph."

"I love you for your whole real self."

She rubbed her nose, but her eyes stayed closed.

Her hair had grown long enough to braid, thick and soft as a paintbrush. I swept it over my cheek as if I could transfer its dark red color to my face. I kissed her breasts. They felt spongy and soft, and her nipples tasted metallic, like frozen yogurt. Her neck smelled like cigarette smoke and beer and Shalimar. She'd nicked a bottle of perfume from her mother.

She pushed me gently away and rolled over. "Mmp. Sleepy."

I curled up against her and closed my eyes, burying my nose in her Shalimar neck. She was over Atti, I could tell. She'd been over him for a while now. Not over his death, but through with him as a boyfriend. Something was going to happen between her and Jem. Maybe something had already happened.

I pictured Jem in his secret sanctuary, drawing and painting, observing his neighbors, sitting on hot days with the window open, drinking a beer, the bottle sweating on his white T-shirt. I wanted to see that room, the real room. Would I ever get the chance? Maybe Carmen would.

I'd nearly fallen asleep when someone pounded on the door. I waited for whoever it was to go away, but they pounded again. I got up and padded through the kitchen in my bare feet. The floor was cold. Through the peephole I saw her: the old lady, clutching her clock. She smacked the door with her palm. I pulled back sharply as if I'd been hit in the face.

I opened the door.

She quivered in her housedress and slippers. The night air seeped in from outside. It chilled the metal and concrete and tile of our building. The wind had a color, blue-green. I could see it whipping around the stairwell like a cyclone, blowing down the hall, right into the apartment. The old lady's eyes were wet.

"What time is it."

"It's two fifteen."

"What time is it!"

I said I didn't know and shut the door and went back to bed. Diego draped his lean furry body over Carmen's head. I settled my arm in the groove of her waist and closed my eyes, but sleep wouldn't come. My mind raced, a dry engine sputtering on toxic fumes. *I'll never do coke again.* Next door, Gergo was photographing a girl. I heard his voice telling her to turn this way and that way, I heard her giggles and murmured protests, the snap of the camera. I kissed Carmen's temple to see if she was awake. She wasn't. I kissed her again. She didn't move.

All those people calling Atti a saint, and Gasper showing off his lack of sentimentality. I thought of the fictional Attila and Caledonia, from Carmen's college stories: by pretending to be tough they only telegraphed their sensitivity.

I rolled onto my back and stared into the darkness until a movie flickered on the bedroom ceiling: Atti walking down Seventh Street leaving purple footprints in his wake. He crossed Avenue B and kept going east, past C, past D, across the river, where the wind lifted him and he started to fly. He flew over Brooklyn, joined by other ghosts, so many ghosts, ghosts crowding pigeons out of the sky, until they reached the ocean and disappeared over the horizon. The sky was a white room over dark water. I searched for my father. I wanted to see him again.

In the morning I passed Kelly Ann, her stringy hair sticking out from under her cap, the baby bundled up in a sling on her back. I smiled at the baby, pleased to see he'd gotten chubbier. "How are you doing?"

"We're just fine." Kelly Ann's voice was cold.

"How's Doug?"

She stopped to face me. "He's supposed to be in rehab."

"What do you mean?"

"Thanks to you he's out shooting up somewhere."

There was an awkward silence as she glared at me, waiting for me to get out of the way so she could move down the hall and out the door.

That fucker. "He told me the baby needed milk."

She and the baby squeezed past me. "I'm breastfeeding," she snapped. The baby faced me now, bouncing on his mother's back as she walked away, his soft blue hat askew on his head. He lifted his hand, a benediction from a tiny bald pope.

"Guess what," I called after her. "My roommate's boyfriend died."

Kelly Ann didn't turn, just let the door slam shut behind her.

18

WRECK ROOM

Carmen never stayed over at Jem's. His apartment was his work space and he fiercely protected the privacy of it. He wouldn't even tell us the exact address. He spent a lot of time at our place.

He rigged up a curtain around the tub in our kitchen and took baths there, shaking his wet hair like a golden retriever on the beach. He made breakfast for all three of us, scrambled eggs, buttered toast, and coffee in a French press that he'd bought for us. Some nights he made dinner too: spaghetti with bottled sauce, or eggs again, or pancakes. I sat on the couch—where I was sleeping most nights now—and watched him hula from the stove to the toaster to the table, hips swaying, humming, *"Teenage kicks right through the night."*

"Zowie, what a cutie." Carmen pinched his ass. He wiggled it happily and called me to the table with a cartoonish bow. "Dinner . . . is . . . uh-served."

"For me it's breakfast," I said.

"We're having breakfast for dinner anyway."

"Night is day and day is night," Carmen singsonged. "Right is wrong and wrong is right."

Since I was working at the club till four most nights, and since she had a boyfriend and I didn't, the bedroom had become hers by default. With three of us the apartment was crowded, but that was better than empty. Also, baseball season had finally begun, and the TV was in the living room, so I could watch the games from my couch bed in the evenings before I went to work.

Carmen seemed incandescently happy—too happy, neon-bright and a little manic. We were doing the same dance, distracting ourselves with nightlife. We went out every night, stayed out as late as we could, and slept as long as possible during the day, to keep any painful thoughts at bay. Carmen took a disco nap after work and then went out with Jem, wherever he wanted to go.

The first time Jem took Carmen to a gallery opening, I tagged along. The show was an installation called *Wreck Room*. The artist had re-created a rec room from hell, complete with Mylar flames licking the walls, bleeding dolls in torn dresses, a white rat in a cage furnished like an elementary school classroom, and a toy tea table set with maggot-infested Twinkies. A grown man dressed in a Boy Scout uniform furiously punched an inflatable clown while *Burl Ives Sings Little White Duck and Other Children's Favorites* played on a Fisher-Price record player. It reminded me of the Swiss dancer I'd seen at Plutonium a few weeks earlier, tripping out of her mind while wrestling with an inflated duck in a pool of what she thought was Jell-O. Maybe the artist had seen that too, and it had inspired this punch-the-clown scene. Or maybe there was simply something in the air that made people want to beat up their toys.

By this time, we'd seen a lot of art like this, exposing the dark side of suburbia. Still, Carmen would never have missed the opening, and neither would I. The art didn't matter as much as being seen as part of the group. Chris Kertesz, the film director whose indie hit *Weird Garden* had launched Bix's movie career, such as it was, occupied a corner in his uniform of black leather jacket, shades, and slicked-back fifties ducktail, sipping a beer and talking to three young women. Bix had told me Chris ordered Brylcreem from England by the case. A girl in a flouncing miniskirt tore herself from Chris's orbit and attached herself to Jem.

"Hey there, Rita," Jem said.

"What do you think of the show?" Rita asked. "It's like the psychic muck of my childhood turned inside out and displayed for everyone to see."

"I didn't have this many toys when I was a kid," Jem said.

Rita laughed. Carmen and I waited for Jem to introduce us to her, but he didn't. It turned out to be a habit of his.

Carmen stepped forward to pluck Rita's hand off Jem's arm, ostensibly so she could shake it. "I'm Carmen. This is Phoebe. Jem, let's get a beer."

The four of us went to the bar. Carmen made herself a barrier between Jem and Rita, who eventually drifted away, only to be replaced by other girls throughout the evening. I'd never seen Carmen behave in this possessive way before. Losing Atti had made her greedy. She held everything close, kept it all for herself, as if she couldn't bear another loss of any kind, no matter how tiny. That night Carmen stuck close to Jem, and I stuck close to Carmen.

Then, as if I'd conjured her myself, the Swiss dancer, Katinka, walked in, wearing the same chain-mail dress she'd worn at the club. "Hi," I said, eager for someone to talk to. "I thought you left that dress at the bottom of the pool."

She aimed her snub nose at me. "Do I know you?"

It wasn't worth the effort to remind her. "I guess not."

She waved to Jem and moved on to the bar. The overgrown Boy Scout had beaten the air out of the inflatable clown and was stomping on its plastic corpse. Chris Kertesz and his entourage headed for the door. Time to go.

"What's happening now?" I asked. Clearly there was some kind of after-party, and everyone seemed to know about it except for me.

"Oh, I'm not sure," Carmen said. "Anyway, don't you have to go to the club?"

"I can get there whenever I want."

Jem pulled a card out of his pocket: an invitation to dinner at Around the Clock, hosted by the gallery and addressed to Jem and guest.

"Come with us," Carmen said. "They can squeeze in one more." As she said this, she took one step toward Jem, as if she were now putting a barrier up against me. I remembered the lesson I'd learned in college: don't show that you want anything.

"Thanks, but you're right, I've got to go to work. Bilan will be waiting for me."

Fortune-telling was my only source of income, and I had developed a following as a sort of house shrink. Bilan, the model, came nearly every Thursday night just to see me, often bringing her friends. She had wonderful, dramatic problems: her best friend stole her boyfriend, her boyfriend stole her jewelry, her bodyguard was in love with her, a photographer wanted to leave his wife for her, she was vying with another model for a perfume ad. The movie ticket oracle never failed to suggest that more drama was on the way.

"Astrid, darling, I must know: Mick promised to take me to Cannes with him this year, but Basia says he promised to take her too! Is he just trying to get me in bed with him?"

"You haven't slept with him yet?"

"No, darling, no! I've been keeping him at elbow's length. I don't want to be another one of his castaways."

"Let's see what the oracle says."

Tess. Seven Beauties. American Gigolo.

Bilan clucked her tongue. "Oh, no no no no no. You don't have to say a word, darling. The oracle knows what sort of man Mick is."

"Yes, I'm afraid it's pretty clear," I said.

"No trip to Cannes for me."

"Unless you go with someone else."

"Ooh! Like who?"

I asked the oracle, and, bizarrely, pulled out (completely at random, I swear) three Chris Kertesz movies: *Punk Kid*, *Jersey Smokes*, and *Weird Garden*.

"Do you know Chris Kertesz?" I asked Bilan.

"The director? I haven't met him."

"Do you know what he looks like?"

"He's the one with the hair?" She mimed slicking her hair back with her hands.

I nodded. "When he comes in, introduce yourself. He's your ticket to Cannes."

Bilan slipped a fifty-dollar bill into my hand, then patted it. "Astrid, this is why I adore you."

Jem and Carmen arrived around two with a group from the gallery dinner. They stopped by my table to say hello. "We're getting out of here, it's too crowded," Carmen said. "Jem wants to see if anyone's at Limelight. You wanna come?"

I gestured at the long line of customers waiting for me. "I'll see you at home later."

"Make lots of money," Carmen said. "Lots of fuck-you-Ivan money."

I did make a lot that night, and shared a taxi home with Bix. Upstairs, the lights were out and the bedroom door was closed. I went to bed on the couch, with Julio and Diego curled up at my feet. The clock on the kitchen wall glowed in the dark, and I found myself staring at the glow for a long time, trying not to think about what was happening on the other side of the bedroom door. To distract myself, I imagined Bilan, resplendent in yellow silk and yellow diamonds, swanning down the red carpet at Cannes on Mick Jagger's arm. "I want to thank the darling Astrid for everything," Bilan said to the cameras trailing her. "Just everything." But Bilan kept turning into Carmen and Mick kept turning into Jem, so in the end I was forced to try naming all fifty states in alphabetical order. I made it to Nevada before I fell asleep.

19

EXPANDING UNIVERSE

In May, Atti's mother invited Carmen to a memorial service in Springfield, Massachusetts, his hometown. I came home from work and found Carmen reading over the invitation, chewing on her lip.

"You forgot all about him, didn't you?" I said, trying to sound light and joking and not mean.

"No I didn't, fuck you."

"Are you going to go?"

"I feel like I should. They're going to spread his ashes over a field or something. I never saw the house he grew up in. It's my last chance." She'd take the bus up there and be gone overnight, she said.

"I'll come with you," I said. "Road trip."

"I don't think Borbála would like it."

"Borbála." I snorted. I'd forgotten that was Atti's mother's name.

"I won't be gone long," Carmen said. "And hey, you'll get the bedroom all to yourself."

"A real bed," I said, as if I cared.

Monday, my night off. I could have watched the Yankee game at home by myself, but it was awful quiet in the apartment without Carmen, so I headed out. Maybe somebody I knew was watching the game at Maher's. I headed over to Second Avenue. When I swung open the door, there sat Bix and Wes, sipping beer, eyes on the TV over the bar.

"Yanks can't buy a hit tonight," Scooter said. *"Some days are like that. You ever hear of this thing called karma, White? Sometimes I wonder who Dave Winfield killed in a past life."*

"Hey, dollbaby, I saved a seat for ya." Bix patted the barstool next to him.

"Yanks are down four-two in the third," Wes said.

I ordered a Guinness. Winfield stepped up to the plate with one man on and swished it.

"Damn." Wes signaled the bartender for another Stella.

"I hate the Royals," I said. "Even when they aren't any good, they're spoilers."

"This year they're good," Bix said.

"What's been going on at Plutonium, Phoebe?" Wes asked. "Got any dirt for me?"

"What do you consider dirt?" It was a nightclub; there was sex, there were drugs—that was no secret.

"Who's funding that place? Where does Toby get the money to redecorate every month? Some of those sets are pretty elaborate."

"Don't tell him anything, dollbaby, he'll just get you in trouble."

"I don't know anything about the money," I said. "All I know is Shan takes the van to discount stores in New Jersey and comes back with cases and cases of candy, plastic leis, shag carpeting, whatever she needs. She buys in bulk."

"Mattingly hits a high fly ball, and while it's in the air, happy birthday to Daphne Lapizana. She turns eighteen today." My ears perked up—the Scooter was in decent form that night. I reached over the bar for a napkin and a pen to jot the line down for Dad. Then I stopped, remembering that I couldn't call him up and trade Scooterisms with him anymore. I went ahead and wrote the line down anyway.

"What are you doing?" Bix leaned over and tried to read my scribbled note.

"Nothing."

"What about you?" Wes asked. "You making money?"

"Sure," I said. I had a steady stream of customers most nights, and was earning more money than I had at the bookstore. Enough to live on. It was hard to save, but I'd managed to stash about five hundred dollars in my secret Ivan revenge briefcase.

"You kidding? She's a superstar," Bix said. "That model Bilan comes in every week and heads straight for her table. She's uncanny."

"Really." Wes turned and studied me with fresh interest.

"Where's your roomie tonight?" Bix asked. "She doesn't like baseball?"

"She went to a memorial service for Atti. In Massachusetts."

"Oh. Man. A little late, isn't it? When'd he die, two months ago?"

"Yeah, in March."

"When's she getting back? I want to talk to her about that script she wrote."

"She should be back tomorrow." I was careful to keep my eyes on the game, so as not to give away my surprise. "What about the script?"

"Tell her if she puts a part in it for me, I'll see if I can get it to Chris. Who knows, right? Anything could happen."

"Sure. I'll tell her."

"Chris writes his own stuff," Wes said.

"If he's not interested, maybe he knows somebody else looking for a good script."

"You think it's good?" I asked.

"Sure, I mean, a little rough maybe, but it's funny. What did you think of it?"

I'd read it secretly, of course—and an unfinished early draft from what I gathered—but I didn't want Bix and Wes to know that Carmen hadn't shared it with me. "I think it's great. Everything Carmen does is great."

"Not sure I'd go that far," Bix said. "But she's a good kid."

The Yanks were having a terrible night. I slid off my stool. "I don't think I can bear to watch the rest of this game."

"I don't blame you." Wes sipped his beer. "If they don't turn it around by the time this beer is gone, I'm leaving too."

"See you around, doll."

It was a cool night for May. I headed east on Fourth Street, stopping at my usual bodega for cigarettes. Brahim reached for a pack of Camel Lights as soon as I opened the door. I added a pack of cherry Lifesavers and started for home.

My head was buzzing. Carmen had finished *Junkie Heaven*—if that was still the title—and recast it as a screenplay without mentioning anything about it to me. She'd showed it to Bix, hoping he could help her get it produced. Who else knew about it?

I lit a cigarette and smoked while I walked. I wondered if she'd really found that typewriter on the street, or if she'd bought it secondhand somewhere with a secret plan to use it. Now that I thought about it, she'd always kept things from me—in college, not telling me that she'd stolen Mark from her roommate until it slipped out, after I'd already started seeing him; or later, using me as an alibi with her parents without asking me first. When the truth came out, she usually claimed she hadn't thought it was important enough to mention. Since Atti's death, though, something had changed. She wasn't simply neglecting to mention things; she was withholding them from me. I felt the barrier thickening between us, and it made me angry, though I wasn't willing to admit that to myself yet.

At Seventh and A, instead of going straight home, I decided to take a turn around the park. It was a nice night, and I felt a longing to see Dad again. So far I'd seen him only once, and was trying to figure out what I had to do to make him appear. I had a Scooter line to share with him. Maybe that would work.

I walked slowly along Seventh Street, keeping an eye out for a mismatched plaid suit. A cluster of homeless people camped in the shadow of Samuel Sullivan Cox's statue. No sign of the rooster that night. *Maybe the homeless people cooked him and ate him.* The thought stirred a mixture of horror and glee in me.

At the corner of Seventh and B, I saw a thin young man doing jumping jacks on a bench inside the park. I paused to peer at him through the trees. He wasn't doing jumping jacks after all; he was waving to me, a large, desperate SOS gesture. I couldn't see him clearly; he was a shadow, he shimmered.

It's Atti, I thought, but then: *No, it couldn't be.*

I sensed movement behind me and whirled around. A tall man in a cowboy hat glided slowly up the street in my direction. He coughed into his fist, a phlegmy sound almost like a laugh. When I turned back to the park, Atti—if it was Atti—had vanished. I tossed my cigarette into the gutter and started quickly up Avenue B. The tall man matched my pace, keeping about a quarter of a block behind me.

It's a cowboy hat, not a ski cap, I thought, trying to reassure myself. But I walked faster. Behind me, the man sped up.

I started running, and felt the tall man running too, as if he could not allow the distance between us to grow more than a quarter of a block. I pumped my legs faster, breathing hard and cursing my pack-a-day habit. He drew closer. I looked back: his hat hid his face. I rounded the corner onto Tenth Street. The man closed in. He had a long stride. He was ten feet away. I glanced back again, not watching where I was going, and crashed into someone.

"Hey!" Strong hands caught me by the shoulders.

"Jem!" He was dressed all in silver. He held me protectively, shielding me from the man in the cowboy hat.

"What the fuck!" Jem barked at him. The man turned and walked fast into the park.

"Are you okay?"

I nodded, out of breath.

"Was that guy following you?"

I nodded again.

"Shit." He wrapped an arm around my shoulders and walked me toward Avenue A. "Why was he following you?"

"I don't know."

"Was he trying to mug you? I didn't get that vibe. I've never seen a mugger in a cowboy hat before."

"I don't know what he wants." I opened the door to my building and he accompanied me upstairs to the apartment.

"Where's Carmen?"

"Springfield, Massachusetts."

"What?" He lifted his captain's cap and ruffed his hair. He was all dressed up in a silver flight suit, Chuck Taylors spray-painted silver to match, dark glasses tucked into his breast pocket, large eyes outlined in kohl.

"She'll be back tomorrow. Memorial service for Atti."

"Shit," he said. "Why didn't she tell me?"

"Spur-of-the-moment thing, I guess."

"I just got invited to a party at Indochine, and I wanted to bring a date."

"Oh." I sat on the couch and pulled the blanket around me. I was shaking.

"You scared?" Jem sat beside me. Julio rubbed against his leg. Jem picked him up and held him in his lap. We both petted him.

"That's the fourth time someone's followed me, that I know of."

"The same guy?"

"I'm not sure." Julio jumped onto the back of the couch and tried to chew on my hair.

"You shouldn't be alone tonight."

"You don't think I'm safe here?"

"Sure you are. But you're shaking." He rested a hand on mine, to still the trembling. "You feel okay to go out?"

"I feel better now."

"Want to go to a party?"

I nodded coolly, hiding my pleasure at being invited.

"All right. Go change."

I asked myself what Carmen would do in my place. She'd go to the party. Besides, it served her right for leaving me here alone.

I slipped into the bedroom to find something to wear—something silvery, to match Jem's suit.

It was Andreas Fischer's birthday. His wife, Chiara, and his dealer, Leo Castelli, had reserved the whole restaurant to celebrate. We paused at the door while a hostess checked the guest list for Jem Farrell plus one. Flashbulbs strobed the room. I suddenly felt like hiding. I plucked the dark glasses off Jem's nose and put them on.

"Afraid your fans will recognize you?" he teased.

The hostess ushered us into a room decorated to evoke colonial Vietnam—wicker furniture, palm fronds, and waitresses in cheongsams slit to the hip drifting by with trays of ice-cold martinis and spring rolls crisp with mint. We squeezed past famous artists, musicians, actors, and models to get to the bar. People noticed Jem, then turned to me, and I could see the question in their eyes: Why is he with *her*? Even with my asymmetrical platinum Japanese haircut, my metallic blue minidress, and Jem's sunglasses, I was outdazzled by him. His height elevated him above the crowd—he was one of the few men in the room taller than the models—but it was more than that: his cowboy grace, his lion's mane of brown hair, his jokey, slangy talk. At the bar, a photographer from the *Post* snapped our picture and asked us our names. I told him my name was Astrid.

Esphyr Collins, in her gold neck cuff and a jangle of bracelets, took Jem's hands in hers, and then, after he introduced me, grasped both of mine. "He is completely and utterly brilliant, isn't he?" she said to me. "Jem, we must say hello to Ross this minute. Off we go, righty-o." She led us to a man in his fifties, one of her stars, holding court in a round booth.

Somehow, inevitably, we got separated. Jem ricocheted around the room between people he knew and people who wanted to meet him. I viewed the party from above, trying to figure it out, looking for patterns in a dream world where everyone knew something I didn't. The revelers swirled through the restaurant, blown this way and that by forces they were unaware of, ensnared in spirals and dead-ends they couldn't swim out of. Jem caught my eye from across the room and waved me over, but at that moment I didn't have the energy to push through all the people between me and him, only to stand there wondering what to say.

Behind me and to my lcft, a man said, "It's called *Expanding Universe*. First you see my hand drawing little black dots on a white balloon. Then you see me slowly blowing the balloon up."

I turned my head to catch a glimpse of him. He was wearing round red glasses. The man with him had shaved off his eyebrows and drawn thick circumflexes in their place with what looked like black marker.

"So . . . what's it about?" the circumflex man asked. "I mean, what would you say it's about?"

"It's about space. It's literally about space, like outer space, but it's also about space as a concept. The balloon is the universe. As it expands it changes the space around it."

"So you're asking a question about a surface."

The man in the red glasses hesitated before replying, "Exactly."

A buzz spread through the crowd as John Kennedy slid past me, towing a young actress by the hand. He found Andreas and Chiara Fischer, kissed them on both cheeks, and introduced his date. I could tell by the way he chatted with them that he was apologizing; he'd stopped in to say hello on his way somewhere else. The young actress pulled away, heading to the back of the restaurant, past a green phone booth, to the bathroom. John said goodbye to Andreas and Chiara and paused at the bar to wait for his date. He took the stool next to mine, shining his vacant smile on me.

"Hello," I said.

"Hello." He asked the bartender for a glass of water.

"You don't remember me, do you."

He hesitated.

"That's okay," I said. "I was a different person then."

"Prep school?" he said. "Or college."

"College."

He nodded and took a sip of water. His date returned from the bathroom. "Nice seeing you," he said to me, and they went on their way. I leaned toward the person next to me and said, "He gave me a piggyback ride once." It turned out to be Lou Reed, who laughed. He thought I was joking.

A waiter announced that dinner was about to be served. I found Jem and we took our places in the round booth with Ross and Esphyr. A woman in a pink kimono sat on Ross's other side. She made a knot of her hair, then grabbed a pair of chopsticks and stabbed them through the knot.

"I want to explore what looking *feels* like," the pink-kimono woman said. "I use patterns to create optical pain."

"It works, too," Ross said.

"Pay no attention to Ross, darling," Esphyr said. "Your work is completely and utterly brilliant."

We ate coconut shrimp and fish wrapped in banana leaves and drank white Burgundy. Esphyr wanted to know how I'd learned to tell fortunes, and if anyone had ever complained that my predictions hadn't come true. I explained how I used movie ticket stubs instead of tarot cards. "I've seen all the movies that I use, so I have a lot of images to draw on. Sometimes the words in the title are enough." No one had complained yet, but then, I only charged five dollars.

"We do live as if life is a movie, or an opera, don't we," Esphyr said. "Especially artists. But how do you connect those images to the person asking the question? You don't usually know the person well, do you?"

"I'm training myself to notice things about people—the things that they try to hide or aren't aware of. I can usually find some clue in what they're wearing or how they present themselves."

"Like what?" Esphyr angled herself toward me, daring me to read her secrets.

"Well, like I've noticed that people who wear a lot of expensive jewelry feel unloved. They want everyone to *think* that they're well-loved, that someone somewhere is showering them with jewels. And people who make a fuss about how important they are are insecure."

"But don't they get defensive when you point these things out?"

"No, they're usually amazed. They think I can read their minds or something. They're not really hiding their insecurity or their need for love—they're broadcasting it, hoping someone will notice."

A waiter interrupted to take orders for coffee, and Esphyr was drawn into conversation with Ross.

"But what about the people who aren't broadcasting their problems?" Jem asked me. "The ones who are really hiding their true selves? How do you read them?"

I tried to think of a way to explain it. "It has to do with light," I said. "Light can reveal things, but it also hides things."

"It can blind you."

"Yes. But also . . . you know how things can seem more real at night? You're alone with your thoughts and dreams and fears; it's quiet, no daytime chores to distract you. In the dark, everything seems clear. Mysteries are suddenly solved, the answers seem obvious, even if you can't quite articulate them . . . but that clarity disappears in the morning. It's as if daylight draws a veil over it."

I reached for a cigarette. Jem took one too. He lit them both, first mine, then his.

"I think some people shine their personalities at us to blind us to their true selves, the mysteries they don't want us to see," I said. "Like, the stars and planets and galaxies are always around us, but we can only see them at night, because sunlight makes them invisible. When I'm telling fortunes, I look for those dark moments when the truth peeks out. They're clues."

"What about me? What do you see?"

"I'm not saying I'm good at this yet."

"Don't be a weasel, *Astrid*."

"Okay." I tugged on the collar of his jumpsuit. "You're wearing all silver—even your shoes! Like you're trying to deflect any deep observation."

He laughed. "But look at you, hiding behind sunglasses."

"I need them to shield my eyes from your glare."

"'Stars hide your fires, Let not light see my black and deep desires . . .' I can't remember the rest."

"That sounds vaguely familiar."

"It's from *Macbeth*." Jem looked embarrassed, and I thought, *He's hiding how smart he is.* "High school play."

"You played the lead?"

He shrugged. "The drama club was short on boys." He leaned close to me and whispered, "What about Esphyr? She's not very sunny."

"She's more like a black hole." I spoke into his ear and smelled mint. "She sucks you in and you can't escape." We snickered over this together.

"What are you two laughing at?" Esphyr asked.

"Astronomy," Jem replied.

"Righty-o." Esphyr shared a glance with Ross, who rolled his eyes. *Young people.*

After dinner we toasted Andreas on the occasion of his fortieth birthday. We drank to his health, to his genius, to his beautiful wife. I leaned against Jem, a bit tipsy. He wrapped his arm around my shoulders.

"We're all going to Ross's after dinner," Esphyr said. She scribbled the address on a napkin.

As the party broke up, I wandered to the back of the restaurant and shut myself in the green phone booth. I didn't intend to make a call. I sat down and waited for Jem to come looking for me. While I waited, I wondered what Carmen was doing that night. I pictured her in Atti's childhood home, which I imagined as a compact brick house that smelled of mothballs. Borbála was hosting a small buffet, but Carmen sneaked away to find her beloved's boyhood bedroom.

A man wanted to use the phone, so I pretended I was talking to someone until he gave up and wandered away. After about ten minutes Jem walked past me on his way to the bathroom. He didn't think to look inside the phone booth, so I opened the door and grabbed his wrist. He jumped slightly and said, "There you are."

I pulled him into the phone booth and sat him on the little stool. I straddled his thighs and shut the door. I pressed my brow to his, and rolled my face down, nose to nose, mouth to mouth. He cupped my ass in his hands and slid me up to his lap. I opened my mouth and kissed him. He let out a small laugh—*ha*. He licked the center of my forehead, which tingled for the rest of the night like a third eye.

We made out in the phone booth for a while. When we came up for air, everybody was gone.

"Let's go to the party," he said.

We walked down to SoHo hand in hand, stopping to kiss at every red light.

Ross's loft was high-ceilinged and huge, with large paintings on the walls, a swing at one end, and a trampoline at the other. Several guests were flipping through the record collection, playing DJ. Danger Dick was there, dressed in a gold daredevil jumpsuit with a matching cape. He passed out flyers advertising his next stunt, on the Fourth of July: a boxing match, Dick versus Mayor Koch, with Dick dressed as the Flying Nun and the mayor as Uncle Sam. He swore the mayor was going to show up and fight.

Jem and Esphyr discussed Ross's paintings while I listened, wearing Jem's arm around my shoulders like a fox fur. "This is a series of portraits. He calls this one *Grandfather*. And this one is *George Washington*." The large abstract canvases were covered in leafy shapes in shades of green.

"They look like plants," I said.

"Exactly," Esphyr said. "Ross is very inspired by Nietzsche. 'Even the wisest among you is only a disharmony and hybrid of plant and ghost.'"

"'You have made your way from worm to man, and much within you is still worm,'" Jem said.

I hadn't read Nietzsche, and the leafy painting looked nothing like George Washington to me. I decided not to say that out loud.

Someone turned the lights down and aimed a spot at the disco ball over the trampoline. A girl rode the swing, letting her skirt fly open as she rose into the air. Her underwear was white. "What do you feel like doing?" Jem asked. I said I wanted to jump on the trampoline.

Stepping onto the trampoline was disorienting, like walking on the moon. Someone put on "Lost in the Supermarket" and Jem and I started bouncing, cautiously. At first our jumps weren't synchronized and we threw each other's rhythm off. I kept landing on my butt. Jem took my hands and we synched up so that we floated up together and bounded down together, up and down and up and down while the bouncy music played and lights popped in our eyes. We laughed very hard. Everything looked like it was moving in slow motion but it felt like fast motion and the difference, the disorientation, exhilarated me. This was the golden world. People were pretty superficial in the golden world, but then, maybe they were superficial everywhere. Like my neighbor, Doug, pretending to be earthy and a good father when he was really just an addict.

The song changed to "When the World Was Young," Peggy Lee's version. The disco ball splashed dots of light like measles all over us. Jem pulled me close and we slow-bounced, my head nestled against the breast of his flight suit, just below the logo patch he'd made for it: Saturn and its rings and some stars around the letters J-E-M.

In the morning, Jem and I ate leftover Chinese food in bed. He curled a shrimp over one of my nipples to compare the two shades of pink, then nibbled it off me. We put on a Michael Jackson record and danced naked all over the apartment. We took a bath together in the tub. Then he left. For half an hour I lay on the bed staring at the ceiling, fixating on a crack in the plaster that zigzagged like a staircase drawn by Dr. Seuss. I listened to the sounds of a weekday morning: the flush of plumbing in the building, footsteps overhead, Gergo humming a tune, a garbage truck down the block, bongos in the park. I imagined telling Carmen about the party and about sleeping with Jem, entertaining her with the story the way she used to like hearing about Ivan. I imagined her laughing, asking to hear more, helping me plot my next move.

As the time of her return grew closer, though, I grew uneasy. Had I done something bad? Carmen would understand. But as the happy haze of the night lifted, I saw that Carmen probably wouldn't understand.

I rose from the bed and mopped up our wet footprints, threw out the empty Chinese food cartons, picked up the sticky tissues off the floor, and put the used rubbers in a bag to throw away somewhere outside. Then I went to the library to figure out how to make myself disappear.

20

INVISIBILITY SPELL

At the library on Tenth Street I skimmed through books on witchcraft and voodoo until I found an invisibility spell. I copied it out for anyone who might find it useful.

YOU WILL NEED:

7 black beans
A bottle of good brandy
A shovel
Water
The head of a dead man

1. *Begin on a Wednesday, before sunrise. Place one bean in each orifice in the dead man's head (eyes, nostrils, ears, mouth).*
2. *Trace a pattern or shape—a triangle, a pentagram, anything you like—on the dead man's forehead.*
3. *Bury the head in the ground, faceup, and water it with the good brandy. (Don't skimp on the brandy; the spirits don't like the cheap stuff.)*
4. *Every morning before dawn, water the head with brandy. Do this for eight days in a row.*
5. *On the eighth day, a spirit will appear before you and ask, "What are you doing?" You must reply, "I am watering my plant."*

6. *The spirit will say, "Give me the bottle. I want to water the plant." You must refuse. No matter how hard the spirit tries to get the bottle from you, you must not let him.*
7. *Eventually, the spirit will surrender. You will know you've defeated him when he shows you the pattern you traced on the dead man's forehead.*
8. *The next morning, the beans will begin to sprout. Pick the new beans.*
9. *Put them in your mouth and look in a mirror. You will see no reflection. You are invisible. To become visible again, spit out the beans.*
10. *Warning: Do not swallow the beans, or you will be invisible forever.*

I would have tried this spell if I had access to a dead man's head.

At six, the library closed. I forced myself to go home. My stomach hurt.

The Sex Pistols snarled on the radio in the bedroom. She was back.

"Carm?"

"Hey." She was unpacking, her suitcase open on the bedroom floor.

"How was the thing?" I asked.

"Sad. And crazy. What else could it be." She lay down across the bed, which was still rumpled. Carmen never made the bed; it would have struck her as weird if I'd made it. "Borbála brought a boom box to the ceremony and played 'Wild Horses' while we tossed Atti's ashes around the field. Then she threw herself on the ground and had a fit—like, kicking and screaming and sobbing. It was horrible." She wiggled her shoes off and let them drop to the floor. "Tell me everything."

"Everything?" My rash-red cheeks blared my guilt to her, surely she could see it.

"The party." She sat up and tossed the *Post* at me, folded to Page Six. There was a picture of me and Jem, captioned "Artist Jem Farrell and Plutonium Fortune-Teller Astrid at Indochine." My sunglasses reflected the photographer's flash. "I missed the big party. I want to hear all about it."

I told her everything, almost everything. How Jem had rescued me from the tall man in the cowboy hat, that he'd come looking for her and only brought me as a last resort, about the people I'd met, that Esphyr said "righty-o" even though she wasn't English, that John-John had stopped in and not remembered me. She listened quietly, trying to hear what I wasn't saying.

"I guess Jem will tell me more." She was meeting him in a few minutes for a drink at 2A. "Want to come?"

A nerve in my neck twanged. "No, thanks." I planned to stay in and watch the Yankees.

I hardly focused on the game—I kept expecting Carmen to burst in, furious at me. I sat on the couch and rolled my father's Scooter bat back and forth over my thighs, thinking it might bring the Yankees luck. When Carmen didn't appear by midnight, I imagined she was with Jem, and felt stabs of jealousy. I was miserable. I didn't want them to be together, because that meant neither one of them was with me. I had a problem with no possible happy outcome. And the Yankees lost again.

I was in the bed, half-asleep, when she finally came home. She crawled in beside me, perfumed with vodka.

"He didn't show up," she whispered. I stirred. "I waited two hours. I called him. Sparky told me where he lives and I went to his place and buzzed his buzzer. He wasn't there."

"Oh." Relief—even joy—but also uneasiness.

"I went back to 2A and waited some more. Sparky got me drunk."

"Gosh."

"He's never stood me up before."

I put one arm over her, carefully, in a half hug. We stayed like that, suspended and still and tense, for a long time, until my arm felt stiff. But I kept it there. I didn't move.

Suddenly she pushed my arm away and sat up, a pair of black Ray-Bans in her hand. "Look what I found under the pillow."

Whoops. I felt a thump in the pit of my stomach. "He let me borrow them."

"How did they get in the bed?"

"I don't know. They were probably propped on my head when I went to bed, and I didn't realize it." My face went hot. Lying to her made me feel sick. *But she lied to me,* I told myself. *She lies to me all the time.*

She read the truth on my face. She threw the glasses at the wall. "Go sleep on the couch where you belong."

"Carmen—"

"Was he here tonight, hiding from me?"

"No! He wasn't here tonight. I swear."

Her eyes were bloodshot from drinking and crying. They burned into me. I held my breath.

"Carmen—he cares about you. I know he does."

"I don't care about his *feelings*," she said. "I don't care about anybody's stupid feelings." She turned her face away now. "One night." She wouldn't look at me. "I went away for *one night*."

I couldn't speak. I floated up to the ceiling, as I'd done so many times before, and watched my cowardly, guilty self below me on the bed, helpless.

"I didn't believe it until this minute." Her voice was thin and wire-taut. "But the guilt is leaking out of your pores. I can smell it."

I tasted it too, sour and bitter as rotten limes.

"You know what? You can have him. You can have him, and this apartment, and the cats. Everything. You can have everything. I'm leaving." She bolted up and paced the room, stuffing clothes into her hard little suitcase.

"What are you talking about? Don't leave!" She'd surrendered so easily. That made everything worse.

Glare from the city outside seeped into the room, so that even with the light off I saw her moving between the closet and the dresser, stooping to pluck things off the floor, scowl at them, and toss them into her suitcase. She balled up a pair of dirty panties and threw them out the window. They were mine, but I didn't have the strength to stop her, or even utter a weak *hey*.

"All I did was go to a party."

"Really? Is that all you did?" She picked up a T-shirt, stared at it, and threw it back on the floor. "Are you even *trying* to be a good person?"

I couldn't remember what I'd been thinking the night before. My thoughts were all tangled up. "I'm trying to be like you."

"Ha. Then you don't know me very well." She pulled a sheaf of paper out of her bottom drawer and dropped it into the suitcase.

"Why didn't you tell me that you were writing a screenplay?"

She stopped, surprised. Then she threw a pair of tights at my head. "You snooped!"

"I didn't snoop. Bix mentioned it."

"Stupid Bix." She swiped the tights and tossed them into her suitcase. "It's none of your business. I don't have to tell you everything."

That stung. "You used to tell me everything," I said. "I thought you did."

"I never did." She clapped her suitcase shut. "And neither did you."

"Where are you going?"

She walked to the door, suitcase swinging.

"Please tell me where you are going."

She slammed the door.

I ran to the living room window and stuck my head out. A few seconds later she appeared on the sidewalk. "Carmen!"

She didn't look up. She hustled down A, turned west onto Ninth Street, and was gone.

Back in the bedroom I blinked at the ceiling, the crazy-staircase crack in the plaster having grown a few steps. Julio and Diego curled up beside me. I rubbed Julio between the eyes, and he purred. Diego flapped his tail. I was weak, morally weak. But weakness begets weakness. I felt helpless to fight it. Jem's Nietzsche quote echoed in my mind: *Much within you is still worm.*

Somewhere out in the world a siren keened. Every siren is a reminder that something bad is happening somewhere, to someone. You may be okay for now, but someday the siren will come for you.

When I was six, my aunt Eilie gave me and Laurel a record called *Darby O'Gill and the Little People*, the soundtrack to a Disney movie Mom wouldn't let us see because it was too scary. Darby O'Gill was an Irishman who caught a leprechaun, which entitled him to three wishes. Side one of the record was all jigs and fiddles and pots of gold—nothing scary about that. But the story darkened on side two, when Darby's beloved daughter, Katie, died, and the banshee appeared.

The banshee was an Irish demon, part witch and part ghost, whose shrieking summoned the Death Coach, driven by a headless coachman, which ferried the living to the Land of the Dead. Once the Death Coach had been summoned to the Land of the Living, it couldn't leave empty. It had to carry a body back to the underworld; the headless coachman didn't care whose. If the coach had been called for your daughter, you could volunteer to take her place. Then you would die but she could live. That's what Darby O'Gill did. He took Katie's place in the coach, and she lived. Then, somehow, he tricked the leprechaun so that he lived, too. But that part wasn't very convincing.

Side two was so scary Laurel and I rarely played it. But once in a while, on a dark afternoon, we found ourselves listening to it over and over. *"It's the wail of the banshee! The same as I heard the night that Katie's mother was taken."* It gave me nightmares, and Mom threatened to throw the record out. We wouldn't let her, even though we didn't particularly like it.

After all these years, the banshee still kept me from sleeping. There was danger out there. I tried to drown out the sirens by turning on the radio and listening to a sports talk show. All the callers agreed that the Yankees needed better pitching and that George Steinbrenner was a moron. I drifted in and out of an unrefreshing sleep.

At around three I got up to pee. On my way back to bed, kicking through the clothes strewn all over the floor, I stubbed my toe on *Edie: An American Biography*, one of Carmen's favorite books. She'd read it three times. My eye fell on an army-green jacket. I picked it up. Mitch.

She'd left without Mitch.

She'd never leave Mitch behind. It meant more to her than ever since Atti had died.

She'll be back, I thought. And if she didn't come back, I'd find her. I would find her and make things right.

In the morning, earlier than usual, I went to Café Lethe. Bix and Wes were sitting at the counter with Page Six open in front of them, analyzing the party pictures. There we were again: Jem in his silver jumpsuit, me in his dark glasses, Andy's profile visible in the background. Bix said I should raise my rates to ten dollars a reading, now that I was famous.

Working behind the counter was a girl I'd never seen before—very young, about eighteen, with a small hoop in her nose. When I asked for Carmen, Bix said she hadn't shown up for work. She didn't call in sick or anything. This girl with the nose ring—her name was

Taffy—happened to walk in looking for a job and Nick, the manager, hired her on the spot. No one knew where Carmen was.

"What happened, you have a fight?" Bix said.

"Kind of."

"Don't worry, she'll come back."

I lit a cigarette and asked Taffy for a cup of coffee. She rummaged around behind the counter until she found the mugs. Then she stared at the empty coffeepot.

"Here darlin', let me give you a demonstration." Bix shambled behind the counter to show Taffy how to brew a pot of coffee. I glanced at Wes's stack of papers. A headline blared SPIKE IN OVERDOSES AS DANGEROUS STRAIN OF HEROIN HITS STREETS.

"I've been thinking. . . ." Wes tapped the *Post* with his pen. "The *Underground* needs some new features, something fun that brings readers back week after week. A horoscope column or something like that. Only hip, not corny."

"Or so corny it's hip?" I said.

"You are getting known around town, 'Astrid.' In certain circles, anyway. We could take advantage of that. Would you have any interest in writing a column for me?"

One night in Jem's company was already paying off.

"I don't know how to do horoscopes," I said. "But I could write an advice column. People could send in their questions and problems, and I could use my movie ticket oracle to find the answers. It's basically what I do at the club."

He closed his eyes, picturing it. "We'll call it Astrid Predicts Your Future. Or Astrid Sees All."

"I'd like to try it."

"Can you write?"

"Sure I can write." *Fake it, fake it.*

"Great. Whip up five hundred words or so and we'll talk."

I finished my coffee and went for a walk, too jumpy and excited to sit still. I had a bit of news and I wanted to share it with someone. I headed down A to Houston, crossed over and skipped east to Clinton. Jem lived somewhere on Clinton, but I didn't know the address. I looked up at the buildings, searching for clues, a window like the one in his painting *Secret Sanctuary*. Maybe I'd get lucky and catch him leaving his apartment. It was quieter down here below Houston, and dirtier, and scarier. I made it as far as Rivington before I turned around to go back.

Javier sat on our front steps, reading the mail. He handed me an electric bill addressed to Carmen. I climbed the stairs, half expecting to find her at the kitchen table drinking coffee. I'd pour myself a cup and say, "Guess what! Wes offered me a column!"

Diego and Julio meowed when I walked in, begging for food. They paced like expectant fathers while I opened a can of 9Lives and spooned it into two bowls.

I turned on the TV to pass the time before I had to leave for work, watching cartoons until the game came on. I heard a bumping sound in the hall and ran to the door, thinking Carmen had come back. I peeked through the peephole. The old lady with the clock was shuffling by in her slippers. I stayed still and quiet and didn't open the door.

I told myself Bix was right: we'd had a fight, so what. She'd be back soon.

Jem showed up at the club around two in the morning. I was getting ready to go home, calling it an early night.

"Where's Carmen this fine evening?"

I wanted to ask him where he'd been the night before, but I bit my tongue.

"I don't know. We had a fight, and she left."

"What did you fight about?"

I looked away. Did he really not know?

"You girls. Always fighting."

"We never had a fight before."

"Before what?"

He was being stubborn, refusing to admit he'd played any role in our troubles.

"Are you going home? Why don't I come with you?" he said. "Make sure you get there safely."

"What if Carmen is back?"

"What if she is?"

I shook my shoebox and pulled out a stub. *The Big Chill.*

"Let's go."

I was quiet and tense on the walk to our place. I wanted the escort, and I wanted to be with Jem, but I also wanted Carmen to be waiting when I got there. And if I walked in with Jem, she might really leave for good.

At the door to my building, I thanked Jem for seeing me home but said I was tired and wanted to go to sleep.

"What? Come on."

"Really, I'm tired."

"Okay." He sauntered off. "See you when I see you."

Once inside the apartment I wished I hadn't sent him away. Carmen wasn't home. I could feel her absence in the very walls.

The next day I called her parents. Len answered. I got scared and hung up. I called again half an hour later and asked for her. "She doesn't live here," Betsy said. "Who is this?" When I went silent she said, "Phoebe? Is this Phoebe?" and I hung up again.

I could taste the guilt in the back of my throat. I drank a glass of milk to get rid of it.

Don't worry, I told myself. *She's a city girl.* She knew how to take care of herself. And anyway, she left *me*.

I found Mitch on the floor, where she'd left it. I picked it up and put it on. It felt good and heavy, like armor.

If she wanted me, she knew where to find me.

21

A SACK OF POTATOES

In the mornings, which were really the afternoons, Jem liked to trace messages on my back with the tip of his finger.

I
C
U
*
U
R
A
Q-T
*
I
H-8
2
GO

But he did go.

It was a hot June. The heat was narcotic. At night I listened to people's wishes and dreams and problems and fears and guessed what would happen to them in the future. Jem met me at the club around 2 a.m., hung out for a drink or two, and walked me home, where we stayed up until dawn, making love until daylight framed the window shades and we were finally ready to sleep. Jem sang to me in the blue morning light, songs he made up. *"Tasty Phoebe yummy Phoebe Slurp you up like Dairy Queenie You give me the Phoebe-jeebies la la la la la . . .*" The words changed from morning to morning, but it always ended with him licking my cheek instead of kissing me.

We slept all day, getting up for breakfast at around two in the afternoon. After that he went home to work. He was painting a lot, using scavenged supermarket posters as canvases, hoping to score a solo show in the fall. A month of this routine, and I still hadn't seen the inside of his apartment.

I spent most evenings alone until ten or so, when I left for the club. On hot nights I went to the supermarket or the movies before work, to bask in the air-conditioning and to add to my ticket collection. I stroked the cats' fur with ice cubes wrapped in a washcloth. I played children's songs on my toy accordion. I watched the Yankees religiously, soothed by the Scooter's voice.

"What a nice-looking young lady," he said as the camera caught a young woman in the stands. *"She reminds me of that old song, 'A Pretty Girl Is Like a Memory.'"*

Bill White: *"Scooter, I think that's 'Melody.'"*

Scooter: *"How do you know her name is Melody?"*

I wrote down the exchange. Maybe if I collected enough good Scooter quotes Dad would come back to hear them.

Every day, I asked the oracle, "Where is Carmen?"

Silkwood. Smithereens. Heaven Can Wait.

One afternoon I pulled *Diner*. I left the apartment immediately, checking every diner in the neighborhood—Veselka, Odessa, Kiev, Little Poland, Second Avenue Deli. No Carmen.

Nashville. Mean Streets. Last Tango in Paris.

Carnal Knowledge. The Last Picture Show. Midnight Cowboy.

• • •

On Mondays, Plutonium was closed, so Jem took that night off too. We biked to Chinatown one muggy evening, the hazy sun setting over SoHo. I loved to see him riding his bike down the street, long legs angled like a grasshopper's. I sat behind him on the banana seat; he pedaled standing up while I clung to his waist. He rode recklessly, darting in and out of traffic, cutting off cars, running red lights. I wasn't afraid. *Let a truck smash into us,* I thought, *let us die in a festival of blood and glass* . . . I felt reckless too. I didn't care if I died, and at the same time, I was sure nothing could hurt me.

We didn't crash; we didn't die. We made it to Grand Street in one piece, two people fused onto a bike. We bought a pound of shrimp at an outdoor fish market, and some potatoes and vegetables at the stand across the street. We stopped at a liquor store for wine, then rode home through the Lower East Side, gray and grimy and beautiful in the dusk. From my precarious seat on the back of the bike I scanned every face we passed, people strolling down the street, people sitting on steps, people dancing in the stream of a fire hydrant, but none of them was her.

I sat on the lid of the tub while Jem sautéed the broccoli and potatoes, singing and rapping out beats on my thighs with a spatula and a spoon. The shrimp sizzled and pinked in the pan. I hopped off the tub from time to time to change the record. When supper was ready, I lit candles and opened a second bottle of cheap cold white wine. We ate until our chins shone with oil, until our bellies popped, storing nutrients for the coked-up club nights ahead. We had cherry Popsicles for dessert, licking the red juice as it melted in tiny rivulets down our knuckles. Then he tugged on my wrist and we drifted into the bedroom, leaving the dirty dishes for later.

I tried to keep my eyes open while he rode me, *stay open* . . .

open . . . open . . . but always a wave crashed over my head and forced my eyes to close. With the wave came a blinding light that flashed like an oncoming headache, or like those blissful moments when sleep overtakes you and you're powerless to stop it . . . like that, only sharper and sweeter. Then I got up and stood in front of the fan, letting it dry the sweat on my chest. Other nights I fell helplessly asleep, drugged by pleasure and guilt. It was too hot. I wished the summer would never end.

On nights when Jem wasn't with me, I walked. I walked alone for hours, taking the long way to work. No matter how hot it was, I would throw Carmen's Mitch jacket over whatever I was wearing and walk. One night in late June I stopped to look at a new flyer—a new Amelia, this one named Yolanda Fermin, eighteen, a runaway. A few weeks later, Yolanda's flyer had faded, but a fresh flyer appeared just below: Linda Suggs, twenty-one. *A junkie,* I thought, studying her scarred and hollow cheeks. The flyers scared me, but not enough to stop me from walking alone, night after night, looking for trouble, tempting fate. I felt that something bad was coming, but all I could do was say, *Come and get me.* I had my armor. Mitch would protect me. I only regretted that Carmen didn't have Mitch to protect her, wherever she was.

One Wednesday night in July, at around eleven, I stepped outside the club for a breath of air and a chat with Zu. Arrayed below me, down three steps and flooding into the street, the bizarrely dressed mob clamored for Zu's attention, chanting "Zu!" and "Looie!" in an endless loop that, after a while, sounded like people booing or cows mooing.

Zu clutched her clipboard and sighed. "It gets old, you know?" Over her leather pants she wore a T-shirt on which she'd stenciled DIE YUPPIE SCUM.

I lit a cigarette. Aviva B. and her entourage rolled up in a baby-blue Cadillac convertible. "Here comes the It Girl."

Zu sneered. "Trust-fund phony." But the crowd parted, the chants of "Zu!" and "Looie!" changing briefly to "Aviva B.!" Several people attached themselves to her train, claiming they were with her, but it was obvious who belonged and who didn't. Zu unhooked the velvet rope for Aviva and Jacky and their friends while Looie banished the hangers-on to purgatory.

"Zuuuuu!"

"Loooooie!"

"Hi, Zu honey." Aviva and Jacky kissed Zu on both cheeks. Aviva shot me a quick, dismissive look—daggers. Then they tramped away through the lobby.

"What did I do?"

Zu shrugged. "She's usually so sweet. Fakey, insipid . . . but sweet."

A siren wailed. A police car zoomed by, on its way to an emergency somewhere else. I stamped out my cig with my combat boot. "I better go back in and earn my five bucks."

Inside, the display windows illustrated July's theme, Martyrdom. In the second window, a model played St. Sebastian: tied to a tree, naked except for a loincloth, his torso punctured with arrows. Andy and Bianca were tapping on the window, trying to make him laugh. Andy borrowed Bianca's lipstick and wrote on the glass—backward, so St. Sebastian could read it—DON'T STAND STILL LIKE THAT FOR SO LONG IT'S NOT GOOD FOR YOU.

"You know," Andy said, "Sebastian is the patron saint of athletes."

In the ladies' lounge, Bix was holding court on the couch in the corner. Five people were lined up near my table, waiting for my services. I greeted them, sat down, and did some readings. I took another cigarette break, and Bix crooked a finger at me. "C'mere, dollbaby. I need you."

On Wednesday nights Bix hosted a talent contest called "Devil's Bell." People volunteered to perform in front of a panel of judges. A large bell dominated the stage; when an act was so abominable the judges could tolerate no more, they rang the bell; they'd ripped off the idea from *The Gong Show*. Bix and a drag queen named Miss Rhea Quaint were two of the judges. The third judge, a DJ named Ilmar, hadn't shown up.

"You want me to be a judge? I'm not a . . ." I groped for a word that described what Bix and Miss Rhea Quaint were. Not stars, exactly. ". . . personality."

"Sure y'are. You're a famous fortune-teller. I saw your picture in the paper once. Come on, honeypie, I'll make it worth your time."

People booed when Bix introduced me—"World-famous fortune-teller Astrid the Star Girl!" But then, that crowd enjoyed booing.

The first contestants called themselves Jesus and the Singing Nun. The nun was a man in a black habit who sang "Is That All There Is?" while a guy dressed as Jesus on the cross—to go with the martyrdom theme, I guess—danced around him. Having his hands tied to a cross made Jesus's dance moves kind of awkward. I gave them a three out of five because I like that song. Bix and Miss Rhea both scored them a two. At least they didn't get the bell.

The next act was called Bonky Roulette Costarring Binky. Two girls wearing tutus, Binky and Bonky, lined up ten squirt guns on a table. Nine of the guns were filled with water, they informed us, but one was filled with ketchup, and they didn't know which one. Binky chose a gun at random, pointed it at her temple, and squeezed the trigger. Water. Bonky took her turn: water again. They continued until the seventh gun sprayed ketchup all over Binky's face.

The crowd loved this act. Miss Rhea gave them a four and Bix a five. "Binky and Bonky are boring," I declared, in an attempt to be controversial, and gave them a one. The crowd booed me again.

Next, a guy dressed as a baby—"Baby Gary"—recited an obscene monologue about his mother while jerking off in his giant diaper. This was my limit. I stood. The crowd screamed. I took a step toward the bell. They screamed louder. Baby Gary groaned. I ran to the bell and pulled the clapper: *BONG*.

Baby Gary was escorted from the stage by a guy in a devil costume. The crowd jeered Baby Gary, they jeered me for stopping him, they jeered Bix for not stopping me. Bix, wearing a powder-blue tux, announced the winners: Binky and Bonky. Their prize: a strip of drink tickets. Show over.

Bix paid me for my judicial services in coke. "Bix," I protested, "coke is great but I need money."

"What do you need money for? You'd only spend it on coke anyway."

"No, I wouldn't. I'm saving up."

"What are you saving up for?"

"Long story."

Ilmar suddenly showed up and demanded his payment. "Fight it out between the two of you," Bix said.

"You can have it all for a hundred dollars," I told Ilmar.

"Forget it," Ilmar said. "I don't have that kind of scratch."

By then it was two thirty. I did a sweep through the club; no sign of Jem yet. Ilmar and I went to the bathroom and did some of the coke off a toilet-paper dispenser. He was the third Ilmar I'd met that summer. Strange how everybody seemed to be named Ilmar lately. I bought a pack of cigarettes from Ruby. I forgot about selling the coke. Ilmar and I went to the bar to get drinks. I asked the bartender if he'd seen Jem; he hadn't. Ilmar asked me if I wanted to dance, so we hopped up and down on the dance floor for a while. Still no Jem. Three twenty-five—he was never this late. Ilmar and I plopped down in the Gold Lounge and did more coke. We went to the hall to look at the window displays. In one of them, the Singing Nun was giving Jesus a blow job. I asked Ilmar if he thought that was a real blow job and he said yes he believed it was. I got tired of looking at that and moved on to the next window, where a blonde in a corset and stockings was smoking a cigarette and reading a *Casper* comic book. "How is that 'martyrdom'?" I said.

"It must be getting late," Ilmar said. "Let's do more coke."

We returned to the bathroom and finished the coke, and then I saw a red drop splatter on the floor and another one on my dress, and then my nose started flowing with blood. "Tilt your head back," Ruby instructed, grabbing a roll of toilet paper. People made way for me and cleared the couch so I could lie down, but my nose would not stop bleeding. I ran through a whole roll of toilet paper in a few minutes and started feeling dizzy. "Does someone have a dime?" Miss Rhea Quaint shouted, and I thought she was going to call an ambulance or something but she needed it for the tampon dispenser. She unwrapped a junior tampon and stuffed the tip into my bloody nostril.

Plutonium was getting ready to close for the night. People drifted out on their way to an after-hours club in Tribeca. I couldn't sit up without spurting blood everywhere, so Bix stayed with me, my head resting on his lap.

"I knew something bad was going to happen," I said.

"You're going to be all right," Bix said.

"Not this." I meant Jem. I'd let myself be vulnerable. Stupid, stupid. I'd learned this lesson in college. Why did I have to keep relearning it?

"You ever shoot up?" Bix asked me.

I shook my head.

"Your friend Carmen has."

Maybe I'd set myself up to get hurt on purpose. Unconsciously. I'd hurt Carmen. I deserved to be punished for it.

"I can always tell," Bix said. "Something in the eyes."

"She didn't do it for long. And she kicked."

"The eyes. You never get it back, the way you used to look."

"What about you?" I asked.

"Honey, I was born on the H train." His mother had been a junkie. He'd never known his father. His stepfather was a boxer who'd punched Bix's mother to death.

"Oh." I squeezed my eyes shut and shuddered, picturing it.

"I'm clean now," he said. "Of junk, I mean—not everything else, obviously. I'm not superhuman. But, you know, you just gotta hope it will last."

The bleeding finally stopped. I sat up and pulled the tampon out of my nose. My dress was streaked with blood. There was blood in my hair and on my neck. I rinsed my face and neck and hands and dried them with paper towels. The bathroom was deserted, except for me and Bix.

"You should maybe take a break for a couple of nights, dollbabe."

"Yeah."

"Where's Jem tonight?"

"He had to go to a thing," I said.

Bix pressed some bills into my hand. "Take a taxi home. It's late."

I tried to give it back to him. "I've got money." I'd made about thirty dollars that night.

"Consider it pay for the Devil's Bell. I been hearing things. Don't you look at the flyers? There's a new Amelia every other week."

"I can take care of myself."

"Take a cab. I'll feel better."

"Okay. Thanks." I took the money, but I intended to walk home and deposit the bills in my Ivan stash.

Varick Street was quiet and dark. Out of the corner of my eye I saw subtle movements in the shadows, in doorways, but when I turned to look, nothing. A blast of noise made me jump, *ratatatatat!* I caught my breath. It came from a few blocks away. Just someone setting off their leftover fireworks . . . unless it was gunshots. I could never tell the difference.

As I crossed Houston, a taxi stopped at the light—a Checker

crammed with laughing, shouting people. Through the open window I glimpsed a shake of dark red hair—*Carmen!* The light changed and the cab sped away.

Was it Carmen? I couldn't be sure.

When I stopped for cigs, a scruffy young man blocked my way into the bodega. I tensed. Park people menaced this corner, asking for handouts, and this was definitely a park guy: bearded and dark blond in torn, dirty clothes. A live rooster—the one who lived in the park, I presumed—perched on his shoulder, surveying the street from on high like a god. "Do me a favor," the guy said. "Buy me a sack of potatoes?"

I hesitated.

"Come on, help me? They won't let me in the store with Fritz."

He was dirty and thin, with a chipped front tooth and blue eyes that burned out of a sun-darkened face. A sack of potatoes. What harm could it do?

"Wait here." I went inside.

"Hello, *habibi*." Brahim reached for a pack of Camel Lights and set it on the counter. "What else? Some candy?"

I looked around the small shop. It wasn't the kind of store that sold produce. A bunch of green bananas, a couple of mealy apples, maybe. Some shriveled limes. Its main business was cigarettes, beer, candy, and soda. "Do you have any potatoes?"

"Potatoes? Sure." He pointed to a dusty sack in a milk crate on the floor next to the ice cream freezer. The potatoes were gnarly and small but they looked okay. Not rotten.

"How much for the whole thing?"

"Is it for you?"

"Well—"

"Is it for that crazy nut with the rooster?" He leaned over the counter. "I see him outside. He's not allowed in here!"

I set the potatoes on the counter. "How much?"

"He steals things! He comes in and takes things, rice and bread. He stuffs them into his jacket! He's not allowed! No roosters allowed!"

"Okay, don't worry. He won't come in." I put the pack of Camel Lights next to the potatoes and added a pack of Starburst. "How much?"

"Two-fifty."

I paid exactly two-fifty, thanked Brahim, went outside, and handed over the potatoes. The rooster guy snatched the sack. "Thanks, girl, thanks." He added something that sounded like, "I'll pay you back." Though of course I didn't expect him to pay me back, or want him to. He trotted off down the street, heading toward the park.

I lit a cigarette and continued up First Avenue to Ninth Street. The circus on St. Marks was winding down for the night. I felt a presence behind me, like someone stepping on my shadow. I glanced back. A guy and a girl stumbled drunkenly into a doorway to kiss. I left them behind but the presence stuck to me. Power of suggestion, I figured; Bix's worry had gotten to me. Nevertheless, the tiny anxious fishhooks started nibbling away.

I turned onto A, scanning the park. No Dad, no Atti. No . . . Carmen. Suddenly chilled, I pushed through the street door of my building—the lock was broken—and ran all the way upstairs, my heart racing until I was safely inside. Damn Bix and his scary stories.

I sat on the living room couch, the windows open to the park, and tried to soothe my speeding heart. I missed crickets. It was summer, and nighttime, and hot, and when I was a child that had always meant crickets. Instead there were moans, and shouts, and alarms, and motors, and sirens, and no Carmen, and no Jem.

Earlier that afternoon, when we were lounging in bed, Jem had absently rubbed my calf. His fingers went back and forth over a small patch below my knee. "You missed a spot," he said.

"What?"

"Shaving. You missed this spot right here." He took my hand and put it on the spot so I could feel the one-inch area of bristly hair.

I didn't think much of it at the time, but now that moment burned with meaning. I should have known.

It was over.

22

CHANCE OF A LIFETIME

It didn't fall apart all at once, of course.

He called the next afternoon to apologize and explain. He'd run into Esphyr at Fanelli's, he said. She finally wanted to talk about representing him, maybe giving him a solo show in the fall, so he couldn't leave, he didn't want to offend her, it's the chance of a lifetime, *you understand, right baby?* And I did understand, I understood all that but I also understood that he was pulling away. He said he wasn't, he swore up and down that he wasn't, but I knew I was right. I told myself not to be upset. I told myself I'd been using him—to meet art world people, to raise my status, to show I could catch a handsome guy that everybody wanted—and now he was using Esphyr. That's the way it goes. I tried to be cool, to face facts, to shrug and let him go—I tried so hard—but I couldn't do it. I was hooked on him. It had been a beautiful summer.

He didn't make it easy for me. He kept me dangling. Sometimes he met me at Plutonium, and sometimes he didn't. I couldn't predict when he would show up. I was afraid to complain for fear he'd feel pressured and pull away from me.

One night I waited for him at the club until 4:30 a.m., when Toby locked the doors. There was no message on the answering machine when I got home. I tried to sleep but kept arguing with Jem in my head, fantasizing about hurting him, except I had trouble imagining anything I could do that would hurt him.

The next day I spotted him perched at the counter at Lethe. I went in and took the empty stool beside him.

"Here she is. Fresh as a daisy like always."

I was rumpled from my restless night and surely not fresh-looking. I ordered a coffee from Taffy and waited to see what else he had to say. Not much, it turned out. He folded open the paper he was reading—the sports section of the *Daily News*, lots of pictures from the Olympics.

"Jem," I said.

"Yes love."

"What's going on?"

He looked up from the paper. "Nothing. Everything's the same." He dipped his head back into the sports section. I stirred milk into my coffee and took a sip.

"Where are Bix and Wes today?" I said.

"I don't know." He turned another page. "Guess they can't come here *every* day."

I picked up someone's discarded *Times* and stared at a picture of Mary Lou Retton's triumphant fireplug body. At a table behind me, a man replaced a cup on a saucer with a clink, then cleared his throat. Taffy padded from table to table in her Tretorns. Was the café always this quiet?

"Jem," I said softly, "please talk to me. Something's bothering you, I can feel it."

He rattled the newspaper, folding it. "You're being paranoid." A hint of annoyance crept into his voice.

"I'm not imagining this. I'm seeing you less and less."

"I'm painting. I'm hoping to score a show this fall, and I'm working hard. Do you want me to feel bad about that?"

"No."

He rose, leaving a dollar on the counter for Taffy. "See you later." I watched him walk out. He turned and waved, but I sensed it took effort, that he did it out of obligation and regret, not because he couldn't resist taking a last look at me.

I spent long days alone, listening for the phone, listening for the door, watching baseball, watching the Olympics, playing sad songs on my toy accordion. I stopped going to Café Lethe because it felt empty now that Carmen wasn't there. I stood at the living room window for hours, studying the foot traffic on Avenue A, looking for people who were as unhappy as I was. I saw lots of them. It didn't cheer me.

"Say, dollbaby," Bix said when I came to work. "You getting any sleep? You look like a dead raccoon."

I opened my Ivan stash and counted my money. Eight hundred and seventy-five dollars. When would I have enough? Throwing money in Ivan's face was the only thing I could think of that might make me feel better.

Then at the end of August, I saw Jem every night for a week. *Maybe it's over with Esphyr,* I thought, afraid to hope but hoping anyway. In the paper I saw a picture of her at a party in the Hamptons. She had a place in Sag Harbor and was staying out there all week. Then, on Sunday night, Jem didn't show up at the club. Esphyr was back in town.

Humiliation and anger boiled inside me like baby spiders—hatching, crawling, biting. That night, I saw Carmen in a dream. She hovered over the bed like an angel, naked. "You're wearing my clothes!" she howled at me. "I saw you. You've taken Mitch!"

"You didn't come back to get it!" I cried. I had to shield my eyes from the bright light she emitted. "If you want your jacket back, you have to come home and get it."

"Why don't *you* come home!" she screamed.

I woke up in a stew of feelings: sadness from my longing for her, stinging from her anger at me, but also, strangely, happy. It was painful not knowing where she was. I couldn't comfort myself by imagining what she was doing. So I was happy to see her again, even if she was mad at me, even if only in a dream. But was it a dream, or a ghost? How could I tell the difference?

"I'll bring fish and corn and wine," Jem said on the phone. "We'll have one of our Monday night dinners."

"Last one of the summer," I said.

It was early September, and he'd finally called.

"I'll be over around six." His voice was soothing, placating, and I wanted badly to believe in him. I knew he didn't love me, but by then it didn't matter. I needed some contact, whatever he would give me, a fix to get me through another week.

When he hadn't arrived by eight, I called his apartment. Stevie Wonder sang on his outgoing message, *"Until the day is night and night becomes the day."* I hung up on his machine. He wasn't coming. And I knew where I could find him.

I walked through the fading late-summer light to SoHo. There was a new Amelia flyer taped to a lamppost, and my heart seized. From a distance, the fuzzy Xeroxed photo of a sharp-faced girl could have been Carmen. All this time I'd been telling myself that Carmen was fine; she just didn't want to see me. After she'd appeared in my dream, I'd begun to feel uneasy. Now I realized—I allowed myself to consider—that something might have happened to her. That her silence might not be her choice.

I hesitated, then summoned the courage to step closer and read the flyer.

MISSING: CATHY CALABRESI

AGE 16

5'4", 115 LBS.

BROWN HAIR, PALE SKIN, FRECKLES

SLIGHT SOUTHERN ACCENT

LAST SEEN ON AUGUST 29

NEAR TOMPKINS SQUARE PARK

I felt a blast of relief, then guilt. To make up for it, I looked hard at the picture. I wished I had seen this Cathy Calabresi, or any of the Amelias. I wanted to help. Maybe I hadn't been paying attention.

Fanelli's neon sign beckoned from the corner of Mercer and Prince. I could see inside the bar through the large plate-glass window. Rowdy artists drank and joked and horsed around, and in the corner, Esphyr and Jem sat with their hands clasped together, deep in conversation. He lifted one of her hands to his lips. She allowed the kiss, then pulled her hand away to reach for her martini.

I'd known all along he'd fallen for Esphyr; of course I had. But he kept denying it, saying that nothing had changed between us, that he was busy working, and until this moment I hadn't realized how fervently I'd clung to that tiny shred of doubt. Now all doubt was gone. I felt a strange, sudden need to cough, as if I had to unblock an air passage. I stood on the sidewalk outside Fanelli's window coughing helplessly. Jem caught sight of me and frowned. I felt ridiculous, my body seizing, my face crumpled, eyes tearing, my throat hacking out some speck of dust, a tiny thing caught inside me, tickling and torturing me, that wouldn't come out. I didn't want him and Esphyr to see me like that, so I ran away.

A few hours later, he banged on the door. "Phoebe! Open up."

I let him in.

"Are you spying on me now? What's wrong with you?"

"You were supposed to come over," I said. "You were going to make dinner."

"I said I might come over. I said maybe." He started pacing, lighting matches and tossing them, aflame, on the floor, one after another, to fizzle out just before landing. The cats hid under the bed, afraid of his boots. "What do you want from me?"

I couldn't say. I knew I should act as if I didn't care. I wished I didn't care.

"You don't know what you want. That's your trouble."

"That's not true." I did know what I wanted. I wanted what Carmen had. I wanted to be her. I wanted her to come back.

"You girls don't get it. This has nothing to do with you. You can be with different people, and it means different things. Esphyr can help me. If I spend time with her, it doesn't take anything away from you."

"Except the time."

"What?"

I wanted to stop my tongue, but I couldn't resist pointing out the hole in his argument. "It takes away from the time you spend with me."

He ran out of matches and tossed the matchbook on the floor. "Look, you're not my first priority, okay? No one is. My work comes first."

"What did you come here for then?"

"You have my Ray-Bans. I need them back."

I gritted my teeth. "I haven't seen them. Get out."

He went into the bedroom and started kicking through the clothes on the floor.

"What are you doing? Get out!"

He found the sunglasses in a drawer and waved them at me. I ripped them out of his hand. He punched the wall. His fist made a hole in the plaster.

I stared at the hole in alarm. I'd never seen him so angry, and it tripped something angry in me too. "GET OUT!"

He grabbed me from behind. I struggled and kicked, but that

only made him tighten his grip, and part of me wanted to stay in his arms. He licked my neck. "Don't lick me! Kiss me!" I said, but he licked me again. He tossed me onto the bed and tore off my panties. I wrapped my legs around his waist and lifted my hips to meet his. He put his head between my thighs and gave my pussy one lick, then lifted his head and grinned, lips shiny. We fucked quickly. I came very hard. I hated myself. I hated the whole ugly, beautiful thing.

He sat back on his knees and looked at me without affection or dislike—just neutral, expressionless. Then he reached for the glasses and slid them on.

"You punched your fist through the wall. I didn't know people actually did that."

"Well, now you know."

After he left, the cats slinked out from under the bed. Julio hid behind the door and ambushed Diego when he trotted by, grabbing him by the neck with his teeth. Diego froze, a gazelle to Julio's lion, then escaped Julio's jaws and fled to the living room. They hissed and scratched. I didn't try to stop them. They were only following their instincts.

23

ASTRID SEES ALL

A couple of days later, I woke up with a headache and a painful itch between my legs. I got up to pee. It hurt. It smelled bad. There was clumpy yellow stuff coming out of me. I started to cry.

I tried to think of someone to call, someone who would know what this was and what to do about it. But who did I know? Zu? Too embarrassing. Bix? Ha.

Who else? Who else?

I went to the clinic on Second Avenue. The doctor diagnosed trichomoniasis and gave me a prescription for Flagyl. He warned me not to take even one sip of alcohol while on the medicine or I'd get violently ill. He added that I should let any recent partners know that they should be treated too. Men often showed no symptoms. They spread suffering without suffering themselves.

I secretly exulted in an excuse to call Jem. VD was gross, but it was something we shared. Something he'd given me. Something we'd have to face together.

I dialed his number. He didn't answer. He had changed the Stevie Wonder song on his machine from "As" to "Ordinary Pain." I hung up on it.

I tried an hour later. The machine again. "Hey Jem, call me, please. It's important."

I waited by the phone, but he didn't call back. I tried a few more times, hoping he'd pick up. "Ordinary Pain" stuck in my head all day long. Late that night, I left one more message: "Jem, I have trichomoniasis. That means you have it too. You need to go to the doctor and get meds. And tell anyone else you've slept with to get checked. This is Phoebe, by the way. 'Bye." I hoped Esphyr would hear it—if he let her into his apartment. I assumed he did. He'd make an exception for her, to show her his paintings.

I stayed home from work and didn't go out for three days. I felt lousy. I couldn't imagine talking to strangers about their lives, pretending to care. I needed rest. And now I had time to work on writing a column for the *Underground.* Over the course of the summer Wes had asked me if I had anything to show him, but I'd been too busy partying and screwing Jem. I had a new plan: I'd work hard, not party so much, and make a name for myself—or at least, a name for my alter ego—with Astrid Sees All. Astrid would be famous, but disguised. Everyone, and no one, would know who she was.

I sat down at the kitchen table to write. Julio walked back and forth over my notebook. I petted him and he curled up in my lap. Diego meowed. It was nine o'clock in the evening, the hour when I normally started dressing for the club.

I heard Gergo's door shut and his footsteps trip down the stairs. The downstairs door slammed. Then a cottony silence.

I glanced at the phone. I'd already checked twice to see if the ringer was on. What the hell, it couldn't hurt to check again.

The ringer was on.

Back at the table, I tapped my pen on the metal spiral spine of the notebook. I wrote:

ASTRID SEES ALL

By Astrid the Star Girl

. . . .

If only Jem would call back, I could have one final talk with him, tie up loose ends, make sure he understood the harm he'd done to me, and then forget about him. When he kept me hanging like this it made me obsess over him more than ever.

My name is Astrid. I'm a fortune-teller.

For inspiration, I pulled three ticket stubs: *American Graffiti. The Seduction of Joe Tynan. Smokey and the Bandit.*

I stared at them for a long time, trying to find some meaning in them. I shuffled them around. I thought about the actors who'd starred in these movies. Alan Alda. Burt Reynolds. Richard Dreyfuss. What did it all mean? I couldn't put anything together.

All the drinking and coke I'd done had addled my brain. I definitely had to cut down, especially on the coke. Too expensive anyway.

I closed my eyes and tried to project images of the future onto a screen in my brain, but it remained blank: a cone of colorless light, swimming with dust motes.

I kept my eyes closed. I kept watching the screen. Finally, a figure stepped onto the screen and began to dance. *"I'll give you fish, I'll give you candy. . . ."* She was only a shadow, a silhouette, but I'd have known that angular face anywhere.

There was a knock at the window. I opened my eyes. *A knock . . . at the window. On the third floor.* Someone on the fire escape?

I crossed the living room and looked out. No one on the fire escape. Across the street, the park was quiet and still.

Let's go to the window and see if we see anyone as unhappy as we are.

I returned to the kitchen table. A few minutes later, I was sure I heard another knock on the window. But no one was there. I told myself an insect must be trying to bash its way inside, but I didn't see any insects big enough to make a knocking sound. Again my eyes were drawn to the park; this time I saw a figure moving slowly through the shadows between the streetlamps.

After an hour, I gave up on the column and switched on the TV. The Yankees were down two-to-one in the third, against Toronto. I picked up my Scooter bat and held it in my pajama-clad lap. It was one of those nights when the Scooter wasn't paying attention to the game.

"I don't like this indoor stadium, White. The stale air makes my head shrink. Look, the mike is getting bigger. . . ."

I wrote down, *My head is shrinking. The mike is getting bigger.*

Around eleven, Zu knocked on the door. "What are you doing in your pajamas? Aren't you going to work?"

"Did you knock on my window a while ago?"

"On your window?" She looked confused. "I haven't seen you around, so I thought I'd check on you."

"I've been sick."

"Poor honey! Toby asked where you were. I'll tell him. Are you okay?"

"I'll be okay in a few days."

"All right. If you need anything, just knock on our door. But not before noon. Unless it's an emergency, of course."

Just before bed, I shook up my shoebox and chanted, "Dear Oracle, give me guidance." I pulled out one ticket: *What's Up, Doc?*

Nineteen seventy-two. Ryan O'Neal and Barbra Streisand. Dad took me to see it, a matinee one Saturday when I was eleven—a rare outing for just the two of us. Mom stayed home with Laurel, who had a cold.

We drove to a mall in Catonsville, in the suburbs, to see the movie. I loved it. Barbra Streisand kept causing trouble for Ryan O'Neal, which somehow made him fall in love with her and leave his uptight fiancée. Afterward Dad asked me if I wanted to get something to eat, and I said yes. We drove to a strange little mill town on a hillside. My memory of the place is blurry, but I remember thinking it looked like something out of *Where the Lilies Bloom*, a book I'd read about four orphans in Appalachia who try to hide the fact that their father has died so they won't be separated and put into foster homes.

"This place is supposed to have the best cheesecake in the city," Dad said. "Even better than Little Italy." One of his patients had told him about it. We climbed a rickety staircase to a restaurant high on the hill, where we ate spaghetti and cheesecake, which was indeed delicious. Dad and I stood out in our plain afternoon clothes; the other customers were dressed for a Saturday night in flouncy dresses and Western shirts. An old lady played polkas and waltzes on her mighty Wurlitzer and everybody danced. Dad and I danced too. I knew how to dance the polka from ballet class, so I taught Dad how to do it. I didn't want to go home, back to practical Mom and snuffling Laurel with her cold.

I hadn't thought of that day in many years. I went to the window to look for Dad. I looked and looked. I waved my sheaf of Scooter notes to entice him.

That night I descended into a strange state, a kind of delirium. I saw visions, hallucinations. I dreamed of waist-high snow as soft and warm as sand. I saw the Yankees hitting run after run, smacking balls out of the stadium, sending them out into space, while Scooter said, *"What a moon, White. Beautiful full moon. Unbelievable. Look, you can see Texas!"*

I opened my eyes and found myself staring at the Dr. Seuss crack in the ceiling. I blinked once, twice, three times. . . . Was I awake? I appeared to be. But everything looked strange. Where had that hole in the wall come from? For a few seconds I couldn't remember who I was or where I was. I felt like a kid who'd stumbled into a time machine and landed in this room, years into the future. Why had the time machine sent me here? Why this room, why this neighborhood, why this summer?

My mind cleared gradually, like a Polaroid developing. I was not a kid. This was not the future, this was now. I was twenty-three, I lived alone in the East Village with two cats, and Carmen was gone. I had to pee badly and eased myself out of bed.

When I came out of the bathroom I noticed a postcard on the kitchen table. The picture on the front was a cartoon of Elmer Fudd. Carmen had found the card in a junk shop and given it to me. On the back was a message in my handwriting.

Dear Mom,

I feel like I'm drifting endlessly through space, past planets and asteroids and moons, but never landing anywhere. I'm full of doubt. Sometimes I'm convinced that I will find love, and a purpose, and I feel strong, sure that all of my doubts were delusions. But before long I'm convinced that the certainty was a delusion and only the doubt is real.

I'm falling through the universe. I don't know what's real and what's not.

I didn't remember writing this. But I recognized the spacey, unmoored feeling.

I threw the postcard away.

The next afternoon, Zu asked me if I'd like to come up to her place for tea. I got dressed and climbed to the fifth floor. Their door was painted raspberry pink. Marie-Claude let me in. Their apartment was beautiful, like a fantasy harem—everything painted pretty colors, gauzy curtains between the rooms and scarves over the lamps to soften the light. Zu and I sat on velvet cushions and drank mint tea while Marie-Claude pinned fabric on a dress dummy. In one corner they'd set up an altar to the goddess Isis, with candles and incense and offerings of jewelry and candy. Nearby, a parakeet fluttered in a cage.

"We let him out to fly around at least once a day," Zu said. "I'm glad you're taking care of Oswald's cats. When's he getting out?"

"I don't know. I hope never."

She looked taken aback.

"Because then I'll have to move out."

"Sure."

"I never met him. Is he nice?"

She shrugged. "He ran with a different crowd." Perhaps she was thinking of Atti, because she added, "Where's your roommate been?"

"We had a fight."

"Oh. That's terrible. Can you afford the rent by yourself?"

"Not really."

"Didn't she work at Lethe?" Marie-Claude said. "You know that girl Taffy? I heard she disappeared. Like those other girls. On the posters?"

"Shit," I said. "Wes Temple calls them the Amelias. After Amelia Earhart."

"What about that girl Katinka?" Zu said. "Do you know her? Kind of a weird girl, skinny?"

"Is she missing too?"

"I don't know. She used to come into the club once in a while, but I haven't seen her in weeks."

"Maybe she went back to Germany," Marie-Claude said.

"I think she was from Sweden," Zu said. "Or was it Switzerland?"

"What do you think is happening to those girls?" I asked.

"Maybe they're OD'ing?" Zu said. "I keep hearing about this bad dope."

"But if that's true, why hasn't anyone found their bodies?" Marie-Claude said.

"Maybe someone's kidnapping them," Zu said.

"I doubt that," Marie-Claude said.

"Have you ever seen that guy who walks around with a rooster on his shoulder?" Zu said. "He's creepy."

"I saw him a few weeks ago," I said. "He asked me to buy him some potatoes."

"Weird," Marie-Claude said.

"Weirdos have to eat too," Zu said.

I felt uneasy. All summer with no word from Carmen. Why had I assumed she was okay?

"How'd you hear about Taffy?" I asked.

"Bix told me. He knows everything."

"I like Bix," Zu said. "He lets it all out. He has no shame—in a good way."

"He's so unhealthy," Marie-Claude said. "Have you looked at his skin up close? It's like corrugated cardboard."

"He's had a hard life," Zu said. "Things other people would be ashamed to admit, he comes right out and tells you."

"Shame is very toxic," Marie-Claude agreed.

I thought of Carmen, of the way she'd taken care of Atti when he was sick. He exasperated her, he broke her heart, but she wasn't ashamed of him.

Maybe Bix knew something about Carmen, what had happened to her or where she might be hiding. "I'm coming back to work tonight," I told Zu.

"Oh good," Zu said. "Bix misses you."

24

GOING UPTOWN

As soon as I got to the club I asked for Bix. He was away for the night, shooting a short film in New Jersey.

I had saved $875. I stayed at my Astrid table all night, leaving only for short breaks, determined to get that last $125. When I had no customers I cased the lounges for people standing alone, or couples not speaking to each other. "It's only five dollars," I said, taking them by the hand and leading them to my table. "Only five dollars for an answer to your most burning questions."

By 3:30 a.m., I had earned $130. Enough, at last.

The next day I took my briefcase full of money, a thousand dollars in small bills, and rode the 6 train uptown to Fifty-Ninth and Lex. I rarely ventured uptown anymore and when I did it looked like a planet inhabited by powdered, coiffed aliens with bland faces.

My heart pounding, I walked to the maisonette where Ivan's office had been, on East Fifty-Sixth Street. I was sure I had remembered the right address, but when I looked for his name beside the door it wasn't there. I went inside anyway, clutching my briefcase. With a shudder I recognized the waiting room, three doors leading to three different doctors' offices, guarded by a receptionist's desk. One patient occupied the waiting area, an old man reading *Field & Stream*. The receptionist looked up warily.

"May I help you?"

"I'd like to see Dr. Bergen please."

"Who?"

"Dr. Bergen?"

"He isn't here." She had a high forehead, a pinched mouth and a paisley scarf knotted around her goose-like neck.

"Do you know where he is?"

"No, I don't."

"Do you know when he'll be back?"

She rested her eyes on the phone as if expecting it to ring. It didn't. "He won't be back. He doesn't keep an office here anymore."

I looked around in confusion. There was his door, the third door, the one he had come out of with a snifter of brandy in his hand. I pointed to it. "That's his office right there."

"It used to be. Now it's occupied by Dr. Peters."

I hadn't anticipated this. He was gone?

"Do you know where he went?"

She shook her head and ostentatiously flipped through an appointment book on her desk. "I'm sorry. No idea. He's been gone for several months now."

I felt like grabbing her by the knot of her scarf and shouting, *Tell me where he is or I'll wring your stupid goosey neck!* But she didn't know. I said, "Thank you," and went outside to light a cigarette and think this over. He'd moved his office, that was all. Surely he was working somewhere else in the city.

I found a phone booth and dialed information, asking for the address of Ivan Bergen, MD. The operator had no listings under that name.

Had I imagined him? My uptown life, the months before my father died, felt distant and hazy. Maybe they hadn't actually happened. Maybe I'd dreamed them.

But I didn't believe that. I hadn't felt all that pain and saved up all this money for nothing. His pied-à-terre was two blocks away. Maybe I could find him there.

I carried my briefcase to Fifty-Eighth Street, reflexively glancing back to see if anyone was following me. The streets were busy now on a weekday afternoon, crowded with shoppers and office workers. So different from the haunted street I remembered.

The doorman stopped me as I entered Ivan's sleek building. "I'm looking for Ivan Bergen, 27A," I said.

A shadow crossed his face, as if he were trying to remember something. "Oh—Dr. Bergen. He hasn't been around for months."

"Did he move out? Do you know where he went?"

"Sorry, miss. No idea. I don't think he moved out, he just hasn't been around."

I stood on the sidewalk, unsure what to do next. People hurried past me, looking preoccupied. I envied them; they had someplace to go, and they knew where it was. The briefcase felt heavy and ridiculous. I found a Chase Manhattan Bank on Fifth Avenue and went inside. I changed the piles of ones and fives into a slender stack of ten hundred-dollar bills. I folded them into the pocket of my jacket—the "Mitch" pocket, as I thought of it, the one with pink stitching. I dumped the empty briefcase in a trash can. Then I walked all the way home, three and a half miles, to ease myself off this alien planet and back to the familiar, comforting world of weirdos.

25

AVIVA B.

"Give me another bump."

Bix was sitting on the lid of the toilet in the stall he called his office, and I perched on his knee. He tapped out a tiny hill of coke onto his fist. I applied my straw and sucked it into my sinuses. My brain thrilled, a dog whose master had finally come home. Carmen was gone, and Jem was gone, and now even Ivan—my dream of revenge, my chance to get rid of the heaviness I still felt deep inside—was gone. Of the three, the only one I wanted back was Carmen.

I asked Bix if he had any idea where Carmen could be, and he said no. "Maybe the park, if she's using. But you shouldn't go into the park."

"But if she's in there . . ."

"If she's in there, what good would it do?" He bounced his meaty thigh. "Get off, my leg's falling asleep."

I switched to the other knee, but he said, "No, dollbaby, go dance or something. Don't you have customers waiting?"

"I can't go out there."

"Yes, you can."

"One more bump."

"Take a rest, sweetie pie. You know how you get, with your sensitive little schnoz, like that scene in *The Shining*, you know, with the blood pouring out of the elevator?"

"I'll pay you. I've got money on me somewhere. . . ." I patted my pocket and realized I still had the thousand dollars with me. I pulled out the money and waved it in front of Bix's nose. "See?"

He followed the money with his eyes. "Put that away." He stuffed the bills back into my pocket and kicked open the stall door. "Look. They're waiting for you."

Six people dawdled around my booth. One of them was Aviva B. A guy with platinum dreads said, "Astrid, I need help."

Bix gave me a gentle shove out of the stall.

"I can't help anyone." I stumbled out to the lounge and asked for a vodka and soda. I took it back to my booth, drew the curtain, and said, "We're closed."

On the table, the crystal ball rebuked me, cloudy as my brain. I plucked an ice cube from my glass and gazed into it, but it melted in my fingers.

Half an hour later, I opened the curtain. The guy with the platinum dreads was still waiting, chewing on a Twizzler. The dreads were short and sprouted gracefully from his head like pineapple leaves. "Will you see me now?"

I let him in and closed the curtain around us. His name was Bob, he said. Bob-o-Phonic Bob. He was a DJ who worked at the club a few nights a week; I'd seen his silver dreads bopping up and down in the booth while he spun soul records. He was around twenty, with a boyish face and sad eyes, wearing a mod suit with a skinny tie.

"Shake the magic box." I put the shoebox in his hands. "Do you have a question?"

He tightened his lips. He had a question, but he wasn't ready to ask it yet. "Okay," I said. "Maybe the box will ask a question for you." I reached in and pulled out a stub. *The Turning Point.*

"Oh my God," Bob said. "That's one of my favorite movies."

"I know. Anne Bancroft. Shirley MacLaine. Ballet. Baryshnikov! It's got everything."

"I can't believe you chose that movie. You're amazing."

"There are no coincidences. What is your question?"

He picked up the movie ticket and turned it over. "I think I'm sick. I'm afraid to go to the doctor."

"What's wrong?"

"I'm tired. I wake up at night sweating, even when the room is cold. I've lost weight. . . ."

"You should go to the clinic."

"I don't want to."

"I know, but I'm not a doctor. I don't know anything about this."

"Can you just tell me . . ." He licked his lips, swallowed. "Should I be afraid?"

"Should you . . . ?" *Yes,* I thought. *We should all be afraid.* But I couldn't say that. People said they wanted to know the future, but I'd learned over the months that my true job was to reassure. "I don't know. Please, Bob, you have to go to a doctor. You know that clinic on Second Avenue? I just went there myself."

"Please—look in the crystal ball or whatever you do. Do you see a sign of doom?"

"Doom?"

"Don't you feel it all around us? This sense of doom? Bad things keep happening, not just to me . . ."

I did feel it.

"It's everywhere I look. Drops of blood on the sidewalk. A dead pigeon on my front stoop. Did you hear that the police found a cooler in a dump near the East River, full of bones? One of my friends is in the hospital, and another one is wasting away. . . ."

I didn't want to hear this. I tapped the movie stub. "*The Turning Point*! Maybe this is it. Maybe from now on things will start to get better."

"Or worse."

I pulled out a second stub. *The Hunger*. He groaned.

"That means nothing. David Bowie's in it! What could be bad?"

"It's about vampires. And *blood*."

"Wait! You get three."

Ciao! Manhattan. Goddammit.

"You have to go to the doctor," I said.

"And if I go, what will they say?"

"I don't know."

"Yes, you do. Come on. Look."

I rubbed the crystal ball, just to make him happy. "The doctor will tell you."

"You're not trying." He stood up, clenching his fists. I think he wanted to punch me.

"I'm sorry," I said. "I don't know anything. I've lost my powers."

He tore open the curtain and stalked away. Aviva B. poked her head in. "Am I next?"

"Sure, why not."

She sat down across from me but did not reach for the shoebox. She'd attached a blue velvet hat to her head, perilously tilted, and lined her eyes in midnight blue to match. "I know who you are."

"Everyone knows who I am. I'm Astrid the Star Girl."

"I said, I know who you are, *Phoebe Hayes*."

The note of menace in her voice made my stomach twist. It wasn't hard to find out what my real name was. But why would she care?

"Okay, so?"

"Do you know who I am?"

"You're Aviva B."

"Guess what the *B* stands for."

"What?"

"The *B*. In Aviva B."

The cocaine thrill in my blood soured. I picked up my cup of vodka and tilted it at my mouth. Nothing left but ice cubes. I crunched on them.

"Can you guess?"

"Just tell me."

"It stands for Bergen."

Some part of me had already, secretly, known that.

"Do you know anyone named Bergen?"

"One person. One person I used to know."

"He's my father."

I nodded. I didn't know what she wanted me to do with this information. It was unnerving to think Ivan had a daughter nearly my age, but I shouldn't have been surprised. Now that I knew, I saw the resemblance: the way she trained her stony eyes on me, expecting obedience.

"Where is he?" I asked.

"What?"

"Do you know where I can find him?"

She looked startled. "He doesn't care about you. Why don't you just leave him alone?"

I realized how my question had sounded and regretted it. I didn't want to give anyone the impression that I cared about him either.

"I owe him something, that's all. I want to repay him so I never have to think about him again."

Now she looked wary. "Repay him? Repay him what?"

None of her business. "How do you know about me, anyway? Did he tell you?"

"Ha. I don't speak to him anymore. I found the pictures in my mother's room—the pictures and the detective's report. Pictures of you with him. Kissing him. Getting into taxis. And everything about you. Everything."

A detective. The thought made me queasy. "Tell your mother she can call off the detective now. She has nothing to worry about from me."

"She called him off months ago, when you left town. She thought you were gone for good. But I found you. You sneaked back, trying to hide under a false name—"

"If you know everything, then you know I owe your father some money. Just tell me where I can find him, and I'll be out of your lives forever."

She hesitated. She didn't trust me, but she was a gossip at heart and couldn't help herself.

"My mother kicked him out, so he rejoined the MSF. He's in Ethiopia, with the famine."

Hiding in Ethiopia, pretending he cared about humanity. I was annoyed.

"Are you talking about the abortion money?" Aviva asked. She really did know everything. "The flowers with the envelope of cash inside? That didn't come from him."

"Where did it come from?"

"My mother sent it. It was the detective's idea."

I absorbed this information slowly. Ivan had not sent the money. So I could never throw it back in his face. He hadn't even been that decent.

"I'm glad you told me this." I plucked the ten hundred-dollar bills out of my pocket and set them on the table. "Give this to your mother for me, please."

Aviva stared at the money. She folded the bills and put them in her tiny purse.

"Or you can keep it for yourself," I said. "I'll never know the difference. Next time you go out, *you* can buy the drinks for a change."

When she stood, her fists were clenched like Bob-o-Phonic Bob's. I had, again, the strong feeling she wanted to punch me. "I no longer have a father. Because of you."

"Only me?" Because I understood, now, that there must have been others. Probably many others.

She flexed her hands open, then re-clenched them. No, not only me. "You did your part."

"You have a father. You just don't want him."

THE MOON AND THURMAN MUNSON

Wes was watching the TV over the bar: Yanks versus Boston at Fenway. Bix sat beside him with a whiskey. They didn't notice that I'd come in. I took a breath and focused on the Scooter.

"Look at that, White: the wind keeps changing direction. I tell ya, it blows Yankee fly balls back into the stadium, but it blows Red Sox hits right out of the park. Strike one to Piniella. Somebody told me the Red Sox control the elements up here. The wind, the rain, everything. I didn't believe them until today.

"Son of a gun, look at this! Piniella whacks one! And it goes . . . foul. Foul ball. How do you like that. The wind again!"

The Yankees' season was basically over. They weren't going to make the playoffs. Neither were the Orioles. Some years were like that. The Scooter accepted it. Dad and I accepted it. Games were won and lost. Players were streaky, hot one day and slumping the next. The wind blew for you or against you, but there was always next spring. In the meantime, baseball and its superstitions, its omens and good luck charms, would get you through. That was the idea, anyway.

I tapped Wes on the shoulder and took the empty stool next to him. He smiled and ordered me a beer. "I heard you got fired."

I glared at Bix. He shrugged and said, "It's no secret, dollbaby."

"I wasn't fired, exactly." But I might as well have been. After my run-in with Aviva B., I'd decided to leave the club early. It had been a bad night. Shan had stopped me on my way out and said Toby wanted to see me. I went to his office and he told me he was getting rid of my fortune-telling table. It took up space in the ladies' lounge, and interest had dropped off. The concept was great for a while, he said, but everything gets stale eventually; that was why they redid the club in a new theme every month. He wanted to put a photo booth in its place. People loved those. He was sure I understood. I was welcome at the club any time, of course, for a drink or whatever.

I suspected Aviva had gotten to him, but it didn't really matter. Nightclub fortune-telling is not the kind of gig that lasts forever.

The next day I finished my tryout column for Wes. I'd lost my only source of income, and Mrs. Lisiewicz had been nagging me for the rent, which I'd skimped on in my rush to pay back Ivan. The *Underground* was my last hope.

In the late afternoon I dropped off the column at Wes's office. He said he would read it and get back to me soon. On my way home, I kicked an empty beer can into the gutter and stopped to look at the latest Amelia flyer, a blurry photo of a young woman with a ski-lift nose, her hair in a severe dancer's bun.

MISSING: KATINKA GELFORS

AGE 20

5'5", 103 LBS. . . .

Taffy missing, now Katinka, and all the other girls too. And where was Carmen? That gnawing feeling returned, the tiny fishhooks eating away at me. The world had always been dangerous, but now I let it scare me.

The evening sky was tart, the sapphire-lemon color of a sno-cone. I entered the park near the statue of Samuel Sullivan Cox and strolled the winding paths, looking for signs of Carmen. I paused at the General Slocum memorial. *They were Earth's purest children, young and fair.* I thought about Doug and his baby. Doug had moved out. It was just Kelly Ann and the baby now. The rooster pecked at a pool of rainwater in the bowl of the fountain, then squawked and fluttered away.

"You know the rooster that lives in the park?" I said to Bix, taking a sip of beer, cool and fizzy and pleasantly sour.

"The park is a jungle these days," Bix said. "All overgrown, people living in there like wild animals. I used to go there to score. Now I won't walk through it. I always go around."

I glanced at the game. Bill Buckner was at the plate, one out, nobody on.

"So . . . you read my sample?" I asked Wes.

"I liked it." Wes had a kind smile, which he bestowed on me now. Somehow I knew that kindness was a bad sign. "I'm just not sure my readers will care about a girl they've never heard of who claims to predict the future with movie ticket stubs—I mean, when they can't see you in person, the whole act and everything."

"But . . . the column was your idea. You asked me to write it."

"I know. But that was when you were the house fortune-teller at Plutonium. Without that club connection, your name alone isn't enough of a draw."

"I'll get work at another club," I said. "I'll tell fortunes at Danceteria, or Limelight."

"I know you will. Let's wait and see what happens."

To hide my disappointment, I concentrated on the game. Buckner drove a bullet of a line drive toward first. Mattingly dove for it and made a miraculous double play to end the inning.

"How do you like that! If Don Mattingly isn't the American League MVP, nothing's kosher in China."

I memorized the line to add to my Scooter notes when I got home.

Wes left a ten-dollar bill on the bar and slid off his stool. "I'd better get going. See you two around." He glanced up at the TV one last time before walking out.

Bix took off his fedora and clapped it onto my head. "Are you going to leave me too?"

"I'll never leave you."

"Good. Let's get drunk." He ordered two Irish whiskeys. We clinked glasses.

"Cheers."

"I heard what Aviva B. said to you the other night, dollbaby. Some of it, I mean. I don't know exactly what she was talking about, but her body language was fierce."

"Yeah." His hat was making my forehead sweat. I took it off and gave it back to him.

"But so, if you're broke or whatever, why not go home and lie low for a while? You got a family someplace, anybody can see that."

"You can? How do you see it?"

"It's all over your face. Why do you think I call you dollbaby?"

I felt so tired, for a moment I actually considered going home. I would crawl into my bed and sleep for days. . . . But that was a fantasy. My mother would not simply let me sleep. She would be driven to find out what was wrong with me, and she would keep me with her until she'd fixed it.

Seventh-inning stretch: the camera panned up to the sky where a big round moon glowed over Fenway.

"Ah, White, look at that moon. Beautiful, beautiful full moon. You know, it might sound corny, but to me it's some kind of a, like an omen. Remember the night after Thurman died? About five years ago. We held a memorial service in Yankee Stadium. There was a moon that night just like this one. A big full moon."

I remembered. The summer before I left home for college, the last year of the seventies. Watching with Dad while the Scooter said a prayer for his dead friend, *"just something to keep you from going bananas."*

I knew what would happen if I went home in this condition, thin and coke-addled and broke, after running away and not telling anyone where I was for nearly a year . . . or I thought I knew. It would be just like the last time, after the funeral. Maybe worse. I thought of my mother as a jailer lying in wait, setting a trap for me. Now I see that I'd set my own trap; she only wanted to help free me. But if you approach a wild animal who's caught in a trap—even to free them—they'll snarl and try to bite your hand off.

"I can't go back home. Can we just watch the game?"

Scooter spoke: *"Both the moon and Thurman Munson, ascending up into heaven. I can't get it out of my mind. I just saw that full moon, and it reminded me of Thurman. And that's it."*

Suddenly my head was swimming. I stepped off the stool and planted my feet, gripping the bar. I felt the Earth turning under me. Nothing was keeping me from being sucked into the void but gravity—which hadn't failed me yet, but who was to say it never would?

"I have to go."

"Hey—are you okay?"

I swallowed, nauseated. "I'm okay. But . . . you know . . . when you're underwater?"

"Say what?"

I couldn't speak, but this was what I was thinking: I'd been living underwater, in an undersea world with its own language and myths, which was great and everything, except that all this time I'd been holding my breath. You know when you're swimming along the bottom of a pool or the ocean and suddenly you can't hold your breath any longer? So you swim for the surface, frantically kicking, but it's a long way off. Maybe you left someone behind who tries to grab you by the ankle and pull you back down. You kick him away and shoot for the surface. When you finally break through . . . relief. You can breathe again. You fill your lungs with salt air. You can look through the mirror of the water at the undersea world you left. You can see it all clearly, the myths the sea people live by, and marvel at how long you are able to hold your breath.

I couldn't articulate this then. Bix said, "Dollbaby, you're talking jibber-jabber."

I stumbled outside. Overhead, the same full moon that the Scooter had admired gazed sternly down on me. The moon reminded him of the dead. It reminded me of my father. And that was it.

27

WHAT HAPPENED AT THE FUNERAL

My father's funeral was held on a bright, blinding December day at the cathedral, even though he wasn't Catholic—he wasn't really anything—but Mom is, and, as she said, you have to have a funeral somewhere. The church was packed. Mom and Laurel and I sat in the front row in our black clothes with our stunned faces. Mom and Laurel wept and wept, but I didn't cry. Everyone said how well I was holding up. Being strong for your mother, they said.

I wasn't being strong. It didn't feel real.

That's why I didn't cry.

I wasn't awake. I was dreaming that I was awake.

At the end of the service, the pallbearers lifted the casket. It floated down the aisle of the cathedral through a haze of incense, *stiff as a board, light as a feather* . . .

After that, my memory gets spotty.

I rode in a long black limousine with Mom and Laurel.

The cemetery grass was surprisingly green for December.

The grave was a neat rectangular hole with a pile of dirt next to it.

I couldn't look at it.

I looked at the sky. It was vast. Vast and empty.

There was nothing up there.

No clouds. Nothing.

I knew there was a universe up there somewhere.

Planets and stars and galaxies,

infinity,
the night world.
The sun hid it all.
I felt the Earth spinning under my feet.
I felt its weight.
Its gravity.
Its dark magnetic pull,
pulling me down,
down to the bottom of the sea.
That's the last thing I remember.

Over the next few weeks, Laurel and Mom recounted the rest of the day to me many times, hoping to trigger my memory.

At the cemetery, they said, I asked, "What's going on?"

Mom said, "Shhh. It's almost over."

Laurel said I gawked at the priest and the mourners, at the casket and the freshly dug grave, with an uncomprehending look on my face.

Prayers were intoned.

The casket was lowered into the ground.

Friends and family surrounded us to express their sympathy.

I whispered to Laurel, "Are we at a funeral? Who died?"

That's when she knew something was wrong. She and Mom hurried me back to the limo.

I asked, "Whose car is this? Where are we going?"

"Home," Mom said. "Everyone's coming back to our house for lunch, remember?"

"Everyone? How many people?"

"I don't know. A lot."

"Is it a surprise party?"

Laurel and Mom looked at each other in alarm.

"For my birthday," I said.

"Phoebe, your birthday is in March."

"What?"

"It's December."

"Oh," I said. "Christmastime."

They reminded me, as gently as they could, that Dad had died. That we had just attended his funeral. I took in the black clothes, the tearstained faces, the limo, the line of cars trailing ours with their headlights on. For a second, they say, my face registered comprehension. "Oh. Oh, yes."

But as the limo turned onto our street, parked cars lining the curb, I cooed, "Someone's having a party," in a teasing singsong voice.

And when we opened the front door and found the house bustling with people, I yelled, "Surprise!" Everyone looked up from their plates of ham and pasta salad. A few people laughed uncomfortably.

"You can't fool me, Mom," I said. "I guessed there was a party as soon as I saw all the cars out front."

Mom led me upstairs. "Where's Dad?" I said. "Dad! Dad!" I ran into my parents' room, where the bed was piled with coats. "Dad?"

They sat me down and told me again: "Dad died. Remember?"

I didn't understand. I didn't believe them. Before this fact had time to sink in, my memory was wiped clean again. I forgot why I was wearing black, forgot why the house was full of people, forgot that it wasn't my birthday, forgot why I couldn't find Dad anywhere.

Mom was afraid I'd had a stroke. She left Laurel to manage the wake and drove me to the emergency room. Laurel told everyone I was drunk.

I hadn't had a stroke. Something at the cemetery—perhaps the sight of the grave—had shocked me into amnesia. Every minute or so I forgot where I was and what I was doing there. Mom would remind me, and I would sort of understand, but then I'd forget again. Over and over I asked: *Why am I in the hospital? Did I have an accident? Where's Dad?* I remembered who I was and who Mom was. But I couldn't remember that Dad had died, or that he'd ever been sick.

The amnesia would dissipate after about twenty-four hours, the doctor said. Much of my memory would return. But I probably wouldn't remember the events of that day. Any memory of the burial or the wake would be lost forever.

They kept me overnight in the hospital. I woke up every few hours to find Mom sitting in a chair beside my bed. I asked where I was and what had happened. She shushed me and told me to go back to sleep. She'd decided it was cruel to keep telling me the bad news when the shock of it hit me fresh every time.

The next morning, a nurse brought a tray of pancakes and juice. I was disoriented. But my minute-to-minute, hour-to-hour memory was working again. I knew that it was December, not March. I understood why I was in the hospital. I remembered that Dad was dead. I even remembered the funeral—up to the part when the sky made me dizzy. I didn't recall Dad's coffin being lowered into the ground, or yelling, "Surprise!" at the wake, or driving to the hospital with Mom, or being examined by doctors the day before. Those memories are still lost to me.

I spent four more days in the hospital while doctors ran tests to make sure my brain was okay. I felt fine. There was nothing wrong with me. The amnesia had been a blip, like an allergic reaction. Like Mom's swollen tongue. I wanted to go back to New York, to my life, but Mom thought I should stay home and rest. I could go back later, when I was well. New York isn't going anywhere, she said.

She was mistaken: New York is always charging forward and threatening to leave you behind. It is going somewhere, always.

The house felt solemn and empty and wrong, as if someone had moved the furniture around just enough so that you couldn't remember how it used to be. I was desperate to get away. I felt the weight in my stomach and remembered where it had come from. Ivan—I thought then—had paid to make the weight go away, but it was still there. I had to return to New York and confront him. Then, maybe, I would feel light again.

But the amnesia had freaked Mom out. She said I had a strange look in my eyes—a dead, dull look. My grip on reality was fragile. I wasn't well enough to live on my own in New York. I needed someone to look out for me.

I argued and fought, ranted and raved, pacing my room like a caged tiger, but she would not be moved. I was the child on the leash, safe but humiliated. Humiliated but safe.

I spent the endless afternoons in the living room playing old records, one after another, in the random order that I found them: *Oscar the Grouch Sings the Songs of Sesame Street*; *Up with People!*; *In the Wee Small Hours*; *The Button-Down Mind of Bob Newhart*; *Piano Concertos by Sergei Rachmaninoff*; *The Sound of Music*; the Disney soundtracks to *Snow White*, *Cinderella*, *Peter Pan*, and the weird and scary *Darby O'Gill and the Little People*. This record now entranced me: the spooky music, the dancing leprechauns, the banshee's wail, and the headless coachman opening the door of the Death Coach and moaning, *"Get in. . . ."* I listened to it at least once a day.

Mom indulged this for a week before she begged me to stop playing that record. So I listened with headphones, waving the album's cover at her and shrieking like a banshee whenever she passed through the room.

I longed for Carmen and wondered what she was doing, remembering scenes from our past: Gossiping in the Blue Room. Dancing at the Gatsby party. Playing the jukebox at the Dublin House. Singing *What's Opera, Doc?* on the lip of the Lincoln Center fountain.

Late at night, in bed, I heard the banshee wailing. In my dreams, I went outside to meet the Death Coach. I woke up to find myself in my nightgown on the front porch.

The next night I sleepwalked in the street, barefoot. A police car picked me up and brought me home. My feet were dirty and cut; I'd stepped on broken glass. Mom took me to the emergency room to have the cuts treated. She told them she was worried about my emotional state. They kept me overnight for observation. In the morning, they released me, but Mom got upset, insisting I needed more treatment. "She's a danger to herself. I can't watch her all night."

The doctor maintained that there was nothing seriously wrong with me. I was an adult. Mom couldn't force me to check myself into the psych ward. So she brought me home.

When I remember those days now, I see the stress lines around her eyes, the tension around her jaw, the fear and the sorrow in her expression. If I noticed it then, I didn't care. I couldn't feel anyone's pain but my own.

She got the name of a psychiatrist from one of her friends and made an appointment for me. "Tuesday afternoon," she said. "Not too early, so you can sleep in."

"I'm not going."

"Phoebe, please. You are not facing this. You're making yourself sick."

"What do you want me to face?"

She sighed and rubbed a knot in the wood of the kitchen table. "Your feelings," she said quietly, as if she knew how weak and silly the word would sound to me.

"I'm feeling my *feelings*," I sneered. "What do I have to do to prove it? Do I need to make my tongue swell up so badly I can't talk? I don't know how to do that! Tell me how to make my tongue swell up and I'll do it. What's the secret?"

"You will go to this appointment," she said through gritted teeth. "Or I will take you to Sheppard Pratt—"

"What!"

"—where they will keep you until you are well enough to come home."

"The mental hospital? It's a prison!"

"It's not a prison. It's a very nice place. Zelda Fitzgerald was treated there."

"You can't do that!"

"If you continue to be a danger to yourself, if you sleepwalk in the street, cut yourself, anything like that, I can and will do it. Or you can see this Dr. Lyons and hope and pray she can help."

No doctors, no hospitals, no talking about feelings could help me, I was sure of it. The only thing that would cure me was throwing money in Ivan's face. I was enraged at my mother: that she wanted to lock me up at Sheppard Pratt, that she thought she could force me to do anything, that she kept me from doing what I had to do.

And then, on Christmas, I got a stolen turban in the mail. Thanks to Carmen, I escaped.

Now it was September. Carmen was gone. And I was trapped underwater at the bottom of the sea, unable to breathe.

28

THE ROOSTER MAN

Every night for weeks, I wandered the streets in search of her. I should have been looking for work, for some way to earn money, but this was all I did. This was my job now. I walked for hours, taking a different route each night: down through NoHo and SoHo to Tribeca, east to Chinatown and Little Italy, up through the Lower East Side, back to the East Village. I passed row after row of posters of a demon-eyed Ronald Reagan and the words

PLUTONIUM. HALLOWEEN.

Toby had come up with the idea. He said that four more years of Reagan was the scariest thing he could think of.

I peered into coffee shops and bars and bodegas and restaurants, parked cars and phone booths and alleys. I was a whale, swimming the streets, beaming out sonar, *beep, beep, beep*. I knew the chances of finding her were tiny—she might not even be in New York—but I felt compelled to look, to scour every corner of the city, to do something good for once.

One night, very late, the feeling of being followed returned. I saw no one, but every doorway loomed in shadow, a hiding place. I tried to convince myself that I was imagining this feeling, that I was paranoid. I was afraid of losing my mind again. Maybe I was sleepwalking. Maybe I was dreaming. It was hard to tell anymore.

I finished my wanderings and returned to Avenue A well after midnight. The park was quiet and still, the park people settled into their tents, dreaming of bongos.

I reached for my keys. Something moved in the shadows near the Eighth Street gate. I peered through the dark.

Plaid sports jacket. Plaid tie.

It was him. I hadn't seen him in a long time.

Come in, Phoebe, come in. . . .

I wanted to join him. I felt the pull of it.

I'll come, I said.

I crossed the street. I hesitated at the entrance to the park.

Where had he gone?

"Dad," I said out loud.

I listened. A breeze rattled the rusty leaves.

"Dad."

Nothing.

I'd lost him.

He was dead. I wouldn't see him again.

Then, from deep inside the park, came a squawk, a flap of wings, and a shout: "Atti!"

I ran along the winding path, leaves crunching under my feet. Dark lumps huddled on benches and on the ground, sleeping or nodding. None of them was Carmen, I saw it instantly, I could tell by their shapes.

At last: in front of the General Slocum memorial, a small figure lay crumpled on the ground, her left sleeve rolled up, a needle on the ground beside her.

"Zowie . . ." she whispered through bluish lips. She rolled her head, her eyes closed. I peeled back an eyelid to check her pupils. Pinpoints. She gasped for air.

"Carmen! It's me." I tried to force her to look at me, but she couldn't keep her eyes open. I rubbed my knuckles on her sternum. Her eyes fluttered.

Wings flapped again, over by the benches. The silhouette of a tall man, watching us. The rooster had landed on his shoulder. He made a phlegmy sound in his throat, a cough or a laugh, it was hard to tell which.

"We've got to go." I pulled Carmen up to a sitting position, wrapped one of her arms around my neck, and hoisted her to her feet. "Come on. Walk."

We stumbled along the path, her feet dragging, her head drooping. She was barely able to stand, incoherent, nearly unconscious. *If Dad were here* . . . I thought, *but he's not. He's not.* It was only me.

I hustled Carmen's slack body across the street to our building. "Stay awake. We're almost home." I dragged her into the vestibule and threw myself against the inner door. It burst open, the lock still broken. I kicked it shut behind me, hoisted Carmen onto my back, and hauled her upstairs. *Help!* I screamed. *Help help help!* But the screams came out in nightmare whispers. I couldn't make enough noise, all my breath went to my legs, to pumping my thigh muscles.

Round the second-floor landing. Up to the third. We'd nearly made it. I pulled out my key.

Then, from below: a slam. Thuds. Panting.

He was in.

I rammed the key into the lock and turned it.

Footsteps running up the stairs. A grunt.

I hauled Carmen into the apartment and threw my weight against the door, turning the bolt. The cats fled.

The doorknob rattled. A fist pounded on the wood. I squeezed my eyes shut.

"Open the door." His voice low but intense. "Open the fucking door."

Carmen lay under the kitchen table, unconscious, turning blue. I ran into the living room. Where was the phone? I kicked aside papers, books, cereal boxes, clothes. . . .

The rattling stopped.

I held my breath. Quiet.

I tiptoed to the door and pressed my ear against it.

In the hall, footsteps, moving away, *clomp clomp clomp clomp* . . . A clinking sound. Footsteps coming back, *clomp clomp clomp clomp* . . .

The knob rattled again. I recoiled. The sound of metal on metal, a key crunching into the lock.

The door burst open. A tall white man in a black knit cap. Familiar face. He grinned and rattled a ring with two keys.

"Hey hey! This is Oswald's place, isn't it? Did you know he kept a spare set hidden out in the hall?" He shut the door and bolted it. "I wonder how old Oz is doing these days?" He grinned, baring a chipped front tooth. "I know you. Don't you remember me?"

"I don't know you." I backed into the living room.

"You bought me some potatoes. A few weeks ago. Remember?" He laughed that cough-laugh again.

He'd shaved off his beard. But it was him.

"Huh, girl? Remember?"

"Yes, I remember."

"You were nice. I asked a lot of people to help me that day. You were the only one who did."

He pocketed the keys and stepped around Carmen, giving her leg a little kick. One of his boots was held together with duct tape. He made his slow, deliberate way toward me.

"You know what I did with the potatoes?"

I said nothing.

"Huh? Do you know what I did? Answer me!"

"No."

"I put them in a soup. You know what else I put in the soup?"

I backed into the cardboard box we used as a coffee table.

"Katinka!" He laughed. "You know why they never found her body? Because I made soup out of it. Then I fed it to those people in the park."

I barely understood what he was saying. I kept backing away from him, blindly scrambling for the phone. My hand landed on an ashtray. I threw it at him.

He ducked. It missed him and smashed against the wall. Ashes rained on the floor. "Hey. Don't do that!"

I threw a book. It smacked him in the chest. He caught it and kept coming. "I thought you were nice."

My leg bumped the couch. I picked up a bowl, cereal dried along the sides, a spoon clattering to the floor, and threw it as hard as I could. It nailed him in the forehead.

He growled.

He sprang.

I dove behind the couch. He pounced, banging his knee on the radiator. I slipped out from under him, my hand rolling over something smooth. The Scooter's bat.

I gripped the bat.

No matter what, I would not let go of the bat.

I crawled out from behind the couch and swung it at him, swishing air. He launched himself at me and knocked me to the floor. My head hit the wall. He bashed his fist into my face. My knee jerked up, a reflex, and rammed his crotch.

He grunted and rolled off me. I sprang to my feet. I saw stars.

He lifted his head. I raised the bat.

I felt the Earth spinning under my feet.

I felt its weight.

And its gravity.

It made me dizzy.

But I did not black out.

I roared

and cracked the bat

down

on

his

head.

He howled and curled up on the floor.

I hugged the bat and fell onto the couch. My eyes filled with some viscous liquid. I blinked and wiped it away.

He crawled toward the door, leaving a trail of red handprints on the floor. He spat, and one of his teeth clattered on the linoleum. Then he collapsed, facedown.

He didn't move.

He still didn't move.

Blood seeped from his nose, forming a little red speech bubble on the floor.

He still didn't move.

Sirens screamed in the distance.

I was afraid to look away, afraid he would spring back to life. I found the phone under the couch. I lifted the receiver to my ear. Dial tone. 9-1-1.

I took in the room. Cushions on the floor. Broken glass. Ashes. Bloodstains. Carmen under the table, her breath a shaky rasp. The Rooster Man's body. His tooth on the linoleum tile.

I crawled over to Carmen and felt her pulse, slow and weak. I rubbed my knuckles over her breastbone. She didn't move.

"Oh Carmen." I lifted her chin and tilted her head back. I pinched her nostrils together and sealed my lips over her mouth. I breathed into her.

I'd watched Carmen take care of Atti. This is what she taught me: to look deeply into a person's eyes, to feel for the blood moving through their veins, to listen to their breath while they are still here, still breathing. To see, hear, and feel as a matter of life and death. Like Dad, with his stethoscope.

She had taught me all this, but had I learned it well enough?

Outside the rooster crowed, a dog howled, and the banshee wailed, on her way. I sealed my lips to Carmen's and breathed.

29

THE FAMOUS ASTRID

That's how I became the famous Astrid.

The police arrived, and three ambulances, and we were all taken to Bellevue. I got stitches over my eye and was told I had a slight concussion. In the morning, two police detectives visited me. They asked me a lot of questions about what I was doing out alone in the middle of the night, how I'd found Miss Dietz in the park, how I'd ended up living in an apartment belonging to a convicted felon, and how I knew William Dankow. How he had gotten into the apartment. How he'd ended up unconscious on my kitchen floor.

It sounded like they were accusing me of something, but they said, No, they just had to ask all these questions. Don't worry, they said.

I told them everything I knew. "Is he alive?" I asked.

Yes, with a severe concussion, they said. The doctors were confident he'd be able to stand trial. He's done a lot of bad things, they told me—really bad—and they'd been looking for him for a long time. They thanked me for stopping him. Then they handed me a copy of that morning's *Post* and said, "You're a hero. A heroine? Anyway, you're famous."

The front page headline screamed PSYCHO AND THE PSYCHIC! over a picture of the Rooster Man posing in the park, grinning mirthlessly under his beard, with Fritz on his shoulder. The caption: "William Dankow, Cannibal Killer of Tompkins Square Park." In the lower right corner was an inset photo of me—a paparazzi shot from Andreas Fischer's party. "Beaten up by a girl!"

According to the press, the police had been looking for William Dankow, known locally as "the Rooster Man," in connection with a cooler full of bleached bones that had turned up near the East River, and with the disappearance of multiple young women, including his sometime girlfriend, Katinka Gelfors, a ballet student from Switzerland. They'd found her skull in a locker at Port Authority, buried in a bucket filled with cat litter. He'd killed her, chopped up her body, and boiled her remains to make a soup that he served to homeless people in the park. A soup that included—in a detail that sent a wave of nausea through me—potatoes, as well as, one witness claimed (more nausea), a human finger.

"When you're ready, there are a lot of reporters out there who want to talk to you," one detective said. They left, giving me a thumbs-up.

A nurse came in to take my temperature. I asked, for the hundredth time, about Carmen. The nurse said she'd check. They kept saying that, but I couldn't get an answer.

"Can I see her?"

"Not yet. She's in intensive care on another floor. We want to keep you under observation for one more day. Tomorrow."

"What about the reporters?"

"You're not ready for that. I sent them away."

My mother arrived just before dinner. She looked at my face and burst into tears. I let her hug me, then sat awkwardly waiting for her to stop crying. She's not a big weeper, so when she cries, it means something.

She hugged me for a long time, then dried her eyes. "I'm so glad you're okay."

"I told you I was. I sent you those postcards."

"Phoebe. For heaven's sake."

Visiting hours ended, but Mom stayed. The hospital grew quiet. A nurse checked on me, telling me to get some sleep, but I wasn't sleepy. Mom sat up with me for a while. She studied the photos of me in the papers, the turban, the sunglasses.

"Why 'Astrid'?" she said, then, "Wait—I know why. *Pippi Longstocking*."

"Correct," I said, both pleased and annoyed. She didn't know everything about me. But she knew some things.

I itched for a cigarette. I felt around in my jacket pocket—the Mitch jacket—and found a pack, but I didn't have a match. I looked at Mom. She frowned.

"I might have some matches somewhere." She dug through her purse until she found a book of matches and tossed them onto the bed. "This doesn't mean I approve." I lit a cigarette. She went into the bathroom and returned with a paper cup half full of water. Then she took a cigarette from my pack and lit it, settling into her chair. She dropped the match into the water and set the cup on the night table between us.

"Mom, whatever happened to Danny Washburn?"

"Who?"

"You know, Dad's old friend Danny Washburn? The one who really knew how to live?"

"Oh, him." Mom nodded. "He died of alcoholism in nineteen seventy-two."

I watched our reflections in the window, blurry against the velvety black outside.

"Remember, when you were three, you used to copy everything I did? You had that toy vacuum cleaner, and you'd follow me all over the house, vacuuming."

"I don't really remember that," I said, mildly horrified. "I remember the Bark Button."

"You were always asking your dad to lift you up so you could press the Bark Button."

I imitated Snookie. "Ra-ra-rarararararah!"

"He had such an annoying bark. You thought it was funny."

"So did Dad."

We smoked.

"Poor Snookie," Mom said.

I shuddered. "Yeah, poor Snookie."

"He lived a good longish life."

"Till you stuffed him in the freezer."

"It was a *heat wave*. Do I have to explain that again?" She tapped a tube of ash into the cup.

We smoked some more. I told her that I'd seen Dad's ghost, more than once, in Tompkins Square Park. I described him, the way he was dressed, the way he beckoned to me. "Do you ever see him?"

"No," she said. "But then, you were always his favorite."

The door opened and the night nurse burst in, waving her hand in front of her face. "What do you think you're doing? Put those cigarettes out before the fire alarm goes off."

"Sorry." I doused my cig in the paper cup. It went out with a *pzzt*. Mom dropped hers in too.

"Don't do it again, or I'll have to ask you to leave," the nurse said to Mom, as if Mom were a bad influence on me. She crossed the room, cracked open the window, and bustled out.

"Whoops," Mom said. "Let's try to sleep."

She fixed my covers for me and settled in her chair with her coat over her for a blanket. We were quiet for a few minutes. Then she said, "You know what the worst part was? For me."

"What?" I asked warily.

"I couldn't picture you in my mind. I didn't know where you were, so I couldn't comfort myself by imagining what you were doing."

"Oh." That's when I felt it, the weight of what I had done. Because not knowing where Carmen was had given me that same unmoored feeling. "I'm sorry, Mom."

She closed her eyes. "Tomorrow I need to see your apartment, so I can picture you there."

"It's kind of a mess." I imagined her walking into the kitchen as I'd left it, grim and bloody, a crime scene, and worried it would scare her.

"If it's messy, we'll clean it up."

In the morning, after I checked out, they let me visit Carmen at last. Mom wanted to come but I asked her to wait for me in the hospital lobby.

They'd just moved her out of the ICU. She was awake and sitting up in her bed, a tray of barely touched toast and eggs, sunny-side up, on the table.

"Hey look, it's Mitch," she said sourly. I realized I was still wearing her jacket. I took it off and draped it over the chair beside her bed.

"You could have come back to get it," I said.

"I was busy." She refused to meet my eyes. She was so thin, her cheeks had caved in, carving even deeper angles into her face. Her thick auburn hair stuck out around her head in all directions, shorter than I'd ever seen it, as if someone had chopped it off with a hatchet.

"What were you doing?"

"Looking for Atti."

"Where? I searched all over downtown for you."

"Everywhere." She picked up her fork and stabbed it into a slice of toast. The fork balanced on its tines and then tipped over with a clank. "I told you, he was the only person I could count on. It was true."

"It's not true. You can count on me."

"Really. The facts tell another story."

"I know they do. But it's true. You can count on me. Now. Now you can."

She freed the fork from the slice of toast and poked its tines into an egg yolk, which bled over the plate.

"I thought I'd proved it to you," I said. "I tried to help you the way you always helped Atti. I learned it all from you."

"Are you waiting for me to say thank you for saving my life? Okay, Phoebe. *Thank you*. Except I don't mean it. Because before I woke up in this hospital bed, I saw him. I almost found him. I could be with him again, right now, if you hadn't saved my life."

I sat down. I swallowed. It took effort.

I'd been so eager to see her, I hadn't expected that she'd still be mad at me. Even madder than before.

"When are you getting out of the hospital?"

"I don't know yet. They're making me go back to the Humph."

"How long?"

"Six weeks, maybe two months."

"I'll visit you every week. I'll bring you those cakes from De Robertis, and *People* magazine and chocolates and anything you want."

She didn't say anything. To fill the silence I sang, *"I'll give you fish, I'll give you candy . . ."*

"'Give Me Back My Man'? Tactful."

"I'll change the words to '*give me back* . . . something else.'"

"You can't change the words. The words are the words."

A nurse interrupted, saying Carmen needed to finish her breakfast and rest.

"I'll visit you," I repeated. "And when you get out, come live with me."

She didn't look up, didn't reply. She hadn't looked at me the whole time I was in the room.

* * *

The lock on the street door was still broken. As we walked up to the third floor, Mom took in the smeared walls, the cracked tiles, the chicken bone on the stairs, the skeleton of a broken umbrella in a corner, the smell of cabbage and pot. I spotted something shiny on the second floor landing and picked it up. A stethoscope.

"That's funny," I said.

"I don't think it's so strange," Mom said. "There's a chicken bone. There's an umbrella. Why not a stethoscope?"

When we reached my door I couldn't open it. The key didn't work. We went back downstairs and I found a note in my mailbox from Mrs. Lisiewicz. She'd changed the locks. I knocked on her door. She smiled at my mother and handed me a new set of keys. She asked how I was feeling and said I didn't look too bad, considering.

I still had the stethoscope in my hand. "I found this on the stairs," I said.

Mrs. Lisiewicz took it and handled it as if it were a dead snake, fascinating and a little disgusting. "The ambulance men must have dropped it this morning."

"This morning? You mean yesterday morning."

"No. This morning."

"What happened this morning?"

"Miss Kulish had a heart attack."

"Miss Kulish?" I didn't know who that was.

Mrs. Lisiewicz hugged the stethoscope to her chest, miming the old lady with the clock. " 'What time is it?' "

"Oh, no. Did she die?"

"Not yet. But she won't be back. She can't live on her own no more." She shook her head. "There have been many ambulances lately." She passed the stethoscope back to me. "You keep it."

The new key opened the door. I braced myself, but Mrs. L. had cleaned up the place and fed the cats. She'd stocked the kitchen with cans of tuna, some kind of Polish cheese, some Oreos, and lots of crackers: Ritz crackers, graham crackers, Triscuits, Goldfish. She'd left a vase of bodega daisies, dyed blue, on the kitchen table. She'd even made the bed. The apartment looked nicer than I'd ever seen it. Julio and Diego greeted us calmly, rubbing against my calves, tails happy and alert, as if nothing bad had ever happened here.

Mom toured the two rooms like a prospective renter. "It gets a nice amount of sun." She noticed the bat, clean and polished and propped up in a corner near the couch. She picked it up, spun it around to the autograph, kissed it, and put it back in its place.

The light on my answering machine was blinking. I had fifteen messages.

"Ms. Hayes, this is Tom Garvin, I'm a reporter for the *New York Post*, and I'd like to speak to you as soon as possible. Call me back at . . ."

"I'm calling from the *New York Times*. We'd like to interview you about your encounter with William Dankow today, if we could . . ."

"Hey. Phoebe. I heard what happened." Jem. "I hope you're okay. Hope Carmen is okay too. I was thinking, remember that night we bumped into each other outside the park? Maybe the guy who was following you was the killer! Gives me chills to think about it. Anyway, give me a call, let's get together."

"Who's that?" Mom asked.

"Nobody."

There were more messages from magazines and newspapers and TV shows, asking for interviews. Then, the last message:

"Phoebe, it's Wes. Listen, let's rethink your Astrid column. You're getting a lot of attention, you're a national hero, I think it would be a hit. We could syndicate it, and you'd make some money. Give me a call when you can. Oh—and—I'm sure you're fielding a lot of requests for interviews. I can help you with that. Call me."

"What's that about?" Mom asked.

"This advice column I'm trying to write."

I waited for her to say that I could write a column from anywhere, from home if I had to, home where I'd be safe, where there were no cannibal killers or junkies or nightclubs and where, after last night—she had made a onetime exception for last night, under special circumstances—I wouldn't be allowed to smoke either. I waited for her to say that so I could tell her she was wrong—the column was about New York, so I had to stay here, and nothing she could say would make me go home anyway.

But all she said was, "I think you'll be good at it."

We were hungry, so I took her to lunch at Odessa. She went home on the three o'clock train.

VISITATION

Carmen gets out of rehab today.

I tried to visit her that first week at Humphrey-Worth. It's in Tarrytown. I read Carmen's copy of *Edie* on the train. There was a photo insert with a picture of beautiful teenage Edie in her room at Silver Hill, lying on a bed, laughing and kicking her graceful legs in the air as if it were the most delightful place in the world. I almost envied Carmen. The Humph was supposed to be just as country-club posh as Silver Hill.

I arrived at the start of visiting hours. The place was impressive, a brick Victorian mansion surrounded by newer buildings and set on acres of fields and woods, like a small women's college. I checked in at the front desk and was asked if I was a member of Carmen's immediate family. No, I said, and the clerk frowned. "No visitors other than family," she said. "I'm sorry."

"Can I just see her for a minute to say hello?"

The clerk shook her head. "These are the rules."

"But I came all the way from the city."

"Sorry."

I glanced around as if there might be a way for me to sneak inside. But that was ridiculous.

"Will you tell her that I came to see her?"

"You may send her a letter if you like."

Frustrated, I turned to go. Len and Betsy opened the door, bringing chilly air in with them.

"Phoebe. What are you doing here?" Len's posture was uncharacteristically stiff.

"I didn't realize only family members are allowed," I said. "I just wanted to see her and sit with her."

They glared at me, jaws tight. "You have a lot of nerve," Betsy muttered. Then, with great control, Len said, "I hope you're well, Phoebe. Goodbye." They pushed past me to the desk. I was momentarily paralyzed by the surprise of seeing them and the change in their manner toward me. Clearly I was no longer Carmen's sweet, trustworthy friend. My face flushed with shame and I hurried out.

I caught a taxi back to the train station, where I paced the platform, fuming at the Dietzes' coldness. It wasn't fair. I'd saved their daughter's life.

When the train arrived, I settled in a seat and lost myself again in the tragedy of Edie Sedgwick. Twenty-eight years of money, drugs, loneliness, and fame; exciting and glamorous and terribly sad. I couldn't separate the glamorous threads from the sad ones. They twined and fed on each other, the glamour impossible without the sadness, and the sadness heightened by the glamour. Toward the end, the book got a little boring: Edie left New York, and the story's energy drained away. She moved back to California and got married, still zonked on pills. One night she swallowed her barbiturates as usual and went to sleep. Her husband found her dead beside him in the morning.

Since I couldn't visit Carmen as I'd promised, I wrote to her. I sent her a gift every week—Swedish fish, chocolates, cakes from De Robertis—and a letter every day. I gave her news of our neighbors, of our friends, of the upcoming trial of William Dankow. Since his arrest, the rooster had vanished. I never saw him in the park, never heard his unnerving squawk again. I wondered what had happened to him.

I described to her my struggles to write the first column of Astrid Sees All. Readers had sent hundreds of questions to the *Underground*, but I felt like a fraud. Who was I to give advice to anyone? I tried to fake it, as Carmen had once advised me, but Wes saw right through that and told me to try again, to be honest this time. I thought I'd gotten good at faking things, but now I realize I never really mastered it.

At the end of every letter I wrote,

> *I am here. Julio and Diego are waiting for you. The apartment is ready to welcome you back. I know that you will need someone to care for you, and I can do it. I stopped partying. I'm learning to cook, if you can believe it! I learned how to care for another person by watching you, Carmen. When you leave the Humph, if you want to, you can come home to me.*

Six weeks of letters. She didn't write back.

Then, in the third week of December, a postcard. On the front: A photo from the nineteen-sixties of four young people playing Ping-Pong in a wood-paneled room with chintz curtains. On the back, a caption: THE HUMPHREY-WORTH CENTER, TARRYTOWN, NEW YORK. PATIENTS RELAX IN THE BUSBY KEANE MEMORIAL RECREATION LOUNGE, COMPLETE WITH CHECKERS, CHESS, AND PING-PONG. And the handwritten message:

> *Getting out December 23. Just in time for Christmas! Holly jolly. L&B taking me home with them. Don't try to visit me—they hate you. They blame you for everything. I know it's not fair, but I don't correct them. I kind of enjoy it. You always wanted to be the bad girl. Now you are.*
>
> *—C*

Her parents will try to keep her with them as long as they can. I understand that. But someday she will get restless and want to leave. Someday soon, I think. When that day comes, I will be ready.

In the meantime, I sit at my window and watch the park. I keep my stethoscope on a hook nearby. Mrs. Lisiewicz said it was dropped by the "ambulance men," but I know that it's a gift from my father. I like to place the eartips in my ears and the chestpiece on my chest and listen to my breath. I whisper a waltz, "One, two, three. One, two, three . . ." I listen to my heartbeat. And when Carmen comes back, I'll listen to hers.

ACKNOWLEDGMENTS

Many thanks to the following:

My editor, Trish Todd, who is not only thoughtful and brilliant, but fun to work with; and everyone at Atria, especially Libby McGuire, Jonathan Karp, Lindsay Sagnette, Fiora Elbers-Tibbetts, Lisa Sciambra, Dana Trocker, Isabel DaSilva, Laywan Kwan, Suzanne Donahue, Felice Javit, Elisa Rivlin, and Polly Watson.

My agent, Sarah Burnes, for her tenacity, wisdom, and heroic willingness to read my terrible early drafts; and everyone at the Gernert Company, especially Sophie Pugh-Sellers, Will Roberts, Rebecca Gardner, Anna Worrall, and Julia Eagleton.

Friends, readers, advisors, bandmates, and partners in crime: Darcey Steinke, René Steinke, Biz Mitchell, Deborah Heiligman, Rebecca Stead, Judy Blundell, Marthe Jocelyn, Margo Rabb, Kristin Cashore, Betsy Partridge, Barb Kerley, Barnabas Miller, Libba Bray, Dan Ehrenhaft, Elise Broach, Bennett Madison, and Maia Danziger.

Ezra, Talia, and Zachary Weiner for being kind and funny souls.

Kathleen, John, and Jim Standiford, Karen Yasinsky, Jon Weiner, and Deborah Heiligman (doing double duty) for being sisters and brothers in spirit as well as by blood and by marriage.

My parents, Will and Betty Standiford, for everything.

And Eric Weiner, for being a miracle.

Gratitude and love to you all.

ABOUT THE AUTHOR

Natalie Standiford is the author of many books for children and young adults, including *The Secret Tree*, which was a *New York Times* Notable Book. *Astrid Sees All* is her first novel for adults. She was born in Baltimore and lives in New York City with her husband.

ASTRID SEES ALL

NATALIE STANDIFORD

This reading group guide for Astrid Sees All *includes an introduction, discussion questions, ideas for enhancing your book club, and a Q&A with author Natalie Standiford. The suggested questions are intended to help your reading group find new and interesting angles and topics for your discussion. We hope that these ideas will enrich your conversation and increase your enjoyment of the book.*

INTRODUCTION

Set in New York's last bohemia, the star-studded, heart-pounding downtown club scene of the 1980s, *Astrid Sees All* unveils the world of its irresistible main character, Phoebe Hayes. Phoebe moves to the city with her best friend, Carmen, just after graduating from college, in search of adventure and a life she can call her own. But there is real pain—from Phoebe's past, from a man who wrongs her, even from her relationship with Carmen—lurking beneath the surface. As much as Phoebe tries to bury it with sex, drugs, and a job telling fortunes at a glamourous nightclub, when Carmen suddenly disappears, Phoebe must confront what she's been desperately living to avoid.

TOPICS & QUESTIONS FOR DISCUSSION

1. We first meet Phoebe at college in Rhode Island, dreaming of a bigger, more adventurous life. How do you think her experiences in college shape that dream for her?

2. Phoebe's relationship, such as it is, with Ivan is one of her first experiences after moving to the city. How do you think this relationship—and the way it ends—affects her? How does it change her perspective on what life might be like when she gets to make her own choices? What does she decide to do about what happens between them, and why do you think she makes that choice?

3. We're initially introduced to Plutonium as "a new kind of nightclub, club as performance art" (p. 87). Art is everywhere in this novel, and the idea of life as performance art is an interesting concept in this context. Later, we're told, "The art didn't matter as much as being seen as part of the group" (p. 156). How much of Phoebe's persona is a performance, meant to be seen by others, and how much of it is true?

4. Phoebe chooses the name Astrid for her fortune-telling alias. How does choosing an alias for her new job help Phoebe become a new person, someone who she's always wanted to be? Do you think she sees herself as that person yet? At what

point does she become the girl she wanted to be when she was younger? Is it like she imagined?

5. Phoebe is low on money or in debt throughout the novel, but this is especially so before she starts the job at Plutonium. She does have the safety net of her mother's home in Baltimore, although she desperately doesn't want to rely on that. Do you think having this safety net there, even if Phoebe doesn't want to use it, affects the story? Do you think Phoebe's experience and choices would change if she did not have that security?

6. Portrayals of drug use and abuse show up several times over the course of the novel. How does the portrayal of drugs for recreational use—like everyone using at clubs, and the "sex, drugs, and rock 'n' roll" lifestyle—contrast with the darker realities of substance abuse at the beginning of the crack epidemic? How do these issues show up in the novel?

7. We're told that Carmen "loved who she loved. Once she loved you, you couldn't shake her. But you couldn't earn your way into her heart, either. So if she loved you, it made you a kind of royalty" (p. 119). In what ways does Carmen make Phoebe feel special? Why do you think Phoebe continues to remain close with her after she discovers, time after time, that Carmen lies to her or hides things from her? Do you think Phoebe wants the relationship with her to be more than simply platonic?

8. Phoebe's sightings of the posters with missing girls appear several times throughout the novel before we realize why or what

is happening. How does having this backdrop of potential loss and fear—even fear for Phoebe's own safety—affect our experience reading the story?

9. Phoebe and Carmen's relationship throughout the novel is tumultuous. At times, they're as close as two friends can be, but at others, Carmen's lies are revealed and Phoebe feels like she doesn't know her at all. Why do you think this portrayal of turbulent friendships is so fascinating? What other works of fiction portray addictive but often damaging relationships between two close friends?

10. At Plutonium, Phoebe brushes up against all kinds of famous people, like Andy Warhol, Sting, Grace Jones, Christopher Walken, and many more. How does including these real people help ground the story and show the scope of Phoebe's world? How are celebrities viewed in the New York bohemia of the time? Are they revered or treated as ordinary people—or somewhere in between?

11. Phoebe feels like she has so much agency throughout the story; she makes her life look the way she wants it to. But at some point, she admits, "I thought about Ivan. . . . When I'd wanted the story to end, I'd declared it over, but by then it had taken on a life of its own and was out of my control" (p. 142). How much of what happens to Phoebe is out of her control? Does this become increasingly so as the story goes on, or was it always that way?

12. Near the end of the book, Jem asks Phoebe about how she tells people's futures when they're hiding their true selves. In what

ways does Phoebe become more perceptive when it comes to reading others throughout her journey? How does this skill serve her amid everything that happens at the end of the novel?

13. Over the course of the novel, we slowly realize that Phoebe's father's death took a much greater toll on her than we'd previously realized. What signs were there, in retrospect, that suggest that Phoebe's grief was affecting her thoughts and actions?

ENHANCE YOUR BOOK CLUB

1. This story is so cinematic that you can almost hear the music and see the clothes and the clubs. If this were a movie or TV show, what would be your dream casting for the characters?

2. Watch classic films set in the 1980s like *Desperately Seeking Susan*, *Bright Lights, Big City*, and *The Last Days of Disco* and discuss them with your book club. How do they intersect with the world shown through *Astrid Sees All*? What does *Astrid Sees All* reveal about that time and place that other books and media have not?

3. You can find the fully designed book club kit at https://www.nataliestandiford.com/bookclubs_.htm. In it, you can find lists of songs, movies, and places mentioned in the book and an eighties playlist created by the author to accompany the read.

A CONVERSATION WITH NATALIE STANDIFORD

Q: New York City in the 1980s is such a vibrant backdrop for the story. What made you decide on that particular time and place for the novel? Do you have a personal connection to it?
A: I graduated from college in 1983 and moved to New York on the last day of August that year. It was such a momentous occasion for me that I still mark the date, privately, every August 31. So I can't help but associate that time and place with coming of age.

I lived on the Upper West Side (where my first job was as a clerk at the late, legendary Shakespeare & Co. bookstore on Broadway and Eighty-First Street) for a year before moving to the East Village. New York City has always been a magnet for adventurous young people, but the downtown Manhattan of the eighties was remarkable for the way it combined a burgeoning arts scene with danger, grit, and a kind of magic. In describing the photographer Nan Goldin's great work from that period (most notably *The Ballad of Sexual Dependency*), the *New Yorker* art critic Peter Schjeldahl wrote that her "photographs of determinedly broken youth . . . preserve the desperate, at times literally deathly, ardors of a generation that stayed up late to fit into each day its maximum quotient of mistakes." I remember that feeling of craving excitement no matter the consequences, of *needing* to live on the edge. The East Village of the eighties drew outsiders of all kinds who weren't afraid of taking risks, and who wanted to live big lives on their own terms . . . which makes a great setting for a novel.

Q: Even though the book is set only a few decades ago, did you do research when writing to add more details to the story? Did you research any of the art exhibitions, clubs, etc. of the time? Did you find anything surprising when you did? How did you choose what details to include?

A: I did do some research. In 2017 the Museum of Modern Art had a show called *Club 57: Film, Performance, and Art in the East Village, 1978–1983*, which thrilled me because that was slightly before my time and I'd always felt I'd missed something big. Club 57 was an influential performance venue/gallery/party space in the basement of a Polish church on St. Marks Place, and the museum tried to re-create that basement vibe. The same year, the Whitney Museum exhibited paintings from the eighties, focused on downtown New York, which brought back memories of the crowded East Village gallery openings I tried to shove my way into on Thursday nights.

I read books like *St. Marks Is Dead*, a history of St. Marks Place by Ada Calhoun; looked at photos by Ken Schles (*Invisible City*) and Nan Goldin (*The Ballad of Sexual Dependency*); and read all the accounts of nightlife I could find. I reread some of the books I'd loved in my twenties, like *Lives of the Saints* by Nancy Lemann, *Breakfast at Tiffany's* by Truman Capote, *Slaves of New York* by Tama Janowitz, *Bright Lights, Big City* by Jay McInerney, and *Elbowing the Seducer* by T. Gertler, which made a big splash in 1984 but seems to be undeservedly forgotten now. I revisited some of my favorite movies from or about the eighties—*Desperately Seeking Susan*, *Smithereens*, *Stranger Than Paradise*, *Downtown 81*, *Basquiat*, *The Last Days of Disco*, *Wings of Desire*, *Paris, Texas*, and Éric Rohmer's *Summer*, to name a few—which helped me remember the look, the sound, and the emotional tenor of the period.

I also reread my journals from those years, which was painful and embarrassing but did yield some juicy details that I probably would have blocked out otherwise. Nothing really surprised me, except perhaps how run-down and dirty the city was in those days. There was a real sense of decay, which, of course, is part of "decadence."

I included only a fraction of all this research in the book, though I suspect that immersing myself in these details enriched the atmosphere of the novel. I used anything that helped illustrate Phoebe's state of mind—what she would notice, what would matter to her or seem new or strange to her—or that contributed to the story.

Q: Why did you choose to start the book with one of Phoebe's experiences with Ivan, before going back to her college days? What about that relationship with him sets the stage for what's to come?

A: To me the Ivan episode illustrates how Phoebe's hunger for experience clouds her judgment. She grew up fairly sheltered, and once she gets to college she realizes how naïve she is compared to many of her peers. She's eager to see the world—the *real* world, the seedy truth her parents tried to protect her from—and she's willing to sacrifice a lot for that knowledge. I thought of her as a Persephone figure, except that instead of being dragged into the underworld by Hades, she hunts for the entrance herself and forces her way in. She feels she needs to do this, that it's part of becoming a full person. The moment she meets Ivan is the moment she finds the door to the underworld.

Then, too, she sees her life as a movie, and a good movie must have drama. If there's no drama in her life, she's willing to create it; and once the story is set in motion, she has to see it through to the end, even if it means getting hurt. (She's not afraid of taking risks, but I don't think she really understands what the consequences might be.) So I opened the novel at the place where, in Phoebe's mind, the movie of her life begins: the relationship that sets her on a downward spiral.

Q: Why did you choose ticket stubs to be the way Phoebe told fortunes as opposed to something more traditional, like tarot cards or palm reading?

A: Originally, Phoebe was a palm reader, but I found it hard to describe palm reading in an interesting way. Head line, heart line, life line . . . there was only so much she could say. One night I was listening to a podcast interview with a tarot card reader and she mentioned that you can use anything you like in place of tarot cards—anything that has meaning for you, even movie ticket stubs. A bell went off in my head. Just mentioning movie titles, plots, and actors evoked so much about Phoebe's state of mind and the flavor of the period, and it was more fun than describing the lines on someone's hand. And the idea of collecting movie ticket stubs fit with Phoebe's sense that her life is a movie, that movies are the standard against which she measures reality.

Q: Were any of the events in the book inspired by things that happened to you or to someone else in real life?

A: The early drafts were full of incidents I remembered from my own life, but they fell away as I revised until the story's connection to my real life grew so blurry as to be unrecognizable. Almost everything in the finished book is made up. (When I'm writing, I know a story is finally on the right track when it starts to pull away from the autobiographical and the "true" and take on a life of its own.)

But there is one real-life incident that I couldn't resist adapting for the novel. My brother John was visiting me here in New York. One day he came home from rambling around the East Village and told me that he'd been stopped on his way into a bodega by a guy with a rooster on his shoulder. I'd seen that guy around; everyone in the neighborhood knew who he was. The guy asked John to buy him some potatoes; they wouldn't let him into the bodega with the rooster, he said. John thought, *What harm could a few potatoes do?* and bought them for him. A little while later the guy with the rooster, Daniel Rakowitz, was arrested for killing his girlfriend, chopping up her body, and boiling it into a soup that he served to the homeless people camped out in Tomkins Square Park. When I heard that I got chills. What if John had unwittingly provided the potatoes for the soup? That's how bizarre the neighborhood was then, and how interconnected everyone was, whether we wanted to be or not.

Q: There are many songs mentioned during the course of the book. Are any of them personal favorites of yours?

A: So many of them! I was obsessed with the Jam, Talking Heads, New Order, Gang of Four, the Clash, and the Pogues, and still love them. I made a playlist while writing the book and listened to it over and over, striving to capture the energy of the music. One of the inspirations for the novel was a simple yet vivid memory. I was living on Avenue A, getting ready for friends to come over for a party. I put New Order's *Power, Corruption & Lies* on the turntable and danced around the apartment to "Your Silent Face" for the sheer pleasure of it. Who knows why that scene felt so evocative to me thirty years later, but it haunted me while I wrote, and kept me connected to that feeling of being twenty-two on a Friday night in New York.

Q: Do you have any favorite books set in a similar time or place that inspired you as you were writing?

A: Tama Janowitz's *Slaves of New York* is like time traveling for me. I used to look for her stories in *The New Yorker* every week and got so excited when they published a new one. I felt like she was writing about me—her recurring character Eleanor was as insecure as I was, even though her life was a lot more glamorous than mine. Other inspirations: Ann Beattie's stories in *Where You'll Find Me*, Laurie Colwin's in *The Lone Pilgrim*, Patti Smith's *Just Kids*, and all the tales of youthful love and folly set at other times, in other places, like Christopher Isherwood's *Berlin Stories*, Françoise Sagan's *Bonjour Tristesse*, the tales of Colette, Nancy Lemann's *Lives of the Saints*, and *No One Belongs Here More Than You* by Miranda July. For starters.

As for poetry: Two poets I love, Alice Notley and Frank O'Hara, were East Villagers. Notley lived on St. Marks Place in the seventies and eighties and published *Margaret & Dusty* in 1985, which includes one of my favorites, "All My Life." A few decades earlier, O'Hara wrote poems like "Avenue A" and "Early on Sunday" ("how sad the lower East Side is on Sunday morning in May . . .") while living on East Ninth Street, right around the corner from the apartment Phoebe and Carmen share on Avenue A.

Q: So much of the story is full of the whirlwind adventure Phoebe has in the downtown club scene, but it becomes increasingly clear that she's hiding from her pain. There is a lot of pain in this novel—grief, overdoses, murders, betrayal, etc. Why was it important to you to portray that, in contrast to the fast-paced nightlife Phoebe experiences?
A: There is a kind of frantic fun that is driven by an unwillingness to face pain, and that's what Phoebe finds on the Lower East Side. But I couldn't truthfully dramatize the appeal of chasing those thrills without also depicting the cost. It's tempting to romanticize the past, but there was real danger in New York at that time. Rents were low for a reason: a lot of people considered the city an undesirable place to live—dirty, crime-ridden, and chaotic. In exchange for excitement, creativity, and glamour, you had to put up with getting mugged, or being awakened in the middle of the night by strangers hoping you'd buzz them into your building so they could shoot up or break into an apartment, or finding blood and needles on your doorstep in the morning, or the sad sight of junkies dreaming on the sidewalk with no idea where they were. Phoebe's experience wouldn't have carried any emotional weight if I'd left all that out.

Q: Carmen is such an interesting character—at times pulling Phoebe in and at others pushing her away. What made you decide on this dynamic for their friendship?

A: I've been in relationships—both platonic and romantic—that had this baffling push-pull dynamic, and I've always been interested in how they work and why they're so common. I'm not sure I'll ever really understand it. What makes a friend pull away, and what makes her come back? What gives one friend power over another? Carmen instinctively knows how to keep people interested in her, which is a skill Phoebe wants, but she learns it by being Carmen's practice dummy. Eventually, Phoebe has to ask herself what she's doing in this friendship and begins to realize that she's been playing games too; she wasn't the faithful friend she appeared to be. She loves Carmen, but she also wants things from her. This kind of lopsided friendship is more complex than it looks on the surface; the one who seems to be taken advantage of is usually in it for reasons of her own.

Q: This story is told as a first-person narrative from Phoebe's point of view. What made you choose this perspective rather than, say, a third-person narrative that showed multiple perspectives? What do you think we gain with this access into Phoebe's mind, and why is that important for the story you tell?

A: Early drafts of the novel were written in the third person, with three protagonists; one was Phoebe, and the others were two of her roommates. The roommate stories were not as compelling as Phoebe's, and in the end she took over the book. I decided to have her narrate it because the story is about how she deludes herself, how her thinking changes over the course of a year, how the events of the story change her, and I thought the reader could see that most clearly if they were inside Phoebe's mind. I wanted readers to understand why she'd make decisions that look so foolish from the outside (though they make sense to her at the time), and why she'd put herself in the way of so much pain. I wouldn't call Phoebe an unreliable narrator exactly, but she's still young when she tells her story; the lessons of it are just beginning to dawn on her. As she reviews what happened, she begins to see the events in a new light, and I hope that witnessing her thoughts as she goes through this process adds a layer to the drama.

Q: This is your first adult novel—congratulations! In what ways did writing this book differ in your process from writing your past novels?
A: In many ways writing is writing. I like to set my books in "Natalie World," which is the world as I see it, filtered through my sensibility. No matter who I'm writing for, my eyes and ears and heart are inevitably drawn to certain images, themes, and details—the odd, the eccentric, maybe a hint of the mysterious or supernatural, the female experience, things that are kind of sad and kind of funny (like a killer with a pet rooster, or a woman's tongue swelling up in reaction to anxiety, or a postcard photo of people playing Ping-Pong at a psychiatric hospital). I think you could draw a line from *How to Say Goodbye in Robot*—a YA novel I published in 2009—to *Astrid Sees All* and find a lot of similarities: a narrator on the edge of a closed world, looking in and feeling drawn to the other outsiders she meets. I could imagine Phoebe going to high school with Bea from *Robot*.

On the other hand, I did enjoy writing about certain subjects (sex, drugs, the pre-internet world, and twentieth-century culture) without worrying that my readers would not have had enough experience to understand what I was talking about. That was very freeing.

Q: Do you have a next project in mind? If so, can you share anything about it?
A: I'm working on a novel about two sisters, set in Baltimore and New York in the late 1990s. It's too early to say much more than that—I'm still writing the first draft and a lot can change in revision!